Captive
Bride

Captive Bride

Johanna Lindsey

Five Star
Unity, Maine

Five Star Romance.
Published in conjunction with Avon Books,
a division of the Hearst Corporation.

October 1996
Standard Print Hardcover Edition.

Five Star Standard Print Romance Series.

The text of this edition is unabridged.

Set in 11 pt. Times by Minnie B. Raven.

Printed in the United States on permanent paper.

Library of Congress Catalog Card Number: 96-86250
ISBN 0-7862-0880-5 (hc)

Captive
Bride

Chapter 1

The weather was pleasantly warm on this early spring day in the year 1883. The slightest of breezes played daintily with the great oak trees that lined the long drive way leading to Wakefield Manor. Two fine white steeds attached to an open carriage stood breathing hard before the huge, two-story mansion.

Inside, Tommy Huntington paced fretfully back and forth across the large drawing room with its gold-brocade furniture, waiting impatiently for Christina Wakefield to come downstairs. Tommy had rushed over to see her after finally reaching a decision concerning her, but now he was getting nervous.

Damn it, she never used to take this long, he mused as he finally stopped pacing and stood before the window looking out at the Wakefields' vast estate, not until she started wearing dresses and putting her hair up. Now every time he came to see her, he ended up waiting a half hour or more before she would join him.

Tommy was having second thoughts about what he wanted to tell her, when two sort hands slipped over his eyes, and he could feel Christina's breasts pressed against his back.

"Guess who?" she whispered playfully in his ear.

Oh God, he wished she wouldn't do that anymore. It had been fine when they were children growing up together, but lately her nearness was driving him crazy with desire.

He turned to face her now, and was enchanted by her uncommon beauty. She was wearing a form-fitting dark-blue-velvet dress with white lace adorning a high collar and long sleeves, and her golden hair was piled in countless ringlets about her head.

"I wish you wouldn't stare so, Tommy. You've been doing that more and more of late, and it makes me nervous. I would think I had dirt on my face if I didn't know better," she said.

"I'm sorry, Crissy," he stammered. "It's just that you've changed so much this last year that I can't help myself. You're so beautiful now."

"Why, Tommy Huntington, are you telling me that I used to be ugly?" Christina teased him, pretending to be affronted.

"Of course not. You know what I mean."

"All right, I forgive you," she laughed as she crossed to the gold-brocade couch and sat down. "Now tell me why you are here so early. I didn't expect you until dinnertime, and Johnsy told me that you looked fit to be tied when you rushed in here."

Tommy felt perplexed trying to find the right words, for he had not prepared his little speech. Well, he had better say something before he lost the courage.

"Crissy, I don't want you to go to London this summer. Your brother will be home in a couple of months, and I plan to ask him for your hand in marriage. Then, after we are married, if you still wish to see London, I'll take you."

Christina stared at him aghast. "You take too much for granted, Tommy!" she said harshly, but calmed down when she saw the stricken look on his boyish face. After all, she had always known this day was bound to come. "I'm sorry I snapped at you. I realize that our families have always considered us a perfect match, and perhaps some day we'll marry, but not now. You're only just eighteen, and I'm seventeen. We're too young to get married. You know I've always been isolated here. I love my home, but I want to meet new people and know the excitement of London. Can't you understand that?"

She paused, not wanting to hurt him. "I love you, Tommy, but not the way you want. You have always been my best friend, and I love you the same way I love my brother."

He had listened to her patiently, knowing how strong-minded she

8

was, but her last words hurt him deeply.

"Damn it, Crissy. I don't want to be a brother to you. I love you. I want you as a man wants a woman." He came over to her and, taking her hands, pulled her up against him. "I want you more than I've ever wanted anything else. Taking you in my arms and making love to you is all I can think about. It's become an obsession."

"You're talking foolishness, Tommy. I don't want to hear any more!"

Christina pulled away from him, and a moment later Johnsy, her old nanny, bustled into the room with tea. So no more was said on the subject.

They had an enjoyable dinner together after going for a long ride to relieve the tension. Since Christina had resumed her normal, carefree manner, Tommy tactfully did not mention his desire for her again.

Later that same night, as Tommy lay in his own bed thinking of Christina and that afternoon, he felt horribly apprehensive. He was suddenly positive that if Christina went to London this summer as she planned, it would change her whole life and ruin his. But there was nothing he could do to stop her.

Chapter 2

A thousand twinkling stars could be seen on this clear summer's eve,
A warm breeze softly tossed the treetops, giving a glimpse here and
there of a full, rounded moon lighting the landscape. But the peace
of the beautiful English countryside was broken by the Wakefield
coach rumbling over the empty, dusty road.

Inside the large, richly upholstered coach, John Wakefield stared
pensively at his own reflection in the window. A lone candle standing
in a sconce on the opposite side cast a subdued light over the
deep-blue-velvet interior of the coach.

He just might enjoy this trip to the city, John thought, he knew
Crissy would. He turned to look at his sister, who was sleeping
undisturbed on the seat across from him.

Christina Wakefield had changed from a mischievous tomboy into
a strikingly beautiful woman, all in the short year that John had been
away from home. He had been shocked to see her so grown-up on
his return a month ago and still couldn't get over the incredible
change. Her figure had filled out to stunning perfection, and even
her face had changed so that John hardly recognized her.

He studied her face now, as she lay dreaming sweetly. Gracing
her high cheekbones were thick lashes that seemed to have grown
longer in just a year's time. Her straight, narrow nose and rounded
chin seemed more pronounced now that she had lost her youthful
chubbiness. John knew he would have his hands full trying to keep
the young bucks at bay when they reached the city.

Crissy had wanted this trip to London for her eighteenth birthday,
and John had found no reason to deny her wish. Christina Wakefield
had always been able to get what she wanted, he mused. She had

had their father wrapped around her little finger, and now she had done the same thing to himself. Well, he didn't mind. John enjoyed giving in to his sister: she was all he had left.

He remembered clearly that fateful day four years ago when Jonathan Wakefield had died in a hunting accident. John had to inform Crissy of their father's death, for their mother took it so badly that she died three weeks later — from grief, the doctor said. But even with John's own grief, he somehow managed to help Crissy through her suffering. Crissy spent most of that time riding wildly across their estate on her black stallion. John let her do this freely day and night, for she had told him only three months earlier that she could forget her troubles by riding with the wind.

John wanted to laugh at her then, for what troubles could she possibly have at her age? Well, he had learned soon enough that troubles come to all ages. The riding helped Crissy through her grief, and she returned to normal sooner than she might have after suddenly losing both parents.

It was up to John to raise Crissy after that, but he couldn't have done it without the help of Mrs. Johnson — Johnsy, they called her. She had been their nanny when they were children, but now she took care of Wakefield Manor and supervised all the servants of the estate. John could still see Johnsy shaking her finger at him before they left for London, her brown eyes wide with concern.

"Now you be keepin' an eye on my baby 'ere, Johnny boy," she had reminded him for the third time that morning. "You don't be lettin' 'er go fallin' in love with none of those London gentry. I don't care for the likes of those London dandies with their uppity ways, so don't you be bringin' any 'ome!"

Crissy had laughed and mocked Johnsy as she got into the coach. "Shame on you, Johnsy. What would I be doin' fallin' in love with a London dandy when I 'ave Tommy 'ere waitin' on my return?" Crissy threw a kiss at Tommy Huntington, who had come to see them off. Tommy lowered his head in feigned embarrassment, but

John could tell that he wasn't happy about Crissy's journey to the city.

Tommy lived with his father, Lord Huntington, on a neighboring estate. Since there were no girls of Crissy's age living nearby, she and Tommy had been constant companions since childhood. John and Lord Huntington had always hoped they might marry someday. But Tommy, with his sandy brown hair and light brown eyes, was only six months older than Crissy and was still just a boy in John's eyes. Crissy was now a young woman, however, and of an age to marry. John had hoped that Tommy would mature as soon as Crissy, but perhaps she would wait for him if she loved him.

Who knows how the mind of a woman works, John thought absently. He didn't even understand Crissy's feelings for Tommy: whether she felt only friendship for him, or something more. He must remember to ask her about it later, but she would probably be so busy the next few weeks that he wouldn't have a chance.

John smiled, imagining the surprised faces of the young men who would seek her out when they discovered that Crissy was not only beautiful but intelligent as well. John chuckled to himself, recalling the heated argument that their parents had had over Crissy's education. They had compromised, and Crissy was schooled like any man but was also taught the feminine arts of sewing and cooking whenever their mother could find her.

Yes, Crissy was educated and she was beautiful, but she had her faults. Her downright stubbornness was one fault that she had inherited from their mother, who would stand her ground on any subject if she felt herself in the right. Another fault was her quick temper, for she could get angry over the smallest thing.

John sighed, thinking how hectic the next two weeks would be. Well, it would only be two weeks. He dozed off then, as the coach continued along the lonely road to London.

Christina and John Wakefield were still asleep when their coach pulled up in front of the two-story house on Portland Place. The sun had just edged over the horizon, turning the sky from pink to soft blue, and the birds were singing cheerfully.

Christina awakened when the driver opened the door of the coach. "We've arrived, Miss Christina," he said apologetically, and went to take down the luggage from the back of the sturdy vehicle.

Christina sat up and straightened her hair, which had fallen in long tresses all about her. She smoothed her dress and glanced at John, who was still sleeping soundly across from her, his blond hair lying softly across his high forehead.

She shook his leg gently. "John, we're here! Wake up!"

Slowly John opened his dark blue eyes and smiled, running a hand through his hair as he sat up straight. Christina noticed that his eyes were bloodshot. He must not have slept very long last night. She was surprised that she had slept so soundly.

"Come on, John! You know how excited I am," she pleaded.

"Slow down, young lady," he laughed, rubbing the sleep from his eyes. "The Yeatses are probably still sleeping."

"But I can unpack and get settled in, then spend the day shopping. You did say I could have a new wardrobe, and what better time to buy it than my first day here? Then I can wear my new clothes during our stay," she said happily as she jumped out of the coach.

"Didn't that etiquette instructor teach you anything at all, Crissy?" he scolded her, shaking his head at her breach of propriety. "I know you're excited, but next time wait until I help you down from the coach."

They walked up the few stairs to a pair of large double doors, and John knocked loudly. "The whole house is probably asleep," he said, knocking again.

But the doors swung open wide, surprising them both. A small, chubby woman with red cheeks and graying hair smiled out at them.

"You must be Christina and John Wakefield. Come in — come in. We've been expecting you."

They entered a small halfway carpeted with an Oriental rug, with a stairway at the end. A mahogany table stood against one wall, laden with small, lacy figurines.

"I am Mrs. Douglas, the housekeeper. You must be tired after your journey. Would you like to rest a bit before startin' your day? Mr. and Mrs. Yeats are still abed," she said cheerfully, leading them to the stairs.

"John probably could use more sleep, but I would just love a hot bath and then some breakfast, if it isn't too much trouble," Christina said as they reached the upstairs landing.

"No trouble at all, Miss," Mrs. Douglas said. She showed them their rooms and left.

The driver followed them up with the luggage, and then went to tend the horses. John excused himself, saying a nap was just what he needed, when a young maid entered with water for Christina's bath.

"I be Mary, the upstairs maid," she said shyly as she pulled out a large tub and poured the water in. "If there's anything you be needin', miss, just let me know," she added.

"Thank you, Mary."

Christina surveyed the room. It was small compared to her bedroom at home, but beautiful. A gold plush carpet covered the floor, and the gold-canopied bed had a small marble-topped commode on one side and an ornate chest of drawers on the other. A green-velvet settee stood in the corner by the single window, which was draped in light-green velvet, and a gilt-framed mirror leaned against another wall.

Mary finished putting away the clothes Christina had brought with her just as more water arrived, and Christina was finally left alone. After pinning up her hair, she undressed and sank into the steaming hot water. She leaned back and relaxed.

For as long as she could remember, Christina had dreamed of this trip to the city. She had always been thought too young before, and last year, when she was sixteen, John had been away with his regiment. He had come home a lieutenant in Her Majesty's Army and now was awaiting further orders.

She had lived her whole life at Wakefield Manor. But she had enjoyed a wonderful childhood growing up in the country, running wild like a tomboy, and often getting into trouble. She remembered how Tommy and she used to hide in the loft of the Huntington stables and listen to old Peter, the head groom. He was always swearing and talking to himself and the horses. Christina learned the most unladylike words from old Peter, most of which she didn't understand. But one day Tommy's father discovered them hiding in the loft. They both got a severe scolding, and Christina was not allowed near the Huntington stables for a very long time.

Christina was no longer the tomboy she once was. She wore dresses now instead of the breeches Johnsy had made for her because she was always getting dirty and tearing her clothes. She was a lady now, and she enjoyed being one.

Christina finished bathing and dressed in a cool cotton dress with a floral pattern. She realized it wasn't in fashion, but she wanted to be comfortable as she did her shopping. She combed out her long golden hair and then pinned it up into a mass of curls and ringlets. Picking up the bonnet she would wear, she went downstairs to breakfast.

She found the dining room through one of the doors off the hall. John was sitting at the huge table with Howard and Kathren Yeats. She could smell the sweet aroma of ham and apple turnovers, for the table was laden with them and with eggs and muffins.

"Christina, my dear. I can't tell you how pleased we are to have you here." Kathren Yeats smiled at her with soft gray eyes. "We've just been telling John of the parties that we've been invited to, and there will be a grand ball for you to attend before your stay is over."

Howard Yeats chimed in. "To start you off, there's a formal dinner

15

tonight at a friend's house. But don't worry — the younger crowd will be there," he laughed.

Howard and Kathren Yeats were in their late forties, a cheerful and robust couple always on the go and loving every minute of it. Christina and John had known them always, for they were old friends of the family.

"I can't wait to get out and see the city!" Christina said enthusiastically, putting something from each dish on her plate. "I want to get my shopping done today. Will you join me, Kathren?"

"Of course, my dear. We'll go to Bond Street. It's just around the corner and simply packed with shops."

"I thought I would join you myself, since I couldn't get back to sleep. There are a few things I have to pick up anyway," John remarked. He wasn't about to let Crissy go out into the dangerous city without him, even if Kathren Yeats was along.

John still looked tired, but perhaps he was as excited as she was, Christina thought. A maid filled her cup with steaming hot tea as she gulped down mouthfuls of savory ham and eggs.

"I'll be just a minute," Christina said, noticing they were all finished eating.

"Take your time, child," Howard Yeats said, an amused expression on his ruddy face. "You have all the time in the world."

"Howard's right, Crissy. Don't eat so fast," John scolded her. "You will have to delay your shopping for a stomachache."

They all laughed, but Christina didn't slow down. She wanted to be on her way. She hadn't expected to have to dress formally their first night here. She had only one evening gown, which she had made for Lord Huntington's last ball.

They spent the whole morning and part of the afternoon going from one shop to another. There were a couple of shops that featured ready-made clothes, but Christina could find only three street dresses that suited her fancy, with slippers and bonnets to match. She could find no evening gowns, however, so they spent the rest of the time having her measurements taken and choosing materials and trims. She ordered three gowns and two more street dresses, all with matching accessories.

The seamstress said it would take at least four days to complete the outfits, but that she would start on the gowns first so Christina might have them earlier. They finally returned home and had a light lunch, then napped.

That evening all tongues were set to wagging when Christina and John Wakefield made their entrance at the dinner party. They were a striking pair with their blond hair and extreme good looks. Christina felt out of place with her deep-violet evening gown, because all the other young women were wearing light pastels. But she was reassured when John whispered, "You outshine them all, Crissy."

Their hosts took them around to meet the other guests, and Christina enjoyed every minute of it. The women flirted boldly with John, and this shocked her a bit. But she was even more shocked by the way the men looked at her, as if undressing her with their eyes. She supposed she had a lot to learn about city people.

The dinner was served in a large dining room, with two huge chandeliers hanging above the table. Christina was seated between two young gentlemen who lavished far too many compliments on her. The man on her left, Mr. Peter Browne, had an annoying habit of taking hold of her hand while talking to her. Sir Charles Buttler, on her right, had limpid blue eyes that wouldn't leave her for a minute. Both men vied for her attentions, each boasting and trying to outdo the other.

After the meal was finished, the women retired to the drawing room and left the men to their brandy and cigars. Christina would have preferred to remain with the men and discuss politics or world affairs. Instead, she was forced to listen to all the latest gossip about people she didn't know.

"You know, my dear, that man has insulted every pretty young girl that his brother, Paul Caxton, has introduced to him. It's not human the way he shuns them," Christina overheard a dowager say to her friend.

"It's true that he doesn't seem interested in women. He will not even dance. You don't think he is ah — odd, do you? You know — the kind of man who doesn't care for women?" the other replied.

"How can you say that when he looks so virile? Every eligible young woman in town would love to land him — no matter how badly he treats them."

Christina wondered slightly who the dowagers were talking about, but she didn't really care. She was immensely relieved when she and John were finally able to leave. In the coach on the way home, John smiled mischievously.

"You know, Crissy, three young admirers of yours cornered me separately in the den to ask if they could call on you."

"Really, John?" she replied, yawning. "What did you tell them?"

"I said that you were very discriminating in your tastes, and that you wouldn't give tuppence for the lot of them."

Christina's eyes flew open. "John, you didn't!" she gasped. "I'll never be able to show my face again!"

Howard Yeats burst out laughing. "You're very gullible tonight, Christina. Where has your sense of humor gone?"

"I actually told them that I didn't dictate to you whom you could or could not see — that the choice was entirely up to you whether you wished to receive callers or not," John said sedately as they pulled up in front of the Yeats home.

"You know — I didn't even think of that. I wouldn't know what to do or say if I had a gentleman caller. I've never entertained anybody except Tommy, and he's like a brother to me," Christina said seriously.

"It will come naturally to you, my dear," Kathren said knowingly. "So don't you worry yourself about it."

The days flew by quickly for Christina, with parties, social gath-

18

erings, and dinners to attend. Peter Browne, her dinner partner of her first evening in London, declared himself instantly smitten, and exasperated her with constant declarations of his love. He even asked her brother for her hand in marriage.

"Peter Browne asked you for my hand yesterday, and Sir Charles Buttler asked me today while riding in the park. These London men are quite impulsive, aren't they? Well, I won't see any more of them! It's ridiculous how they think every girl who comes to London is looking for a husband. And to declare they're in love, when they hardly know me — it's absurd!" Christina stormed at her brother, who was more than amused at her outburst.

Tonight was Christina's first ball. She had been looking forward to dancing ever since last month, when she had coaxed Johnsy's husband to teach her how. She had saved her prettiest new gown for this night and was as excited as a small child with a new toy. So far, her London season had not been what she had dreamed it would be. But tonight would be different! And she hoped Peter and Sir Charles would be at the ball, for she was determined to ignore them.

Chapter 3

Paul Caxton sat staring moodily out the window of his study. He was brooding about his older brother, Philip, for Paul had never understood him. Philip had been a silent, withdrawn child, and living with their father these past years had not improved his disposition.

Philip had been discontent since returning to London a year ago for Paul's wedding. Paul talked him into staying in England, hoping Philip would find a wife for himself, settle down, and start a family. But Philip had become a barbarian after living with their father in the desert for so long. Paul and his wife, Mary, introduced many young ladies to Philip, but he showed contempt for them all.

Paul couldn't understand Philip's attitude. He knew Philip could be charming and polite if he chose, for he treated Mary with the greatest respect. But Philip just didn't give a damn what society thought of him. He refused to play the gentleman, no matter how it embarrassed Paul.

Philip had arrived last night from a month's stay at their estate in the country. He had uncommon control of his temper, but went into a rage when Paul told him of this night's ball.

"If you are planning on foisting some more of your pert little society misses on me, I swear I'll leave this town for good!" Philip had stormed. "How many times must I tell you, Paul, that I don't want a wife! I have no desire to have a frilly-skirted, obnoxious woman underfoot and making demands on my time. I have better things to do than contend with a woman." Philip paced back and forth vigorously. "If I want a woman, then I'll take her, but only for a night of pleasure with no strings attached. I don't want to be tied down. Damn it all, when will you get that through your head?"

"But what if you should someday fall in love — as I have? Then will you marry?" Paul had ventured, knowing his brother's bark was worse than his bite.

"If that day ever comes, then of course I'll marry. But don't get your hopes up, little brother, for I've seen what this town has to offer. The day will never come."

Well, Philip might be surprised at the ball tonight, Paul thought, smiling to himself. He jumped out of his chair and ran up the stairs three at a time. He was in a jubilant mood as he knocked loudly on his brother's door and stuck his head inside. Philip was just sitting up on the bed, wiping the sleep from his eyes.

"It's time to get dressed, old man," Paul said mischievously. "And wear your best regalia. You want to charm all the ladies, don't you?" Paul closed the door swiftly as a pillow slammed against it. He laughed boisterously as he went down the hall to his room.

"What's so amusing, Paul?" Mary asked as he came into their room still laughing.

"I think Philip will meet his downfall this night, and he won't even know it," Paul answered.

"Whatever are you talking about?"

"Nothing, my sweet — nothing at all!" he exclaimed. He picked her up and swung her round and round.

Philip Caxton was annoyed. He had had an argument with his brother only yesterday about women and marriage, and now Paul was at it again.

"Look at all the beauties you can choose from in this ballroom," his brother was saying with a twinkle in his green eyes. "It's about time you settled down and gave the Caxtons an heir."

Paul was going too far. Philip wondered at the game he was playing. "Do you expect me to pick a wife from one of these simpleminded young ladies of society?" he said sarcastically. "There's not one here I would care to invite into my bedroom."

21

"Why aren't you dancing, Philip?" Mary said, coming up to them. "Shame on you, Paul, for keeping your brother from all these pretty young things." She put her arm on Paul's.

It always amused Philip when Mary referred to girls her own age as young things. Mary was only eighteen years old herself, and very lovely, with big cat-like eyes and light brown hair. Paul had married her only last year.

Philip replied teasingly, "When I find a maiden as beautiful as you are, my dear, I will be more than happy to waltz the night away."

Just then Philip saw Christina standing only three feet away. She was a vision! He didn't know a woman could be that beautiful!

She glanced at him before turning away, but in that moment her image was etched in his mind forever. Her eyes fascinated him — dark rings of sea-blue surrounding light-blue-green centers. Her hair was a shimmering golden mass of curls, with a few loose curls dangling softly against her neck and temples. Her nose was straight and narrow — her lips, soft and alluring and made to be kissed.

She wore a dark-sapphire-blue-satin ballgown. Her soft rounded breasts swelled above the décolletage, and light-blue ribbons emphasized her slim waist. She was perfection.

Philip's gaze was interrupted by Paul's hand waving back and forth before his eyes. He finally looked at his grinning brother.

"Have you gone daft?" Paul laughed. "Or is it Miss Wakefield who has caught your eye? Why do you think I insisted you come tonight? She lives with her brother in Halstead and is here for the season. Would you like to meet her?"

Philip smiled. "Do you have to ask?"

Christina noticed a man staring rudely at her. She had overheard him earlier insulting all the ladies in the room. Perhaps he was the same man whose bad manners were the talk of London.

She turned away when she saw him coming toward her. She had to admit he was the handsomest man she had ever seen, but reminded herself that she had lived a secluded life and had met very few.

"Excuse me, John," she said to her brother, "but it is extremely warm in here. Could we take a turn in the garden?" She took a step, but was stopped by a voice behind her.

"Miss Wakefield."

Christina had no choice but to turn around. She looked into a pair of forest-green eyes with hundreds of yellow flecks in them. They held her spellbound. It seemed an eternity before she heard voices again.

"Miss Wakefield, we met in the park yesterday — you mentioned you would be attending this ball. You do remember, don't you?"

Christina finally turned to the tall young man and his wife. "Yes, I remember. It was Paul and Mary Caxton, was it not?"

"That's right," Paul said. "I would like to introduce you to my brother, who is also visiting the city. Miss Christina and Mr. John Wakefield — my brother, Philip Caxton."

Philip Caxton shook John's hand, then kissed hers lightly, sending shivers up her arm.

"Miss Wakefield, I would be more than honored if you would consent to have the next dance with me," Philip Caxton said, without letting go of her hand.

"I'm sorry, Mr. Caxton, but I was just leaving for a stroll with my brother. It's so stifling hot in here." Why was she explaining herself to this man?

"Then you must let me escort you, with your brother's permission, of course." He looked at John.

"Certainly, Mr. Caxton. I have just seen an acquaintance I would like to speak with, so you will be doing me a service."

Oh John, how could you, she thought angrily. But Philip Caxton was already leading her through the crowd toward the doors. When they stepped outside, Christina immediately withdrew her hand from his. They walked a few paces before she heard his deep voice again.

"Christina, your name is enchanting. Was your excuse of the heat a feminine way of getting me outside alone?"

She turned to face him very slowly, with her hands on her hips and sparks flying from her eyes. "Why, you insufferable cad! Your conceit overwhelms me. Are you quite sure this simpleminded young lady of society is worthy enough to invite into your bedroom?"

Christina missed the shocked look on Philip's face when she turned and stalked back into the ballroom. She also missed the slow grin that replaced the shocked look.

I'll be damned, he thought, shaking his head. She's no simpleminded young lady. She's a little spitfire. Damned if she didn't tell me off. He closed his eyes and saw her before him, and he knew he must have her. But he certainly was off to a bad start, for she had taken an immediate dislike to him. Well, he wouldn't give up. One way or another, he would have her.

Philip walked back into the ballroom to find Christina safely with her brother. He watched her all night, but she managed to avoid meeting his eyes. He decided to keep his distance, for there was no point making matters worse than they already were. He would give her a chance to calm down tonight, and would start anew tomorrow.

Chapter 4

The sun was high over the trees when Christina finally crawled from her bed. She put on her slippers and robe and walked over to the window, wondering what time it was. She remembered how she had tossed and turned all night after coming home from the ball.

She kept seeing those unusual eyes staring at her insolently from that handsome face. Philip Caxton was taller than most men, more than a foot taller than her five feet, four inches, and lean and muscular. He had black hair, and a deep rich tan that stood him apart from the lily-white London dandies.

What's the matter with you, Christina, she scolded herself. Why can't you get that man out of your thoughts? He insulted you, but you continue to think about him. Well, you won't be seeing Philip Caxton again if you can help it.

She threw off her robe and slippers and took out one of the new street dresses from her wardrobe. After she was attired to her taste, she descended the stairs to look for her brother.

Christina walked into the dining room to find Mrs. Douglas and one of the downstairs maids clearing away what looked like the remains of lunch.

"Why, Miss Christina, we were beginning to wonder if you had taken ill. Would you be caring for some breakfast? Or perhaps some lunch would be more to your liking?" Mrs. Douglas said.

Christina smiled as she sat down. "No, thank you, Mrs. Douglas. Some toast and tea will be fine. Where is everyone?"

"Well, Mr. John said he had some errands to run, and left just before you came down, miss," Mrs. Douglas said as she poured Christina a cup of tea. "And Mr. and Mrs. Yeats are taking an afternoon nap." The maid came in with a plate of toast and jams.

"I almost forgot, Miss Christina," said Mrs. Douglas, "there's been a gentleman come round to see you this morning. He's a persistent one — come three times already. A Mr. Caxton, I believe." She was interrupted by a knock at the door. "That must be him again."

Christina was annoyed. "Well, if it is the same gentleman, or any other, tell him I am feeling poorly and won't be receiving callers today."

"Very well, miss. But this Mr. Caxton's an awfully handsome gent," Mrs. Douglas replied before she left to answer the door.

She came back shortly, shaking her head. "It was Mr. Caxton again. He said to tell you, miss, that he's sorry you're feeling ill, and he hopes you'll be better tomorrow."

John and she were returning home tomorrow, so she wouldn't have to see Mr. Caxton again. She missed the country, and she missed her daily rides on her stallion, Dax. She would be glad to be home.

Dax and Princess had been born at the same time, and her father had given Princess to her for a birthday present. But Princess was white and gentle, while Dax was a fiery black colt. So Christina had coaxed her father into giving her Dax instead, promising to train him to be gentle.

But Dax was gentle only for Christina. She laughed aloud when she remembered John trying to ride Dax two years ago. The stallion would allow no one on his back but Christina. At home she could soon forget about that rude Philip Caxton, and Peter Browne, and Sir Charles Buttler.

Christina heard the front door open and close, and John appeared in the doorway.

"So you finally managed to pull yourself out of bed. I waited for you this morning, but gave up at noon." John leaned against the doorframe. "I ran into Tom and Anne Shadwell while I was out. He was in my regiment, you remember. They have invited us for dinner tonight, along with a few of their friends. Can you be ready to leave by six?"

"I suppose so, John."

"I also met Mr. Caxton outside. He said he had called for you, but you weren't feeling well. Is anything the matter?"

"No. I just didn't want to see anyone today," she replied.

"Well, we'll be leaving tomorrow, so today is your last chance to find a worthy husband," John teased.

"Really, John! You know that's not why I came to town. The last thing I want is to be tied down and enslaved by wifely duties. When I find a man who will treat me as an equal, then perhaps I shall consider marriage."

John laughed, "I warned father that giving you an education would be your downfall. What man will want a wife who's as smart as he?"

"If all men are so weak and timid, I will never marry — and be content!"

"I can't say I would pity the man who wins your heart, Crissy," said John. "It will make a most interesting marriage." Then he left.

Christina sat thinking over what John had said. She doubted she would ever find the kind of love that would make her happy: the kind of love her father and mother had had for each other. Theirs had been the perfect marriage until they died four years ago. John and she had grown even closer since their deaths.

Then, last year, John purchased a commission in Her Majesty's Army, and was now on leave awaiting further orders. Christina suddenly determined to go with him wherever he was sent. She would miss Dax and Wakefield, but she would miss her brother more.

She hoped John wouldn't be sent too far away. He didn't plan to make the army his career, but he wanted to do his part for his country before settling down. They would be at Wakefield tomorrow, and soon they would be leaving again. She hoped it wouldn't be too soon.

Christina went upstairs to order a bath. She loved leisurely baths. They relaxed her and improved her frame of mind, just as riding did.

Christina decided to take special care with her attire, since this would be her last night in London. She chose a dark-burgundy evening dress and had Mary pile her blond curls into an elaborate new style. She arranged blood-red rubies in her hair and clasped a matching necklace around her neck. Her mother had left her rubies, sapphires, and emeralds to Christina. The diamonds and pearls were for John to give his wife when he married. Mother had told her once that her complexion and hair were too fair to wear diamonds, and Christina quite agreed.

Christina admired her reflection in the mirror. She loved to wear pretty clothes and jewelry. She knew she was pretty, but she couldn't believe she was as beautiful as everyone was fond of telling her. Her hair was such a light blond color that her high white forehead seemed to merge with her hairline. However, she was happy with her figure. Her breasts were full and perfect in shape, and her hips were slim, accentuating her long legs.

A knock at the door interrupted Christina's primping. John called from outside, "If you are ready, Crissy, I thought we might drive through the park one last time before going to dinner."

Opening the door, she saw John's admiring gaze. "I just have to get my cape and we can be off," she replied gaily.

"You are beautiful tonight, Crissy, but you are always beautiful."

"You're such a flatterer, John, but I like it," she teased. "Shall we go?"

Christina and John took a leisurely drive through Regent's Park before stopping before a lovely town house on Eustin Street. Tom and Anne Shadwell met them at the door, and John introduced them to Christina. Anne Shadwell was the smallest woman Christina had ever seen. She looked like a china doll, with her black hair and eyes and white complexion. Her husband was a big man like John, with rugged features.

"John, you're the last to arrive. My other guests are in the drawing

28

room," Tom Shadwell said as he led the way.

When they entered the drawing room, Christina couldn't help but see him. He was the tallest person in the room. Oh damn, she thought, he would spoil her last evening in London!

Philip Caxton saw Christina as soon as she entered the room. She turned away with contempt when she saw him. Well, he didn't expect an easy conquest. She had seemed to hate him last night.

It had been sheer luck running into John Wakefield this afternoon and learning from him that he and his sister would be here tonight. Paul knew Tom Shadwell and was able to get Philip and himself an invitation.

Philip also learned from John Wakefield that this was their last night in London, so he had to work fast. He hoped that Christina wouldn't be too affronted by his boldness, but he had no choice other than trying to win her over tonight. He would much rather take Christina to his home and make her his wife whether she protested or not, in the manner of his father's people. But he knew he couldn't do that, not here in England. He had to try to win her affections the civilized way.

He sighed, cursing the lack of time. But perhaps Christina Wakefield was just playing hard to get. After all, young women came to London to look for husbands. And he wasn't such a bad catch. But still, with only one day's acquaintance, the odds were against him. Damn, why hadn't he met her sooner?

Anne Shadwell drew Christina toward Philip. "Miss Wakefield, I would like to introduce —"

She was cut off abruptly.

"We've met," Christina said contemptuously.

Anne Shadwell looked startled, but Philip made an arrogantly graceful bow, took Christina's arm firmly, and walked her out onto the balcony. She resisted, but he was sure she wouldn't cause a scene.

When they reached the railing, she whirled to face him defiantly.

29

Her eyes sparkled wildly, and her voice was cold and heavy with contempt.

"Really, Mr. Caxton! I thought I made myself quite clear last night, but since you don't seem to understand, let me enlighten you. I don't like you. You are a rude, conceited man, and I find you quite intolerable. Now if you will excuse me, I am going back to join my brother." She turned to leave, but he grabbed her hand and pulled her back to him.

"Christina, wait," he demanded huskily, forcing her to look into his dark eyes.

"I really don't think we have anything to say to each other, Mr. Caxton. And please refrain from using my first name." She turned to leave again, but Philip still grasped her hand in his. She faced him once more, stamping her foot in fury.

"Let go of my hand!" she demanded.

"Not until you've heard what I have to say, Tina," he answered, pulling her closer to him.

"Tina!" she glared at him. "How dare —"

"I dare anything I damn well please. Now shut up and listen to me." He was amused at the disbelief written on her lovely face. "I spoke rudely about the young ladies last night simply to quiet my matchmaking brother. I never wanted to marry until I first saw you. Tina, I want you. I would be honored if you would consent to be my wife. I would give you anything you want — jewels, beautiful gowns, my estates."

She was looking at him in a most unusual way. She opened her mouth to say something, but the words wouldn't come out. And then he felt the sting of her hand across his cheek.

"I have never been so insulted in my —"

But Philip didn't let her finish. He gathered her in his arms and silenced her words with a deep, penetrating kiss. He held her tightly against him, feeling her breasts pressed against his chest, crushing the breath from her body. She was struggling to free herself, but her

30

efforts only increased his desire.

Then, unexpectedly, Christina went limp in his arms and threw him off guard. Philip thought she had fainted but winced when he felt a sharp pain in his shin. He released her instantly to grab his leg, and when he looked up, Christina was running into the drawing room. He saw her go to her brother, who left to get her cape and say something to their host. Then John escorted his sister out of the room.

Philip could still feel her lips on his. His desire had not yet ebbed as he turned to face the street and saw Christina and her brother enter their carriage and drive off. He watched until they were out of sight, then went to find Paul and ask him to make his excuses to Tom Shadwell. He was in no mood to suffer through dinner.

Paul started to protest, but Philip was already on his way out of the drawing room.

He should have known better, Philip told himself. He had pleaded with her like a fool. Well, that would be the last time. He'd never explained himself to a woman before, and he never would again. To think he actually thought to win her in one night. She was not some scullery maid who would jump at the chance to be rescued from drudgery. Christina was a lady born to luxury. She didn't need the wealth he could give her.

He should have gone to her home in Halstead and courted her slowly. But that wasn't his way. Besides, he had never courted a woman before. He was used to getting what he wanted immediately, and he wanted Christina.

Christina was shaking uncontrollably when she ran back into the drawing room. She could still feel Philip Caxton's lips on hers, his arms holding her pinned against him, the hardness between his legs pressing against her. So that was how a man kissed a woman. She had always wondered what it would be like. She hadn't expected the strange feeling that Philip Caxton had aroused in her: a feeling that both frightened and excited her.

31

Luckily she had remembered what her mother once told her: if a man accosted her and she wished to get away, pretend to faint and then kick him as hard as she could. It had worked, and she thanked her mother silently for her advice.

Christina calmed herself while her brother went for her cape. She told him she had a splitting headache and wished to leave immediately. When he came back they left for their carriage.

Looking up, she saw Philip Caxton on the balcony watching them leave. To think the man wanted her and had asked her to marry him knowing she disliked him! Of all the nerve, the outright audacity!

Now that she was safely away from Philip Caxton, she was furious. She had met him only yesterday, and today he had asked her to marry him — without one word of love. He declared only that he wanted her. He was even more impulsive than Peter or Sir Charles. They, at least, were gentlemen.

Thinking about it made her angrier. He was no gentleman! He acted like a barbarian! She wanted to go right back to that balcony and slap his arrogant face again.

Christina's feelings showed on her face, and John, who had been scrutinizing her quietly, finally interrupted her thoughts.

"Crissy, what on earth is the matter with you? You look fit to be tied. I thought you had a headache."

Focusing her attention on John, she absentmindedly put her hand to her forehead as if to feel for a pain, then burst forth heatedly.

"Headache! Yes, I had a headache, but I left him back on the balcony. John, that insufferable cad asked me to marry him."

"Who did?" John asked calmly.

"Philip Caxton, that's who! And he had the effrontery to kiss me — right there on the balcony."

John was amused. "It seems, dear sister, that you have encountered a man who knows what he wants and goes after it. You say he asked you to marry him, and after only one day's acquaintance? At least Browne and Buttler knew you a little longer than that. It looks as if

Philip Caxton truly wants you."

Remembering his words vividly, Christina stormed more. "Yes, he wants me. He even told me so, with no mention of love — just lust!"

John laughed. It wasn't often that he saw his sister so angry. If Caxton had tried to molest Crissy, John wouldn't be so amused, and he would have had to call the man out. But he could hardly blame Caxton for a kiss and a proposal of marriage. He would have done the same if he had found a woman as beautiful as Crissy.

"You know, Crissy, more times than not, desire does come before love. Had Caxton said he was in love with you, it probably would have been a lie. What he did state was the truth — that he wanted you. When a man finds a woman he can't live without, then he knows he's in love. I believe that love has to grow slowly and takes more time than just two days, or even two weeks. However, it seems that Philip Caxton was prepared to love you, since he proposed marriage. Instead of getting so angry, you might have taken it as a compliment."

Calming down slowly, Christina leaned back on the seat and stared moodily off into the distance.

"Well, it doesn't matter, anyway. I'll never see Philip Caxton again. I should never have come to London in the first place. The men here don't know their own minds. They all just compete for attention: each one boasting that he's better than the next. And men like Philip Caxton think anything can be theirs for the asking. This isn't the life for me. I guess I'm just a country girl at heart." Christina took a deep breath and exhaled slowly. "Oh, John, I'm glad we're going home."

33

Chapter 5

A pleasant breeze ruffled Christina's skirts as she and John boarded the ship that would carry them to Cairo. Christina was shown to a small cabin that she would have to share with another woman. John would be in the cabin directly across from hers. After their luggage was brought aboard, Christina went on deck for a last look at her beloved England. As she watched the seamen preparing to cast off, she recalled the frantic haste of the morning.

Christina had been awakened from another restless sleep by loud pounding on her door. Her brother entered the room and stood beside her bed, a forlorn expression on his handsome face. She noticed the paper he was holding as she wiped the sleep from her eyes.

"They came this morning, Crissy. I'm afraid I'll have to leave immediately."

"Who came?" she yawned. "What are you talking about?"

"My orders. They came sooner than expected," he replied, handing her the paper.

Christina read it slowly, shaking her head in disbelief. "Cairo!" she exclaimed. "But that's more than four thousand miles away."

"Yes, I know. I have to leave in an hour's time. I'm sorry I won't be able to escort you home, Crissy, but Howard said he would be glad to go with you. I'm going to miss you, little sister."

A smile crossed her lips. "No, you won't, big brother. I'm going with you! I decided a long time ago."

"That's ridiculous, Crissy! What would you do on a military post in Egypt? The weather is miserable. It's blazing hot and very unhealthy. You'd ruin your complexion!"

Throwing back the covers, Christina jumped from the bed and

faced John, hands on hips and a stubborn tilt to her chin.

"I'm going, John Wakefield, and that's all there is to it
miserable at home last year with you gone. I won't stand
Besides, we won't be in Egypt all that long." She spun about, ──
her belongings scattered about the room. "Oh, I'm wasting time! You
get out of here while I pack and get dressed. I won't be long, I
promise."

Christina pushed John out of the room and called Mary to help
with the packing. She had to hurry so John would have no excuse to
leave her behind.

She was dressed and ready to leave in less than an hour. John made
no more objections and even told her he was glad she was coming.

And now they were about to cast off for a strange land that
Christina knew very little about.

Looking over the other passengers, she thought it strange that her
brother was the only army officer on board.

"Crissy, you should have waited for me. I don't want you on deck
alone again!"

Christina was startled at his words, but relaxed as John joined her
at the rail. "Oh, John, you're being a mother hen. I'm perfectly all
right up here alone."

"Nevertheless, during the journey I'd rather you not come on deck
without an escort."

"Very well, if you insist," she gave in. "I was just thinking how
strange it is that there are no other officers on board. I thought
replacements usually traveled together."

"They usually do, I was wondering the same thing, but I won't
know the answer until we reach Cairo."

"Maybe they want you for something special!" Christina ventured.

"I doubt that, Crissy, but we'll find out when we land." John put
his arm around Christina's shoulder, and they watched England fall
behind them as the ship sailed out to sea.

It was a long, boring journey for Christina. She hated confinement, and the ship offered few pastimes. She made friends with her cabinmate, a Mrs. Bigley. Mrs. Bigley had been visiting her children at school in England, and now was returning to Egypt. Her husband was colonel of the very regiment where John was posted. But Mrs. Bigley couldn't tell Christina why her brother was being sent to Cairo. She knew only that the other replacements wouldn't be leaving for a month.

Since there could be no answers until the journey was over, Christina put the mystery out of her mind until then. She spent much time reading in her cabin or on deck, When she had exhausted all the books she had brought with her, she made frequent visits to the ship's small library.

Christina attracted three young gentlemen admirers early in the voyage who did their best to monopolize her time.

One was an American. His name was William Dawson, and he was a nice young man with soft gray eyes and dark brown hair. His face was lean and rugged, and his voice was very deep, with the strangest accent. Christina could sit and listen to him for hours as he told her exciting tales of the wild western frontier.

Though she liked Mr. Dawson, Christina wasn't interested romantically in any of her three beaux. She had decided that most men were alike; they only wanted one thing from a woman. None seemed willing to respect her as an equal.

The days rolled slowly by without incident. Christina could hardly believe it when they finally reached Egypt. The weather had turned much hotter as they moved south, and she was grateful for the summer clothes she had brought. John had sent for the rest of their clothes, but the trunks wouldn't arrive until next month.

Their ship docked in Alexandria the following morning. Christina couldn't wait to put her feet on solid earth again, but the dock was so crowded with Egyptians that disembarking passengers had to fight their way through the crowded mass.

John and Christina were standing on deck with their luggage when Mrs. Bigley came up and took Christina's hand. "My dear, do you remember when we discussed your brother's orders at the beginning of our voyage? Well, it has puzzled me ever since. My husband, Colonel Bigley, will be meeting me here, and it will be the first thing I ask him. If anyone knows why your brother was sent here early, my husband does. If you care to stay with me until I locate him, then you can learn the answer, too."

"Yes, of course," said Christina. "I'm dying to know, and I'm sure John is, too."

Mrs. Bigley waved to a portly gentleman in his late forties who must be her husband, the colonel. They walked down the gangplank toward him, and he met them on the dock. He embraced his wife and kissed her full on the lips.

"Godawful lonely here without you, love," the colonel said, holding his wife closely.

"I've missed you, too, love. I would like you to meet Lieutenant John Wakefield and his sister, Christina Wakefield." She looked to her husband. "Colonel Bigley."

John and the colonel saluted each other. "What on earth are you doing here a month early, Lieutenant? The replacements aren't expected to arrive until next month," Colonel Bigley said.

John said, "I was hoping you could answer that question for me, sir."

"What? You mean to tell me you don't know why you're here? Do you have your orders with you?"

"Yes, sir." John pulled his orders from the inside of his coat and handed them to the colonel.

After Colonel Bigley read the orders, he looked at John with a puzzled expression on his sunburned face. "Sorry, son, but I can't help you. All I can tell you is, *we* didn't send for you. Do you have any enemies in England who might have wanted you out of the country?"

John looked shocked. "I hadn't thought of that, sir. I have no enemies I know of."

"This is most unusual, but now that you're here, you must join us for some refreshment," Colonel Bigley said, drawing his wife's arm through his. "The train for Cairo doesn't leave for another two hours."

Colonel Bigley led the way through the crowd to a small café. They had a leisurely lunch in an open patio, and then left for the station.

William Dawson was there to say good-bye to Christina. He would call on her when he came to Cairo in a week's time, he said, and asked her not to promise *all* her time to other swains.

The train ride was hot and uncomfortable. It amused Christina that, with all the trains in England, she had had to come halfway across the world to ride on one. She much preferred the cool comfort of a coach, however, though it was a bit bumpy at times.

Mrs. Bigley and Christina shared a seat in the overcrowded salon. "I've heard there are many dangerous outlaws in the desert. Is it true that the Bedouin tribes make slaves of their captives?" Christina asked Mrs. Bigley nervously.

"It's all quite true, my dear," Mrs. Bigley returned. "But don't worry about it. The outlaw tribes fear Her Majesty's Army, as well they should! They hide in the Arabian Desert, which is quite far from Cairo."

"Well, that certainly is a relief," Christina sighed.

The train pulled into Cairo before nightfall. The Bigleys showed Christina and John to a hotel.

"After you get settled in your quarters, I'll show you the city in its entirety, and we can go to the Opera House," said Mrs. Bigley kindly. "Did you know that it was right here that the famous opera *Aida* was first produced, to celebrate the opening of the Suez Canal?"

"I didn't know, but I haven't read too much about this country," Christina replied. She was too tired to be overly interested in anything tonight. She and John thanked the Bigleys for their kindness, and bade them goodnight. John ordered a light supper, but Christina could eat very little, and retired early.

Her room was at the opposite end of the hall from John's, and a hot bath awaited her. She quickly shed her clothes and slid into the tub. This is heaven, she thought! The heat and crowded railway car had made her feel sticky and dirty. But now she luxuriated in the steaming hot water.

She lay there for an hour before rinsing off and donning her nightdress. The hot water had relaxed her, and she had no trouble falling off to sleep.

Chapter 6

Sometime in the middle of the night Christina was awakened from a peaceful sleep by a noise in her room. She opened her eyes to see a tall figure standing above her. Christina wondered what on earth John was doing standing beside her bed looking down at her in the dark. But then she realized it couldn't be John. This man was taller than John, and he had something covering his face.

She started to scream, but before she could make a sound, a huge hand clamped down over her mouth. She tried to push him away, but the man was too strong for her.

Suddenly he pulled her to him and kissed her painfully, crushing her body against his and running his free hand boldly over her breasts.

My God, she thought frantically, he's going to rape me! Christina started to struggle violently, but her attacker dropped her back onto the bed and quickly bound a gag over her mouth, tying it tightly behind her head. He pulled a sack over her head and pushed it down over her body, tying it around her knees. He picked her up and threw her over his shoulder.

Christina tried kicking her feet to throw him off balance, but he bounced her up in the air, so that the breath was knocked out of her as she landed back on his shoulder. She could tell he was walking, and she heard the bedroom door open and close.

They seemed to be descending stairs, and then she felt a slight breeze touch her bare feet. They must be outside. Oh God, what is this man going to do with me? Did I come to this Godforsaken country just to die — and how will I die? Will I be raped brutally first? Why did I ever leave England? Poor John, he will blame himself for my death. I have to get away!

Once more, Christina kicked and squirmed, but the man crushed her to him to still her efforts. He walked faster for a few minutes, then suddenly stopped. He spoke in the native language, then threw her over something. Christina squirmed, but stopped when she felt a painful whack across her buttocks.

A different voice muttered something, followed by a loud burst of laughter, and Christina felt herself bounced up and down. She knew then that she was lying across a horse, like a sack of potatoes. She almost laughed hysterically when the man pressed a hand into her back. Was he afraid she might fall off and hurt herself before he could hurt her?

Christina's heart was beating so fast she was afraid it would burst. Where is he taking me? she wondered, and then it dawned on her. Of course — they would be going into the desert. What better place to rape a woman than the desert — where her screams could not be heard. And there seemed to be several men riding with them. How many rapes would she have to endure before they killed her?

They rode for hours, but Christina lost track of time. Her hair was tangled over her face, and her stomach ached from the position she was in. She couldn't understand why they were taking her so far into the desert. Then they stopped.

It's going to happen now, she thought frantically as she was lowered to the ground. When she felt no hands on her she tried to run, but she forgot the sack was tied about her knees and fell forward onto the sand.

This was all the humiliation she could stand. She began to whimper. She would have been crying hysterically if she hadn't had the gag in her mouth. Someone picked her up and put her on her feet again. Her toes sank slowly into the cold desert sand.

Christina felt the rope being untied at her knees, and she lunged forward again. But she was pulled back and caught to a man's broad chest. He held her imprisoned in his powerful arms for what seemed like an eternity, then chuckled deeply. He lifted her up onto the horse, then mounted behind her. It seemed the man was at least going to let her ride upright with some dignity.

But why were they riding again? Why hadn't they done anything to her? Did they think to make her suffer more by keeping her in suspense? Then it came to her. Maybe they weren't going to kill her after all. Maybe they would sell her as a slave after raping her. Of course. She would probably bring a handsome sum at a slave auction. She would make an unusual attraction, with her long blond hair and slim white body. That was probably it, she thought miserably. They will use me and then sell me for a profit. That would be worse than dying.

Christina always said she would be a slave to no man in marriage. But now she would be a real slave — to a master who could do anything he wanted with her. She would have no say in the matter. She prayed they would kill her instead, for she couldn't bear to be a slave.

The hours dragged on slowly until Christina began to see light through the rough material of the sack and knew it must be dawn. She thought of John and of his misery when he found her gone. She doubted he would ever be able to find her, for they had been riding all night.

Where were they taking her? Christina could feel the sweat pouring down her sides and legs as the day grew hotter. She would curse this bastard to the devil if only he could understand her. She was exhausted.

Finally they stopped, but Christina didn't care anymore — she didn't want to think anymore. She was lowered to the ground again, her legs crumpling under her. She wasn't giving up, but she knew it was useless to run. The sun blinded her for a minute as someone dragged the sack up over her head. When she could see again, a short native was standing in front of her. He handed her a robe and a square piece of cloth with a cord, which was for the Bedouin headdress.

"Kufiyah," he said, pointing to the cloth. He untied the gag from

42

her mouth and walked away.

There were three of them. Two medium-sized young men, and one huge man who was watering the horses. The young man who gave her the robe and *kufiyah* came up again, smiling sheepishly, and handed her some bread and a skin of water. She was very hungry, for she had eaten little the night before.

When Christina finished eating, the big man came toward her and took the waterskin from her, tossing it to one of the other men. His *kufiyah* covered the lower half of his face, so she couldn't see what he looked like.

He was a big man for an Arab. She thought that Arabs were generally small, but this man dwarfed the other two.

He helped her on with the robe and pulled back her hair, which was hanging to her hips. At least he was helping her dress instead of taking her clothes off. He arranged the *kufiyah* on her head, then led her into the shade of a rock outcropping and pushed her down onto the cool sand.

Terrified, Christina shrank from him. But the big man just laughed harshly and walked away to help the others with the horses. They removed the rough blankets from the horses, rubbed them down, and left some grain for them in the shade. The shorter Arabs ate a little and lay down to rest, completely hidden under their black robes.

Christina looked around and saw the tall man climbing up the rocks, rifle in hand, to stand guard. She could not escape. She let her exhausted body relax, and slept.

The sun was low on the horizon when Christina awoke. The horses stood ready, and the tall man swung her up onto the horse in front of him.

Christina could see mountains in the far distance and an ocean of sand in front of them. She gave up and leaned on the man behind her. She thought she heard him laugh, but she was still too tired to care. She slept again.

They rode three more nights, resting during the hottest part of the days. Finally they started to climb out of the desert. Christina could see trees around them, and she felt the air becoming cooler. They must be climbing high into the mountains if it was getting colder, she thought.

She wished desperately that this living nightmare were truly just a bad dream. Soon she would wake up at her home in Halstead to the cool morning breezes, have breakfast, and then go for a leisurely ride on Dax. But she knew that it wasn't a dream. She would never see Dax or her home again.

A fire blazed up ahead of them. One of the men with her shouted something, and then they rode slowly out of the trees that had shrouded them and into an encampment. There were five tents, one larger than the rest, circled around the fire. The fire was the only source of light, and it cast dancing shadows upon everything within its reach.

Four native men with smiles on their dark faces approached, and all started talking and laughing. The women of the camp came out of their tents with curiosity shining in their eyes, but they hung back from the group of men.

Christina was lifted to the ground. She realized that she must be at the end of her journey. She had to try to save herself from the fate that awaited her. Perhaps she could hide in the mountains and then somehow find her way back to civilization.

More men joined the group by the fire. They all crowded around her tall captor, talking and gesturing. Christina was momentarily standing alone. Did they expect her to stand there calmly and await her fate?

Lifting the robe and nightdress up to her thighs, Christina started to run. She ran for her life, with a speed she didn't know she had. She didn't know if they were chasing her. All she could hear was the loud pounding of her heart. The *kufiyah* came off her head, and her hair flew wildly in the wind behind her.

Christina stumbled and fell headlong. She looked up and saw two

44

feet straddled in front of her. She threw herself on the hard earth and started to cry. She couldn't help her tears, but hated to show this man her weakness. He had won a victory by making her cry. He pulled her roughly to her feet and dragged her back into camp.

Christina was taken into the largest of the tents and deposited unceremoniously on a backless couch with low, rounded arms at each end. She immediately tried to compose herself, pushing her tangled hair away from her face and wiping the tears from her cheeks.

The tent was quite large inside and was curtained on three sides with a sheer material through which the fire outside brightly illuminated the room. Multicolored rugs covered the floor, and the fourth side of the tent was of a heavy material. Christina could see another room where the material was drawn aside.

The main room was sparsely furnished. Another light-blue-velvet couch faced the one she was sitting on near the back of the tent, with a long, low table between them. A small cabinet stood in one corner at the back of the tent, with a single jeweled goblet and a goatskin bag on top. Many small pillows in bright colors were scattered on the two couches and on the floor beside them.

Christina watched her captor. The tall man had his back to her as he removed his *kufiyah* and robe. He laid them on top of the cabinet and poured something from the goatskin into the goblet. He wore knee-length suede boots, a short tunic, and loose-fitting trousers tucked inside his boots.

Christina was startled when the man spoke to her in perfect English.

"I can see that you're going to be very difficult to manage, Tina. But now you're here and you know that you belong to me, perhaps you will not try to run away so often."

Christina couldn't believe what she heard. The man turned around to face her. Her eyes widened in shock, and her mouth fell open.

He burst out laughing. "I've waited a very long time to see that

45

expression on your face, Tina, ever since you left me that night in London."

What was he talking about? He must be crazy!

Her cheeks flushed red with anger, and her body shook with rage. "You!" she screamed. "What are you doing here, and how dare you kidnap me and bring to this Godforsaken place? My brother will kill you, Philip Caxton!"

He laughed again. "So you're no longer afraid of me, Tina. That's good. I don't think I would care to hear you begging and pleading with me for mercy."

"I would never give you that satisfaction, Mr. Caxton." Christina stood up and faced him, her hair flowing to her hips. "Now would you kindly tell me why you've brought me here? If it's ransom you're after, my brother will give you anything you want. Only I'd like the matter handled quickly, so I may leave this place and your company."

He smiled at her. His unusual eyes held her hypnotized. Why did he have to be so damned handsome, she thought irrelevantly.

"I suppose I should enlighten you about why I've brought you here." Philip sat down on the couch across from her and motioned for her to do the same. He drained his goblet, and studied her intently before continuing.

"I don't usually explain myself to anyone, but I suppose I can make an exception in your case." He paused, as if to find the words he wanted to use. "Christina, the first time I laid eyes on you at the ball in London, I knew I wanted you. So I tried it your way. I declared my feelings to you and offered you marriage. When you refused, I decided to have you my own way, and quickly. I arranged for your brother to be sent to this country the night you refused me."

"So it was *you* who had my brother sent here!" she gasped.

"You will not interrupt again until I am finished. Is that clear?" Philip asked brusquely.

Christina nodded her head, only because her curiosity demanded she hear him out.

46

"As I said, I arranged for your brother to be sent here. It was only a question of knowing the right people. If you had decided to stay in England, I wouldn't have had too much trouble taking you away to my home with your brother gone. You would have found it easier to escape me there, but I could have had you sooner. Here you will have less chance to get away from me. It's the way of the land here to take captives, so don't expect any help from the people of my camp." Philip smiled wickedly at her. "You're mine now, Tina. The sooner you realize that, the better it will be for you."

Flying off the couch, Christina paced the floor in fury. "I cannot believe what you've told me! How could you possibly imagine that I'd marry you after what you've done to me?"

"Marry!" he laughed. "I offered you marriage once, I will not again. I don't have to marry you to have you in this land!" He came to her and took her in his arms. "You may call yourself my slave, but not my wife."

"I will be no man's slave! I'll kill myself before I'll submit to you!" Christina screamed, and fought to escape his embrace.

"Do you think that I'd let you kill yourself, after I've waited so long for you?" Philip murmured huskily. He lowered his lips to hers and kissed her passionately, holding her head with one hand and both of her arms with the other.

Christina felt a strange sensation creeping through her body again. Did she enjoy his kiss? But that was impossible. She hated him!

She went limp in his arms, but before she could manage to kick out, Philip picked her up, and his laughter rang through the tent.

"That little trick of yours won't work again, Tina."

Philip carried Christina through the heavy curtains to his bed. When she saw his intent, she began to fight in earnest, but he dropped her onto the bed and lay down beside her. She beat at his chest with her fists until he pulled both of her arms above her head and held them there with one hand.

"I think I'll see now if your body matches your beautiful face."

Philip untied the robe she was wearing. He threw his leg over her to still her kicking and, with one rending tear, ripped her nightdress apart.

Christina screamed, only to find his lips on hers and his tongue probing deeply in her mouth. But this time his kiss was soft and gentle, making her head spin with mixed feelings. He moved his lips to her neck and with his free hand boldly caressed her full, ripe breasts.

Searching her eyes for a response, Philip smiled down into her face. "You're even more beautiful than I had dreamed possible. Your body was made for love. I want you, Tina," he whispered huskily. Then he lowered his lips to her breasts, kissing each one in turn. Christina felt on fire.

She had to say something to make him stop. She was no match for his strength. "You're no gentleman, Mr. Caxton. Must you rape me against my will," she asked coldly, "knowing that I hate you?"

Philip looked at her then, and she could see the desire fade from his dark green eyes. He released her and stood up beside the bed. He gazed down at her, and his mouth was hard, matching the cold glint in his eyes.

"I've never claimed to be a gentleman, but I will not rape you. When I make love to you, it will be because you want it as much as I. And you will want me, Tina. I promise you that."

"Never!" she hissed, pulling her clothes across her body. "I will never want you. I hate you with all my being."

"We shall see, Tina," Philip answered, and turned away.

"And would you stop calling me Tina? It is not my name!" she yelled at him, but he had already left the tent.

Christina tied the robe across her torn nightdress and glanced about the room. But there was nothing to see, only a single chest beside the huge bed with its heavy sheepskin cover.

Sliding under the cover, Christina mused over what he had said. So — he would not rape her. If he was a man of his word, she would

48

be quite safe, for she knew she could never want him. Why should she ever want any man? Desire was a man's emotion, not a woman's.

But what if he didn't keep his word? She hadn't the strength to stop him if he decided to take her by force. What then? And what the devil was he doing in Egypt, anyway? He acted like a native, and the tribe seemed to accept him as one of them. She couldn't understand it, and the question kept going through her mind without answers.

When she thought of the lengths Philip Caxton had gone to, to get her here, she became furious again. To think that she had come all the way across the ocean only to be abducted by a madman! Well, she wouldn't be here long if she could help it. With thoughts of escape running through her mind, Christina finally went to sleep.

Chapter 7

Damn, but Christina could be a bitch when she wanted to, Philip thought. Well, her day would come, and he would take great pleasure in making her admit her desire for him.

Late as it was, Philip left the tent to visit Sheik Yasir Alhamar, his father, for he knew the old man would be waiting for him.

Yasir Alhamar had been sheik of the tribe for over thirty-five years. He had captured his first wife, an English lady of noble family, while raiding a caravan. She lived with Yasir for five years, giving him two sons, Philip and Paul.

During those days, the tribe lived a nomadic life on the desert, and the climate and hard life aged Philip's mother quickly. She begged to go home to England with her sons. Yasir loved her very much and let her go. But she promised him to let his sons return to Egypt when they came of age, if they chose.

Philip was raised and schooled in England. When he was twenty-one years of age, his mother told him about his father. Philip decided to find Yasir and live with him. When Philip's mother died five years ago, he inherited the estate. He left it in the care of the Caxtons' estate manager, since he didn't want to live in England and his brother was still in school.

Philip lived with his father's tribe eleven years, but finally went back to England a year ago to attend his brother's wedding. Paul had talked him into staying for a while. Then he met Christina Wakefield, and decided to make her his.

Philip had followed Christina and John Wakefield to the dock and waited patiently until their ship departed. It was sheer luck that he managed to obtain passage on a cargo ship. He left the same day, but docked a week before Christina's ship.

When he arrived, he contacted Saadi and Ahmad, and had them bring his horse, Victory, to meet him in Cairo. Saadi and Ahmad were good comrades; they were also distant cousins of his. The whole tribe was distantly related to him.

Philip had a half-brother here who was eight years younger than he. But they didn't get along too well. He could understand why, since Rashid would have become head of the tribe if Philip had stayed in England.

Yasir Alhamar was sitting up on the sheepskins that served as his bed. He still lived the traditional nomadic way, with little furniture and few comforts. Philip could remember how his father had laughed at him when he carted his bed and furniture up to the hillside encampment.

"So, you are still an Englishman, Abu. I had thought you would be used to sleeping and eating on the ground after so long," Yasir had said.

"At least I stole the items, father," Philip had returned.

"Ah, so there is still some hope left for you," Yasir had replied, laughing.

When Yasir saw Philip, he motioned him to enter and sit down beside him. "It has been a long time, my son. I have been told of the woman you brought into camp tonight. Is she your woman?"

"She will be, father. I first saw her in London and knew that I had to have her. I arranged for her brother to be sent here, and now she is mine. She fights me now, but it will not take too long to tame her."

Yasir laughed. "You are truly my son. You have stolen your woman, just as I stole your mother. Your mother also fought me in the beginning, but I believe she grew to love me as I did her, for she married me. Perhaps if we had lived in the mountains then, she would have stayed with me, but she couldn't survive in the desert climate.

51

I would have gone with her, but I have lived all my life here, and I could not survive in your civilized England," he said. "Perhaps you will give me grandchildren before I die."

"Perhaps, father, we shall see. I will bring her to you tomorrow, but now I must return."

His father nodded, and Philip went back to his tent. He entered to find a meal awaiting him, and sat down to eat and muse over the girl sleeping in his bed.

He wouldn't be able to wait very long to have her, with her now-constant nearness. It had been too long since he had bedded a woman, and Christina's body was driving him crazy. He remembered her breasts, full under his caress; her tiny waist and slim smooth hips; her long legs, perfectly formed; her skin like satin; her hair — he could lose himself in that golden mass of curls.

Christina's eyes fascinated him. They had turned a dark, stormy blue when she discovered it was he who had abducted her. He had waited a long time to see that reaction. He laughed again as he remembered the shock on her face that had quickly turned to anger.

Well, perhaps he would give her a little time to get used to her new home, but not too much time. Tomorrow would do.

He undressed and gently eased his way into the bed. Christina was curled into a ball with her back to him. Philip considered undressing her, but that would only wake her and he was too tired to suffer her rage. He smiled when he thought of her reaction when she found him in bed beside her in the morning. Well, at least Christina was here beside him, even if it was against her will. She would have to accept the situation eventually. Philip closed his eyes and let sleep overtake him.

Chapter 8

When Christina Wakefield awoke the next morning, a smile on her lips, for she had been dreaming of running through a field at home in Halstead. Her blue-green eyes widened in surprise when she saw the man lying in bed beside her. Then she remembered where she was and how she had come to be in this predicament.

What audacity! she thought furiously. She never expected he would share the same bed with her. This was too much to bear; she had to escape from this man!

Easing herself from the bed, Christina turned to see if she had awakened him, Philip Caxton slept soundly, an innocent, self-satisfied expression on his face. Cursing him silently, she cautiously tiptoed around the bed and between the heavy curtains that hid the bedroom from the rest of the tent.

Smelling the aroma of food coming from somewhere in the camp, Christina realized how hungry she was. She had eaten nothing the night before. But she couldn't think of food now. She had to get away while Philip was still asleep.

Christina pulled back the material covering the tent entrance and peered out. Luckily she could see no one about the camp. Well, it is now or never, she thought.

Gathering courage, Christina started walking out of the camp. As soon as she passed the last tent, she started running wildly, veering off the main path in case Philip came looking for her. The rocks cut her bare feet as she hurried through the wild olive trees.

She prayed silently that no one had seen her leaving the camp. If only she could reach the bottom of the mountain, she could hide herself and hope for a passing caravan to take her back to her brother.

Then Christina heard the sound of a horse trampling the brush behind her. All her hopes shattered when she turned to see Philip galloping his beautiful Arabian stallion up to her. His eyes were a dark, turbulent green, and his expression was full of black rage.

"Damn you!" she screamed. "How did you find me so fast?"

"You damn me! I was the one who was awakened from a sound sleep to be told by Ahmad that you were running down the mountainside. What do I have to do, woman? Must I tie you to my bed at night to ensure that you'll not escape me while I sleep? Is that what you want?"

"You wouldn't dare!"

"I told you once, Christina, that I dare anything I damn well please." Philip jumped off his horse with the ease of a mountain cat. His face was hard, his eyes dangerous and cold as he grabbed her by the shoulders and shook her roughly. "I should beat you for running away from me! That's what any self-respecting Arab would do to his woman."

"I am not your woman!" she said, her eyes flashing murderously at him. "Nor will I ever be!"

"That's where you're wrong, Christina, for you are and shall remain my woman until I tire of you."

"No, I won't! And you have no right to keep me here. My God, can't you see how much I hate you? You're everything that I despise in a man. You're a — a barbarian!"

"Yes, I suppose I am. But if I were a civilized gentleman, I wouldn't have you here where I want you. And like it or not, I will keep you here, tied to my bed if necessary," he replied coldly. He picked her up and deposited her roughly across the back of his horse.

"Why must I ride this way?" Christina demanded indignantly.

"I'd think that you'd be happy with this light punishment," he said. "You deserve much worse."

Philip mounted the horse behind her, and when she started to struggle he brought his hand down hard across her buttocks. Christina

54

stopped her kicking but fumed silently all the way back to camp.

Damn him, she thought vindictively. Someday she would take extreme pleasure in seeing Philip suffer. Why was this happening to her? She had always been proud — proud of her family, proud of their estate, proud of her own fiery beauty and independence. It was doubly painful to be brought so low now. It was degrading to be just a toy for this hateful man. She didn't deserve this. No one deserved this!

When they reached his tent, Philip dismounted, lifted Christina off the horse, and pushed her inside. She sat down on one of the couches to await whatever would happen next.

Philip spoke to someone outside the tent, came in, and sat down beside her. "There is food coming. Are you hungry?" he asked, the harshness gone from his voice.

"No," she lied. But when a young girl brought in a platter of food, nothing could have stopped Christina from eating her fill.

Philip finished eating before she did, and leaned back on the couch behind her. She felt him gather her hair in his hands and play with it gently. Christina stopped eating and turned to look into his smiling green eyes.

"Would you like to bathe, my sweet?" Philip asked her, rubbing a lock of her golden hair between his fingers.

Christina couldn't deny that she would love a bath. While she finished eating, Philip left the tent and came back shortly with a skirt, a blouse, a pair of slippers, and what she assumed was a towel. She wondered who they belonged to, but she was not about to ask.

Philip led Christina from the tent and across the camp. There was a young woman about Christina's age playing with a small child in front of the tent to the left of Philip's. Goats and sheep grazed on the hills above the camp, and a corral housed ten or twelve of the finest Arabian horses she'd ever seen, including two new foals. She wished that she could stop to look at the horses, but Philip led her out of the camp and up a path into the mountains.

Christina pulled away from him. "Where are you taking me?" she demanded. But he grabbed her arm again and continued walking.

"You wished to bathe, did you not?" he asked, leading her into a small clearing that was surrounded by tall juniper trees.

A large pond in the middle of the clearing had been formed by the mountain rains. It was a beautiful place, but Christina wondered why Philip had brought her here. He took the clothes from her and handed her a bar of sweet-smelling soap.

"You don't expect me to bathe here, do you?" she asked haughtily.

"Look, Tina, you're not in England anymore where you can have a nice hot bath sent up to your room. You're here now, and if you wish to bathe, you will do as the rest of us do."

"All right. I must wash after that horrible journey. If this is the only way that I will be able to bathe, then so be it. You may leave now, Mr. Caxton."

Philip grinned at her. "No, my lady, I have no intention of leaving." He sat down on a log and lazily crossed his legs. She noticed that the yellow flecks in his eyes brightened in the sunlight.

A slow blush crept into Christina's face. "You can't possibly mean that you are going to stay here and" — she paused, not wanting to finish — "and watch me!"

"That's exactly what I intend to do. So you may proceed if you will." He was staring at her intently with a wicked grin on his lips. Her blood boiled.

"Well, turn around so I can disrobe!"

"Ah, Tina. You will have to learn that I will not be denied the pleasure of looking at your body, even if I haven't possessed it yet," he replied.

Christina glared at him with stormy blue eyes. This man left her no dignity.

"I hate you," she hissed. She turned around and untied her robe. The robe and torn nightdress slid down over her body and dropped to the ground. Christina stepped out of the clothes and walked into the water; deeper and deeper until it covered her breasts.

She'd give him no pleasure if she could help it. She kept her back to Philip and washed herself under the deliciously cool water. She submerged to wet her hair, but it took a long time to build up enough lather to give it a thorough scrubbing with the bar of soap. When she finally succeeded, she heard a large splash.

Christina turned around quickly, but she couldn't see Philip anywhere. Suddenly he was standing directly in front of her. She was all too aware that they were both naked underneath the cool water.

Philip shook the water from his thick black hair and reached to take Christina in his arms, but she was prepared and threw the bar of soap at him. She swam away quickly. She stopped when she heard him laughing, and turned around to see that he hadn't moved, but was washing himself with the soap.

The relief showed openly on Christina's face as she finished rinsing her hair and emerged from the water. Quickly she toweled herself dry and wrapped the towel around her hair. She wrapped the long, dark-brown skirt around her waist, tying it in front. Next, she put on the dark-green sleeveless blouse with a low, rounded neckline. The rough cotton material irritated her skin, but she would have to make do with whatever he gave her.

Christina sat down and was trying to comb the tangles from her hair with her fingers when Philip came up behind her.

"Feel better now, my sweet?" he ventured softly.

She refused to answer him or look at him, and busied herself with braiding her hair while Philip dressed. Christina couldn't keep quiet for long, however, because her curiosity was stronger than her unwillingness to talk to him.

"Philip, what are you doing in this land, and how do these people know you so well?" she asked.

His laughter rang through the clearing. "I was wondering when you would start asking questions," he said. "These are my father's people."

Christina was stunned. "Your father! But you're English!"

"Yes, I'm English through my mother, but my father is an Arab and these are his people."

"You're half-Arab, then?" Christina interrupted, finding it hard to believe.

"Yes, and my father captured my mother, just as I have captured you. He let her return to England later with my brother and myself. So I was raised in England until I came of age. Then I chose to come here and live with my father."

"Your father is here?"

"Yes, you will meet him later."

"Surely your father doesn't approve of your kidnapping me?" she asked, hoping his father might help her.

"I have done nothing to you yet — but yes, my father approves," he said, a smile playing on his lips. "You forget, Tina, this isn't England. It's the way of my people to take what we want if we can. And I made sure you were available for the taking. You will understand better after you have been here awhile."

He escorted her back to his tent and left her there alone.

Would she ever understand Philip Caxton? Christina looked around the tent, wondering what she was supposed to do with herself. She suddenly felt quite lonely, and it annoyed her.

Without thinking, Christina raced out of the tent to see Philip mounting his horse along with four other riders. She ran to him and clutched his leg. "Where are you going?" she demanded.

"I will be back shortly."

"But what am I supposed to do with myself while you're gone?"

"That's an absurd question, Christina. Do whatever you women usually do when you're alone."

"Why, of course, Mr. Caxton," she said flippantly. "Why didn't I think of that? I can make use of your sewing room, though it's not really necessary — I'm used to wearing hand-me-downs. Or perhaps I could take care of your correspondence. I'm sure you must be a

58

busy man and can't find time to do it yourself. But if you'd rather, I could just browse through your well-stocked library. I'm sure I can find some thing interesting to read there. I do have a mind as well as a body, Mr. Caxton!"

"Sarcasm doesn't suit you, Christina," Philip said angrily.

"Of course, you're a better authority on what suits me than I am," Christina retorted.

"Christina, I will not tolerate this tirade of yours any longer. You may act as you please in our tent, but in public you will show me respect!" he replied, the muscles twitching dangerously in his jaw as he stared down at her.

"Respect!" She stood back to look at him, slightly amused. "You want respect after the way you've treated me?"

"In this land when a woman shows disrespect to her husband she is beaten."

"You're not my husband," she corrected.

"No, but I'm the same as a husband to you. I'm your master, and you belong to me. If you'd like me to find a whip and bare your back in public, I'll be happy to oblige you. Otherwise, return to my tent."

He said it so coldly that Christina didn't wait to see if he would carry out his threat. She scurried back into the tent and threw herself onto the bed to cry out her frustrations.

Must she now fear a beating as well as rape? That devil wanted respect after what he'd done! But she'd be damned if she'd show him anything but hate and contempt.

She detested feeling sorry for herself, but what was she supposed to do whenever he left? For that matter, what was she going to do when Philip was around? She cried herself to sleep.

Christina was rudely awakened by a hearty whack on her behind. She turned quickly to see Philip standing by the side of the bed, hands on his hips and a taunting smile on his handsome face.

"You spend a lot of time sleeping in that bed, my sweet. Would you like me to show you another way to use it?"

Christina jumped off the bed. She was finding it easier to understand his crude meanings.

"I'm quite sure I can do without that kind of knowledge, Mr. Caxton." Christina faced him with her arms akimbo, feeling safe with the bed between them.

"Well, you'll learn soon enough. And I'd prefer you to address me as Philip or Abu, as I am called here. I think it's time you dispensed with the formalities."

"Well, I'd prefer to continue the formalities, Mr. Caxton. At least your people will know that I'm not here willingly," she said flippantly.

Philip grinned devilishly. "Oh, they know you're not here of your own free will, but they also know that I'm not a man to be kept waiting. They assume you were deflowered last night. Perhaps tonight you will be."

Christina's eyes flew open and turned a darker shade of blue.

"But you — you promised! You gave me your word you wouldn't rape me. Don't you have any scruples at all?"

"I always keep my word, Tina. I will not have to rape you. As I told you before, you'll want me as much as I want you."

"You must be crazy. I will never want you! How could I want you when I detest you with all my being?" she stormed. "You've taken me away from my brother and from everything I love. You keep me prisoner here with a guard at the door when you leave. I hate you!"

Christina stalked from the room, silently cursing him with every horrible word she could think of. Suddenly she noticed two stacks of books and at least a dozen bolts of cloth lying on a couch. She forgot her anger and ran over to examine the goods.

There were silks, satins, velvets, and brocades in some of the most beautiful colors she had ever seen. There was even a bolt of semi-transparent cotton that she could use to make chemises. Threads of every matching color, scissors, intricate trims, and everything she

60

would possibly need to make beautiful dresses were lying before her.

She turned to the books, picking them up one by one. There were Shakespeare, Defoe, Homer. . . . Some she had read before, and some were by authors she'd never heard of. Lying beside the books was a beautifully carved ivory comb-and-brush set.

Christina was delighted. She felt like a small child on her birthday receiving an abundance of presents that would last until another birthday came. Philip had been standing behind her, watching her joy at the surprise. She swung around to face him now, her eyes a soft blue-green again surrounded by their dark ring.

"Are these for me?" she inquired demurely, running her hand over a bolt of soft blue velvet that matched her eyes.

"They were, but I don't know if I should give them to you after the way you have been acting," he said.

His eyes gave no clue whether he was teasing her or not. She suddenly felt desperate.

"Please, Philip! I'll die without anything to occupy my time."

"Perhaps you could give me something in return," he replied huskily.

"You know I can't. Why must you torture me so?"

"You jump to conclusions, my sweet. What I had in mind was a kiss — an honest kiss with some feeling in it."

Christina took one more look at the bounty of goods on the couch. What harm could one little kiss do, she thought, if it would get her what she wanted? She came to him and waited, eyes closed, but he did nothing. She opened her eyes and stared into his amused ones.

"I asked you to give the kiss, my lady, with feeling." He smiled down at her.

After a moment's hesitation, Christina put her arms around his neck and drew his lips down to hers. She opened her mouth to his. The kiss began softly, then his tongue penetrated deeply. The butterfly feeling came over her again, but this time she didn't fight it. His arms went around her, crushing her body to his. She could feel the hardness between his legs as he lowered his lips to leave a trail of fire across her neck.

Philip picked her up and began to carry her into the bedroom. Christina started to struggle.

"A kiss was all you asked for! Please put me down," she begged.

"Damn you, woman! The time will come when you'll gladly go with me. I promise you that."

He set her down and went outside. A smile crossed Christina's lips when she saw that she'd won again. But how long did she have before her luck ran out? Philip's kiss stirred something in her that she didn't understand. It left her empty, wanting something more, but she didn't know what.

After a few minutes, Philip came back into the room, followed by a girl who brought in the evening supper. When she left, Philip spoke harshly.

"We will eat now, and afterward I'll take you to meet my father. He has been expecting us."

They ate silently, but Christina was too nervous to enjoy the meal. She was a little afraid of meeting Philip's father. If he was anything like his son, then she had much to fear.

"Couldn't this meeting be put off for a few days until I can make something more presentable to wear than this?" she asked.

Philip frowned at her. "My father has lived his whole life here. He's not used to fancy gowns and dresses on women. What you're wearing will be quite suitable for the occasion."

"And whose clothes am I wearing? Did they belong to your last mistress?" Christina asked distastefully.

"You have a sharp tongue, Tina. The clothes belong to Amine, the girl who brought in the food. Amine is the wife of Syed, one of my distant cousins."

Christina felt ashamed, but she wasn't about to admit it.

"Shall we go? My father is eager to meet you."

Philip took her hand and led her to a smaller tent to the right of his. They entered, and she saw an old man sitting on the floor in the middle of the tent.

"Come in, my children. I have been looking forward to this meeting." The old man beckoned them to enter.

Philip led her across the room and sat down on a sheepskin across from his father, pulling her down beside him.

"I would like you to meet Christina Wakefield," Philip said to his father, then looked to her. "My father, Sheik Yasir Alhamar."

"You must stop calling me sheik, Abu. It is you who are the sheik now," Philip's father scolded.

"I shall always think of you as sheik, my father. Do not ask me to stop addressing you with respect."

"Well, it does not matter between us. So this is the woman that you could not live without," Yasir said, staring intently at Christina. "Yes, I can see why you had to have her. You are a pleasure to look at, Christina Wakefield. I hope you will give me many beautiful grandchildren before I die."

Christina's eyes flew open wide, and her face quickly turned a becoming shade of pink. "Grandchildren! Why, I —"

Philip cut her off abruptly. "You will say no more." He glared at her, daring her to disobey him.

"It is all right, Abu. I can see that your Christina still has a lot of fight in her. Your mother was the same way when I first brought her to my camp. Only I was not so kind as you, for I had to beat her once."

Christina gasped in horror, but Yasir smiled at her knowingly.

"This shocks you, Christina Wakefield? Well, it did not sit well with me, either, after the deed was done. You must understand that I had been drinking heavily at the time and was in a blind rage because she was flirting openly with the men of my camp. She admitted to me afterward that she had been purposely trying to make me jealous enough to marry her.

"I never raised a hand against her after that, and we married the very next day. I had five treasured years with her, and she gave me my sons, Abu and Abin. But she could not endure the desert heat, so when she begged to go home, I could not refuse her. I still grieve over her death. I always will."

Philip's father had a sorrowful look in his dark-brown eyes, as if he were remembering those long-ago years of happiness. He only nodded, without looking at them, when Philip said they would come again.

Christina felt sorry for Yasir, who had had only five years with the woman he loved, but she had no such feelings for Philip. When they returned to his tent, she faced him with flashing dark-blue eyes.

"I will not give him grandchildren!" she stormed.

"What?" Philip laughed at her. "That's just an old man's dream. I don't expect you to give me any children. That's not why I brought you here."

"Then why did you bring me here?" Christina yelled at him shrilly.

"I have already told you, Tina. You're here for my pleasure. Because I want you," he replied simply.

He reached for her, and Christina moved away swiftly, her anger replaced by fear. "Where can I put these bolts of material?" she asked to distract him.

"I'll see if I can find you a chest next week. For now, you can leave them where they are. Come, let us go to bed," he said, and started to walk into the bedroom.

"It's only just dark, and I'm not tired. Besides, I won't sleep in that bed with you. And you have no right to force me!" She sat down and started to unbraid her hair.

Philip came over to the couch and picked her up in his arms. "I did not say we were going to sleep, my sweet," he chuckled wickedly.

"No!" she cried. "Put me down this instant!"

Philip smiled down at her as he carried her into the bedroom and threw her on the bed. "I told you you'd give me pleasure. Take off your clothes, Tina."

"I will do no such thing," Christina retorted indignantly.

She started to get off the bed, but it was a futile gesture, because Philip swiftly pulled her over to the middle of the bed and straddled her hips with his knees. He pulled the blouse over her head, pinning her arms with one hand, though she fought him with all her strength. He untied her skirt and rolled her over to pull it off.

"You can't do this. I won't stand for it!" she cried, trying desperately to push him away.

He laughed heartily. "When will you learn, my little one, that I'm master here? What I wish to do — I do."

Looking into her dark-blue eyes, Philip could see her fear, but he would not stop.

"Damn it, Tina. I gave you my word I wouldn't rape you, but I made no promise that I wouldn't kiss you or touch your body. Now be still!" he said harshly. He brought his lips forcefully down on hers.

Philip kissed her long and brutally. Christina felt so strange. Did she actually enjoy his kisses? Her breasts, her belly, her whole body tingled and felt tautly alive.

Philip released her and stood up beside the bed. He caressed her body with dark-green eyes as he removed his clothing piece by piece and threw it aside. Christina's eyes widened when she saw his naked desire. Fear gripped her, and she jumped from the bed, trying one last time to escape. But Philip grabbed her long braid as she ran, and pulled her forceably into his arms.

"You have nothing to fear from me, Tina," he said, pushing her down onto the bed.

He moved his lips over her face and down her neck, but when they nibbled at her breasts, she began to fight him again. He caught her arms and pulled them firmly above her head with one hand.

"Don't fight me, Tina. Relax and enjoy what I can do for you," he whispered deeply.

While Philip continued to kiss her peaking breasts, he rested his free hand on her upper thigh. When he moved his hand upward to the golden triangle of hair below her navel, Christina moaned and begged Philip to stop.

"I have only just started, Tina," he murmured, and pushed his knee between her legs to open them.

Christina felt on fire as Philip stroked her delicately between her legs. He covered her mouth with his as she began to moan softly. She didn't want him to stop now. She wanted to know the end of this strange tingling feeling inside her.

Philip released her hands and rolled on top of her. He held her head between his huge hands and kissed her hungrily. She could feel his hardness between her legs, but she didn't care anymore. Her mind cried out for him to stop, but her body demanded that he go on. Christina knew then that Philip was right. She hated her body for betraying her, but she wanted him.

She felt him start to enter her slowly. But he stopped and looked into her eyes.

"I want you, Tina. You are mine, and I want to make love to you. Do you want me to stop now? Do you want me to let you go?" He was smiling down at her, knowing that he had won. "Tell me, Tina, tell me not to stop."

She hated him, but he couldn't leave her now. She circled her arms around his neck. "Don't stop," she whispered breathlessly.

She felt a searing pain as he pushed deep into her. His lips muffled her scream as she raked her nails down his back.

"I'm sorry, Tina, that had to happen. It will never hurt again — I promise." He started to move slowly inside her.

He was right. It didn't hurt anymore. Her pleasure rose as Philip quickened his pace. Christina abandoned herself to him completely as she met each thrust. He took her higher and higher until her eyes flew open and she became one with him.

Philip showed her pleasure that she never knew existed. But now that she lay exhausted beneath him, she hated him all the more. She cursed herself for her newfound weakness. She said she would never give in to him, but she had, and she could not forgive herself.

Christina opened her eyes to find Philip staring at her, an unreadable expression on his face.

"I will never give you up, Tina. You will always be mine," he murmured softly. Then he rolled off her, but pulled her to him until her head rested on his shoulder. "And I give you warning. If you ever try to run away from me again, I will find you and whip the hide off your lovely back. I give you my word."

Christina remained silent. Soon she could hear his deep, even breathing and knew that Philip was asleep. She edged herself away from him and slipped off the bed.

Picking up Philip's robe, Christina put it on and left the tent. The fire in the middle of the camp burned brightly and cast dancing shadows that mocked her everywhere she looked, but she could see no one about. She walked carefully in the direction Philip had taken her that morning until she came to the little clearing. She dropped his robe and walked into the warm water.

She had made it this far without being seen. She thought briefly of stealing one of the horses in the corral and escaping while Philip slept. But her luck was no longer with her, and she was sure someone would hear her leave. She wasn't anxious to learn if Philip would keep his word and whip her. So Christina put the thought from her mind and let the warm water take the smell of him from her body.

Chapter 9

The sun was just clearing the mountains, taking away the sharp chill of the night past, when Philip awoke from a pleasant sleep. He looked to see if his captive still lay beside him. He frowned when he saw Christina lying on the far side of the bed and wearing his robe. He would have to speak to her, for he would allow no clothes between them in bed.

Remembering his victory of the night before, Philip smiled and played with the loose ends of Christina's braid. He noticed the deep red stain of blood on the sheet and felt the scratches on his back.

What a woman he had found! She had abandoned herself completely to him last night after admitting defeat. She had matched his own wild passion. Perhaps he should make her his wife to make sure she would never leave him. But she had refused him once, and there was no way he could force her to marry him.

Getting out of bed, Philip opened the chest that contained his clothes and donned a pair of light-tan trousers and a white, long-sleeved tunic. He left the tent and, seeing Amine by the fire, asked her to bring in the morning meal. Philip checked on his horse, Victory, and on two recently captured horses in the corral. He enjoyed working with horses, and breaking in the new ones would give him something to do besides raiding the passing caravans.

Philip remembered the incredulous look on the fat old merchant's face during yesterday's raid when he had asked if there were any books in the caravan. Philip had taken only the things he wanted for Christina and had ordered his men to take only foodstuffs and other necessities.

Philip had no need of the riches that could be accumulated by raiding caravans, for he had all the wealth he could ever need in England. His mother left him a very rich estate, and a title as well.

His half-brother Rashid took everything when he raided, and didn't care very much if anyone died in the process. Rashid was a hard and bitter man. Philip was glad he had not been in camp since his return.

Giving Victory a last rub on his velvety gray nose, Philip went back to the tent. He found Christina sitting on the couch eating breakfast. She had removed his robe and had on the skirt and blouse she had worn yesterday. As he approached, she shot him a look of hatred that would have frozen any other man.

"I was hoping that your disposition might have improved after last night, but I can see it hasn't," Philip remarked casually.

"And I was hoping that you'd have the decency not to mention last night. But you throw it in my face, like the cad you are! I promise I'll never let it happen again!"

Philip grinned wickedly as he calmly sat down beside her. "Don't make promises you won't be able to keep, Tina."

Christina swung viciously at his leering face, but he swiftly grabbed her wrist.

"This is hardly the time for a quarrel, my sweet. I suggest you put your energy to a better use and finish your meal. Afterward, I'll take you to bathe."

"No, thank you. I bathed last night," she said haughtily.

Philip's eyes narrowed dangerously. Christina winced when he seized her shoulders and turned her to face him.

"So that's why you were wearing my robe this morning!" he stormed, shaking her violently. "You little idiot! Do you think we're the only tribe in these hills? There are at least a dozen others, and we share our water and our bathing hole with Yamaid Alhabbal. His tribe doesn't speak English as mine does. Do you know where you'd be this morning, had one of his tribesmen discovered you? You'd be at a slave auction — bringing a healthy price. After Yamaid Alhabbal and all his men had sampled your charms, that is."

69

Philip pushed her away and stood before her, his eyes cold and unrelenting. "Never will you leave this camp unescorted again. Do you hear me?"

"Yes," she whispered meekly.

Seeing how frightened she looked, Philip calmed down. "I'm sorry, Tina. It's just that if you were sold, I probably wouldn't be able to find you. The fat old buzzard who could pay the most for you would hide you away for fear of losing you. I wouldn't want that to happen any more than you would."

"I'll be sure to heed your warning and be more careful in the future," Christina replied, smoothing imaginary wrinkles from her skirt. "If you'll excuse me now, I have some sewing that needs to be done."

She picked up a bolt of material and disappeared into the bedroom. Philip shook his head. She certainly could compose herself quickly, he thought: frightened dismay to cool disdain.

After he had eaten his fill, Philip sauntered over to the bedroom and pulled back the heavy curtains. "By the way, my sweet, don't waste your time making nightdresses to sleep in, for you'll have no use for them here."

Philip ducked as a pillow came flying at him. He laughed deeply as he turned and left the tent. He would start breaking the wild horses today: they might prove more tamable than Christina!

That evening after dinner, Philip reclined on the couch lazily watching Christina. She sat across from him sewing on a piece of light-green material and ignoring him completely. Her neglect irritated him, but he decided not to give her the satisfaction of knowing it.

Closing his eyes, Philip let his mind wander. He'd spent the latter part of the afternoon with his father telling Yasir about Paul and his new wife. Although his father hadn't seen Paul for many years, he was still close to his heart. Philip hoped Paul would come at least once to visit his father. The old man didn't have much time left.

People died before their time in this land.

When Yasir had decided to move his tribe into the foothills, Philip had been delighted. He had never liked the nomadic desert life, constantly roaming from one oasis to the next. The tribe had lived in the hills for eight years now. Philip might not have stayed so long with his father if they had not moved permanently to these hills. The climate was considerably cooler. There was enough water even for regular bathing. And their camp was situated so they could hold off an attack if necessary.

Philip didn't know if he would stay in Egypt after his father died. But now that he had Christina, he'd probably decide to stay. He couldn't take her back to England, because she'd be able to escape him there.

Stretching languidly, Philip opened his eyes to find Christina dozing on the couch. He arose and quietly walked around the table to stand above her. His eyes caressed her unbraided hair; its glowing mass covered the pillow and rippled to the floor behind her. She was curled in a ball like a little girl dreaming innocently. She hardly seemed the sensuous woman of the night before.

Philip bent to scoop Christina into his arms. But she jumped up and scurried to the other end of the tent. She turned to see if he were pursuing her.

"So — you were only feigning sleep." He straightened, giving her an amused glance. "It's rather late for games, my pet."

"I can assure you, I do not play games," she retorted stiffly, pushing back the hair that had fallen all around her.

"I was only going to carry you to bed. But now that you're awake — I can think of better things to do," Philip teased as he slowly came toward her.

"No!" she snapped, backing away from him. "And I won't sleep in that bed with you. It's indecent! I'd rather sleep on the floor!"

He chuckled softly as he cornered Christina at the end of the tent.

"You wouldn't like sleeping on the floor, Tina. It can get very cold here at night, and you'd better have the warmth of my body next to you. Winter is coming soon!"

"Better to suffer with the cold than with your advances," she replied tartly. She tried to run past him.

"You didn't feel that way last night, Tina," he said. He caught her in his arms and threw her roughly over his shoulder.

She struggled fiercely as Philip swiftly crossed the tent and tossed her onto the bed.

"I think it's time I taught you a lesson, Tina. You're a very passionate woman, even though you refuse to admit it!"

Christina fought him furiously while he tried to remove her clothing. Amid her kicking and useless struggles, she spat curses at him that he had never dreamed a lady would know. He finally managed to pull her blouse over her head, and the skirt followed easily. He quickly dropped his own clothing to the floor and pinned her to the bed with his body.

"Your language certainly doesn't befit a lady, my sweet," he laughed. "You must tell me sometime how you acquired such an outlandish vocabulary."

Christina made one last effort to push him from her, then changed her tactics and lay perfectly still beneath him.

Opening her mouth with his, Philip kissed her intensely, but felt no response from her. So — she was playing at a new game, he mused. But she wouldn't be able to hold out for long.

Moving to her side, Philip brought his lips down to her full breasts, sucking and teasing each one in turn. He moved his hand down over her belly until it rested between her legs. Gently his fingers moved back and forth across her soft flesh until she moaned with passion.

"Oh, Philip," she breathed. "Take me."

Philip mounted her. Her arms encircled his neck, and she met his kisses eagerly. He entered her slowly, then rode her fast and hard until their passions exploded, sending them soaring into ecstasy.

Chapter 10

The dawn came slowly for Christina. She had slept fitfully through the night, awakening fully with the tent still in darkness. Now, as the daylight slowly illuminated the bedroom, Christina stared boldly at the man who had robbed her of her will last night.

Christina had fought desperately to quell the urgings sweeping through her body as Philip caressed her, but she couldn't resist his touch. She had surrendered to him completely. She had begged him to take her.

What has he turned me into? Christina thought angrily. I was like a bitch in heat the way I wanted him.

She let her eyes roam over the length of his naked body. He was perfectly formed: lean, muscular, and powerful. She studied his face: so rugged and handsome when he was awake; boyish and charming when he slept. His black hair curled softly at the nape of his neck, disheveled by the night's sleep. Philip looked like the Prince Charming she had childishly dreamed of, but his character was that of the devil!

Suddenly Christina was startled by a deep voice.

"Abu," the man said. "I only just learned of your return. Wake up!"

A tall man of slight build that Christina had never seen before entered the bedroom, but he broke off when he saw her.

The man looked at Philip, who was just coming awake, and back at Christina. A wide grin slowly spread across his dark features as Christina jerked the covers over her, ashamed at being seen in bed with Philip.

"A thousand pardons, brother. I did not know you had married," he said innocently. "When did the happy event take place?"

Philip sat up on the side of the bed and glowered at the man.

"There has been no wedding, as I am sure you already know. Now if your curiosity has been adequately appeased, will you kindly leave my bedroom?"

"As you wish, Abu. I will wait and have the morning meal with you," he replied. He grinned as he swung around and left the room.

Cautiously Christina came out from under the covers and turned to Philip.

"Who was that man?" she demanded angrily. "How dare he enter your bedroom like that? Am I to have no privacy here?"

Philip stood up and stretched lazily. He donned his tunic and trousers and sat down on the bed to pull on his boots.

"Will you answer me, damn it?" she flung at him.

Philip turned around to face Christina and chuckled at her anger.

"This won't happen again, my pet. That was my half-brother, Rashid, and this was just one of the games he plays to annoy me. My bedroom is the one place you may be assured of privacy — except from me. Now get dressed," he said, picking up her clothes and handing them to her. "He's waiting to meet you."

As he walked from the room, Philip didn't see the tongue Christina childishly stuck out at him. Brother indeed, she thought while she dressed hurriedly. How many more surprises am I expected to endure? Now I have his brother to contend with — another barbarian, no doubt.

She brushed the tangles from her hair and tied it back with a piece of lace she'd cut from some Philip had given her. Christina wished she had a mirror but was not about to ask Philip for one.

Both brothers were seated on the couch eating the morning meal when Christina opened the curtains. They're so uncivilized that they can't even stand up when a lady enters the room, Christina thought. She crossed the tent to stand before them.

"I am Rashid Alhamar," Philip's brother said, his eyes roving over her body from head to foot. "And you must be Christina Wakefield."

She nodded, picked up a piece of bread, and sat down on the opposite couch.

Except for his height, Rashid didn't look anything like Philip. He was much darker in complexion, with black hair and brown eyes. His face was boyish, almost effeminate, with smooth, soft skin, where Philip's was rugged and heavily bearded. Philip was broad and muscular, but Rashid was actually skinny.

"Your brother has posted a very large reward for your safe return, Christina," said Rashid. "I have heard that he and his men search for you among all the caravans and desert tribes."

"And pray tell, do you wish to collect that reward, Mr. Alhamar?" Christina inquired icily.

The question brought a scowl from Philip.

"There will be no more talk of a reward," Philip said to Rashid, his voice heavy with malice. "I will tell you once only. Christina is here to stay because I wish it. As head of this tribe, no one will question me about her. She is my woman and shall be treated as such. And you are never to enter my bedroom again."

Rashid laughed. "Nura said you were being overly protective of this one. I can see she was right. Nura is jealous of your new woman, you know. She always hoped to become your wife herself."

"Ah, women," Philip shrugged. "I never gave Nura any reason to hope for marriage."

"But she is just like all the other young women of the tribe. They all want your attentions." Christina thought she heard envy in his voice.

"Enough talk of women," Philip replied sourly. "Where have you been, Rashid? And why weren't you here when I returned to camp?"

"I was in El Balyana, where I heard of a large caravan stopping. It was there that I learned of Christina's disappearance. The caravan was two days late in arriving or I would have been here to welcome you back."

75

Taking a small sack from the inside of his robe, Rashid opened it and poured the contents on the table.

"This is the reason I waited so long. I knew where they would be hidden, so it was quite easy to steal them."

Christina's eyes opened wide as she saw the magnificent jewels roll onto the table. There were huge diamonds, emeralds, sapphires, and other precious stones that she didn't recognize. But the most beautiful stone was a huge ruby shining with many blood-red facets. The ruby alone was truly worth a king's ransom.

"Of course, since you are head of the tribe, they are yours," Rashid said reluctantly.

"What would I do with a sack full of jewels?" Philip laughed. "I have no need for wealth here, nor do I wish it. You may keep the jewels, since you went to the trouble of stealing them."

"I hoped you would feel that way, Abu." Rashid scooped the jewels back into the sack and hid them in his robe.

"I just hope you use the gems wisely," Philip said. "Have you been to see our father yet?"

"I will go see him now. He became very ill a few months ago. Maidi pulled him through, but he has not been strong since. I fear he will not live long," Rashid said flatly.

Philip saw his brother out and stayed at the entrance staring into the camp. What kind of man was he, Christina wondered, that he could so casually hear that his father was dying? What kind of man could turn away a fortune in jewels as if they were ordinary stones? Would she ever understand this man who had made her his mistress? Did she want to understand him?

Slowly Philip turned around, raising both hands to brush back the hair that had fallen into his face. Christina could read the sadness in his dark-green eyes.

So — he did feel pain after all. Suddenly she wanted to go to him and put her arms around him. She wanted to wipe away his sadness. What was the matter with her? She hated him. Besides,

76

he would only laugh at her.

"I think it's time you met the people of my tribe," he said quietly, crossing the tent to stand before her. He cupped her chin in his hand and lifted her face to his. "That is — if you have nothing better to do."

"My sewing can wait," she replied.

Philip's hand dropped to her tiny waist as she stood up. They were standing only a few inches apart, and his nearness made Christina's pulse beat warmly. She felt herself melting, losing control. She hated his effect on her. She had to say something to break the mood between them.

"Do you wish to go now, Your Highness?" she said sarcastically.

"There is no Highness here, Tina. I told you to call me Philip." His hand tightened on her waist.

"Yes sir, Your Highness," she returned demurely.

"Enough!" he roared. "If you want me to turn you over my knee and wale the vindictiveness out of your hide, then you may persist. Otherwise, go put your slippers on."

Christina didn't wait around to find out if Philip would carry out his threat. She scurried into the bedroom and, finding her slippers under the bed, donned them quickly and came back into the main room.

Philip, with a hand on the small of Christina's back, escorted her outside. They stopped at the first of the tents to the left of theirs.

"Said, are you there?" Philip called from outside.

"Come in, Abu. You do me honor to visit my home," a short, sturdy man said, opening the entrance of his tent.

When they entered, Christina saw that the whole family seemed to be present. The women were on one side of the tent: one kneading dough, another on the floor feeding a baby, and an older woman preparing meat. The men sat on the opposite side cleaning their rifles and an assortment of knives.

"This is Christina Wakefield," Philip said to the group at large.

They all stared at her. "Christina, this is my old friend Said, and his wife, Maidi." He motioned to the old woman preparing the meat. "Maidi takes care of my father, now that he's ill, and also prepares our food. The young woman on the right is her daughter, Nura."

Christina's eyes widened at the sight of the beautiful dark-haired girl who looked no older than she. She thought she saw hostility in Nura's eyes, and remembered she had hoped to become Philip's wife.

"And the young woman with her babies is her sister-in-law, Amine."

Christina returned the smile of the dark, pretty girl who seemed to be in her early twenties. She was the one who had brought their food yesterday and whose skirt and blouse Christina was wearing. Perhaps Christina could become friends with her if given the chance.

"These are Maidi's sons — Ahmad, Saadi, and Syed, Amine's husband," Philip finished.

Each of the sons nodded in turn. Christina recognized Ahmad and Saadi as the two young men who had helped Philip kidnap her. Syed was Philip's age and had a long scar running down his right cheek.

"I am very pleased to meet all of you," Christina said.

"It is we who are honored to meet you, Christina Wakefield," Said returned, smiling warmly at her. "I can see why Sheik Abu went to so much trouble to bring you here. You have a most unusual beauty."

"You flatter me, Said, but I —"

Philip cut her off. "It was no trouble at all, as Ahmad and Saadi can attest to, but Christina still has to meet your brothers, so we'll be going." He pushed Christina from the tent.

"I understand. Another time perhaps," Said called after them, looking disconcerted.

Christina turned on Philip with her hands on her hips, eyes flashing angrily.

"Why did you cut me off like that?" she demanded.

"You'd better lower your voice if you know what's good for you, Tina. I wasn't teasing when I warned you that we beat our women

78

for showing disrespect," Philip said harshly. "I cut you off because you were about to say that you were here against your will. Everyone here already knows that. But if you had said so in public, it would have been an embarrassment to me. A good lashing is probably just what you need to tame you down." Philip grasped her shoulder roughly.

"No!" Christina gasped, pulling away from him. "I'll be good, I — I promise!" she said frantically, her whole body trembling.

"Christina, stop it," Philip demanded softly. "I'm not going to beat you now. You haven't pushed me that far yet."

He took her in his arms and held her tenderly until she stopped shaking. She would never be able to comprehend this man. One minute he threatened to beat her, and the next, he was holding her with tenderness and love.

Love? Why did she think of that? Philip didn't love her. He only wanted her. And love and wanting were as different as night and day. She could never hope to leave this place unless his heart softened toward her and he let her go, as his father had released his mother.

"Are you all right now, Tina?" he inquired huskily, lifting her face up to his.

"Yes," Christina replied softly, without opening her eyes.

He took her then to meet Said's two brothers and their large families. Christina noticed that all the young women watched Philip with longing in their eyes. So Rashid was right, she thought. They had all hoped to win Philip's attentions before he brought her all the way from England to flaunt in front of them. They all must hate her — and Nura most of all.

That afternoon, Christina finished the skirt she had been making, and was quite pleased with her work. She had fashioned the skirt after the one she was wearing, using a pale-green silk and trimming it around the hem with dark-green lace.

She could wear the green silk skirt with Amine's dark-green blouse while she worked on a matching top. She had decided it would be faster to make simple skirts and blouses first, instead of dresses. She didn't care if the clothes she made were too fine for camp life. Christina enjoyed wearing beautiful clothes. They made her feel good, wherever she was.

Before dinner, Philip came to take Christina to bathe, with a knife strapped to his leg for protection. He joined her in the warm water but didn't try to touch her this time.

After bathing, Christina donned her new skirt. But Philip only commented, "You're fast with your hands, Tina."

Rashid joined them for dinner, and he couldn't keep his eyes off Christina all evening. His attentions annoyed Philip, so she retired early, leaving the two brothers to discuss tribal affairs. When Philip came to bed later, she feigned sleep, expecting him to try to take her again. But he only pulled her to him and presently fell asleep.

Chapter 11

In the slow days that followed, Christina and Philip fell into a routine. He took all his meals with her, but left her to herself during the morning and afternoon. He took her to the pond to bathe each evening before dinner and stayed with her after the meal, cleaning his weapons, reading, or just meditating.

Each night Philip made love to her, and each night she fought him until her passions overcame her resistance and swept her away. Christina could not deny that his lovemaking gave her pleasure, but that only made her hate Philip more than ever.

Philip made her feel strangely mixed emotions. She was nervous whenever he was near. She could never predict what he would do next. He made her lose control of herself, sending her into a fit of anger and then turning that anger to fear. And she was afraid of him, for she really believed he would beat her if she provoked him too far.

A week had passed since Philip had brought Christina to his camp. With nothing else to do, she had completed the green silk blouse and two more skirts, but she was tired of sewing. She was tired of being inside the tent all day long, every day.

Philip had left without a word right after breakfast that morning. She knew he was angry with her for not telling him why she had cried the night before. How could she tell him she cried because her body deceived her? She had been so determined to be unmoved by his caresses and to lie placidly beneath him. But Philip patiently brought her to life, snatching away her will as he did every night.

But Philip was not satisfied by breaking her down once. He had asserted his power over her again, mercilessly, and she had loved every minute of it. But when he was finished with her and rolled to his side of the bed, she started to cry.

When Philip tried to comfort her, she just cried harder and told him to leave her alone. She was disgusted with herself for enjoying the act, more than angry at him. But when she wouldn't explain herself, he became coldly angry. Christina cried until she finally fell asleep.

Now, as the morning wore on, Christina felt stifled by inactivity. She put her sewing aside and walked to the entrance of the tent. The sunlight looked so inviting as it filtered through the juniper trees that Christina forgot her fear of Philip's reaction to her leaving the tent. She meandered toward the corral, basking in the warmth of the sun.

She stopped dead in her tracks when she saw Philip. He was in the large corral with Ahmad, who was astride a beautiful Arabian horse. The other horses were grazing peacefully on the hillside with the sheep. Bravely she continued walking. When she reached the corral fence, the horse shied away.

Philip turned to see what was bothering the animal, and his eyes narrowed menacingly when he spied her. He soothed the horse, then came to her with quick strides.

"What are you doing here?" Philip asked angrily. "I gave you no permission to leave the tent."

Christina fought to control her rising anger.

"I couldn't stand it another minute in that tent, Philip. I'm not used to being confined. I need to feel the sun and breathe the morning air. Can't I stay here and watch you? I'm interested in what you do every day," she lied.

"I train these horses, among other things," he said.

"What for?" Christina asked, stalling for more time.

"Do you really want to know, Christina? Or are you playing at another game?"

"I can't win the game when you are the opponent, as you well know," she pouted. "I'd really like to know how you train your horses."

82

"Very well. What would you like to know?"

"What are you training them to do?"

"To follow directions with the pressure of the knees and not the hands. Sometimes our hands are not free to direct the reins, as in battle or after a raid. Also it serves another purpose, for our horses cannot be stolen unless they are led away. They will not carry a rider who uses the reins to direct them."

"That's ingenious," Christina said, her interest growing. "But how do you teach the horses these pressures?"

"The horse is led in a certain direction, say to the left, while the rider uses the pressure for that direction. We continue with one direction at a time until the horse learns it."

"How do you stop the horse?"

"Since we don't ride with saddles, we use our feet to stop him by digging them into his sides. Are you satisfied now?"

"Yes. May I stay and watch you for a while?" she asked meekly.

"If you are quiet and don't disturb the horse," he said. He looked at her quizzically for a long moment before walking away.

So — she had won. She was free of that damnable tent for a while. Christina let her mind wander while keeping her soft, blue-green eyes on Philip.

How she wished that she were astride that beautiful animal. Perhaps she could persuade Philip to let her ride one of his horses or, better yet, give her an untrained horse. It wouldn't be like riding Dax freely through the lush green fields of home, but it would be better than not riding at all.

Christina suddenly realized that she was thinking of a future in this camp. Oh damn, why didn't John rescue her? But John probably thought her dead already. She had to find a way to escape, but she couldn't go alone. She must have a guide to help her cross the desert and protect her from outlaw tribes. She must have food, water, horses.

Could she wait until Philip tired of her? How long would that be? And Philip might not send her to her brother when he no longer wanted her. He might sell her as a slave for someone's harem.

Perhaps she could persuade Philip to let her go if she made him fall in love with her! But how could she manage to win him over when he knew she hated him? Besides, he had told her he only desired her body.

"Christina."

She looked up into Philip's smiling green eyes.

"I called you twice. You have a strange way of showing that you're interested in what I do."

"I'm sorry," Christina smiled back at him. "I was just thinking of my horse, Dax, and how I would love to be out riding."

"Did you ride often at your home?"

"Oh yes! Every day, for long hours at a time," she said enthusiastically.

They walked back to the tent, where steaming dishes of porridge, rice, and sweetmeats were on the table for their midday meal. There was a pot of tea for Christina and a fresh skin of wine for Philip.

"I'll be leaving the camp this afternoon for a while," Philip mentioned as they sat down to eat. "I'll leave Ahmad to guard the tent while I'm gone. It is for your protection that you're guarded, nothing else."

"But where are you going?"

"On a *ghazw*," he said irritably.

She had obviously hit on something Philip didn't want to talk about. But her woman's curiosity wouldn't let her stop.

"A *ghazw*? What's that?"

"Christina, must you always ask so many questions of me?" Philip's voice was edged with anger, making her shiver despite the warmth. "It's a raid, if you must know. Syed spotted a caravan this morning. Since our food supply is getting low, we'll take what we need to hold us over for a while. Does that answer your question, or is there something else you'd like to know?"

"You can't be serious!" Christina was appalled. She stopped eating

84

and looked into his cold green eyes. "Why can't you buy what you need? Rashid had all those jewels you turned down. You must have wealth of your own. Why must you steal from other people?"

Philip stood and faced her, the yellow flecks in his green eyes disappearing as he looked at her wrathfully.

"I will not stand for your questioning my actions anymore, Christina. I will tell you once, and once only. Raiding is the way of my people. We rob to survive as we have always done. We take only what we need. I have no wealth here, because I have no need of it. Rashid has a grievance against me that I understand, so I don't curb his greed for riches. What he steals, I let him keep. Do not question me about it again!"

He turned on his heel and stormed from the tent. Christina was shaken. She felt as if she were hopelessly falling into a bottomless pit.

Philip was an outlaw! No doubt he killed men mercilessly when he went on raids. He probably enjoyed killing! And she — Christina Wakefield — was at his mercy.

Christina shivered uncontrollably, thinking of the rage he had just shown. Would he kill her if she pushed him too far? He was an outlaw, and she knew where his camp was. Would Philip ever let her go with that kind of knowledge?

She heard horses galloping out of the camp. He was off to pillage and plunder and only God knew what else, Christina thought. She couldn't live with this new fear. She had to know what he intended to do with her. If she was to die, then she wanted to know it.

Walking quickly to the entrance of the tent, she found Ahmad sitting on the ground outside the entrance. He was meticulously cleaning a long silver sword with a curved handle.

"Ahmad," she ventured slowly, "may I ask you a question?"

He looked at her strangely.

"It is not right. Women do not ask questions. It is not their place."

This was too much. These people were barbaric!

"But Ahmad, I was not raised as your women are. I was brought up to be equal to men, can't you understand that? I just wanted to know if Abu ever brought another woman here before me," she said, hoping he would just think her jealous.

Ahmad grinned. "No, you are the first woman Sheik Abu has ever brought to camp."

"Thank you, Ahmad," she smiled back at him.

Going back into the tent, Christina paced the floor. That was no help at all. If there had been another woman, Christina might have discovered what had happened to her after Philip tired of her. Now she would have to face Philip with the question that was tormenting her. She prayed he would be in a better mood when he returned.

Chapter 12

The sun was still above the horizon when they reached the foot of the mountains. They rode hard now, for the caravan was many miles away. Philip hoped this wasn't a slaver's caravan, for they usually carried little food.

Damn that woman and her curiosity! How could she so easily make him lose control? He had always prided himself on his cool reactions toward women — until he'd met Christina.

She'd angered him the night before by refusing to tell him why she was crying. He couldn't understand it. She had never cried before after making love.

Would he ever understand her? Christina continued to fight him each night, but he knew she enjoyed his lovemaking. Why did she fight what was so pleasurable?

When she came to the corral this morning, he knew her feigned interest was only an excuse to leave the tent. But could he blame her? He'd have done the same thing. He was positive she wouldn't try to escape again, she feared him too much. Perhaps he could trust her enough to give her the freedom of the camp.

Philip recalled the look of horror on Christina's face when he told her he was going raiding. He hadn't intended to tell her about that part of his life. He didn't enjoy it himself, and he knew it would appall her. But he was so angered by her inquisitiveness that he wanted to shock her.

He wasn't used to so many questions about his life, especially from a woman. Ah, but what a woman! Philip thoroughly enjoyed having her around. He found pleasure in just gazing at her uncommon beauty. He looked forward to entering his tent knowing she would be there — willing or not. Before, his tent had been a lonely place that he avoided as much as possible.

As they approached the caravan, which had camped at an oasis for the night, Philip saw five camels, their packs piled on the ground, and six men gathered around a small fire. Philip and his men galloped up to surround the camp, brandishing their guns, and Syed fired off two shots to see if the caravan intended to fight or surrender its goods.

Slowly, one by one, the caravan guards threw down their rifles. Philip dismounted and walked forward cautiously flanked by his men, but the six guards put up no resistance. They would rather stay alive than fight and die for another man's property.

Syed guarded the prisoners while the rest of them opened and ransacked the packs. They soon made themselves comfortable for the night, and broke open some wine and dried meat for supper.

The next morning, they loaded the foodstuffs and other goods they wanted on one of the camels, sent the rest of the caravan on its way, and set off for the mountains. They rode into camp about midafternoon amid the cheers of the rest of the tribe. They led the horses into the corral, unloaded the camel, and sent it off into the hills to graze. Philip left the men to divide the spoils among themselves, and carried one large chest to his tent.

He hoped he'd find Christina in a gentler mood than she'd been in the afternoon before. He found her sitting demurely on the couch with her towel and new clothes lying across her lap. She didn't say a word as he went into the bedroom to dispose of the chest.

"We can go bathe in just a minute, my pet," he said cheerfully. He came back into the main room and removed a small bundle from the corner cabinet. "Is something the matter, my sweet?" Philip inquired, hoping her silence didn't mean she was still angry with him.

But she just turned away from him and shook her head. Well, he wouldn't press her to answer him. Without another word, Philip pulled her to her feet and took her up the hillside to bathe.

Christina had not yet lost her shyness at disrobing in his presence. She turned her back to Philip and slowly removed her blouse and skirt. He controlled his desire with great effort as he watched her wade into the water.

But turning his attentions to the bundle he had brought with him, Philip unwrapped a finely honed razor and proceeded to shave his week's growth of beard.

After he was satisfied with the results, he took a new bar of soap from the bundle and joined Christina in the water.

It was dark when they finally returned to camp. The newly kindled fire illuminated the tent brightly, making dancing shadows in the corners.

Philip pondered Christina's sullenness as they finished the evening meal. This attitude of hers couldn't continue, for he was aching to take her to bed. But she would succumb to his advances after her usual resistance, he knew.

Reclining on the couch behind her, Philip played with the loose curls dangling at the nape of Christina's neck. He leaned forward and grazed the soft flesh behind her ear with his lips, and watched the gooseflesh run down her arms.

Downing the rest of his wine, Philip stood up and took Christina's hand in his.

"Come, Tina," he murmured, and led her into the bedroom, surprised that she didn't resist him.

While taking off his clothes, he watched Christina move to the opposite side of the bed and unbind her hair. It fell gloriously about her body. He was astonished as she slowly, seductively removed her garments. She sat naked on the bed, as if inviting him to join her. But as he came to her, she put up her hands to stop him.

"Philip, I must talk to you," Christina said, searching his eyes with her dark, sapphire ones.

"Later, my pet," Philip replied huskily and silenced her words with his kiss. But, with an effort, she pushed him away.

"Please, Philip! There's something I must know."

He looked down at her and saw her trembling lips and deepening blue eyes.

"What is it, Tina?"

"What do you intend to do with me?"

"I'm going to make love to you. Did you think otherwise?" He smiled beguilingly and toyed with the curls dangling over her breasts.

"I mean in the future — when you no longer want me. What will you do with me then?"

"I haven't really thought about it," he lied, for there was nothing to think about. He'd never let her go.

"Would you let me return to my brother?" she ventured timidly.

Philip knew now what was troubling Christina. Did she actually think he would do away with her? Of course she did, for she thought the worst of him.

"When I tire of you, Tina — then, yes, you may go back to your brother."

"Will you give me your word, Philip?"

"You have my word. I swear it."

He could see relief flood her features as she relaxed into the pillow. She smiled up at him invitingly.

"Are all your fears forgotten now, my sweet?" he whispered, branding her throat with his fiery lips.

"Most of them," she breathed. She pulled his face to hers and accepted his passionate kiss willingly.

Philip wondered fleetingly what else could cause Christina to fear him. But she wasn't fighting him right now, and it both puzzled and excited him. He didn't ponder long, for he was not about to waste this moment on trivial questions.

As dawn crept over the horizon, Christina slowly awakened to the sweet song of a nightingale. A grimace crossed her pretty features

90

when she remembered the night past and the lengths she had gone to.

She didn't have to play the whore. She had already made Philip promise to return her to her brother. But she had struck a bargain with him, and she had given herself willingly to seal the pact. It was a small thing to do — he would have taken her, anyway.

Christina smiled as she recalled how her caresses had driven Philip wild with desire. His fervid passions had carried them higher than ever before. And she had been caught in the same whirlpool of desire until the tide swept them both into a sea of mutual bliss.

Well, the evening was behind her now. She had given herself to Philip for a reason. But with her worst fears put to rest, Philip wouldn't find her so willing in the future. Indeed, she would be more obstinate than ever.

It's going to be a glorious day, Christina thought as she slipped from the bed and donned her new mauve velvet skirt and her green blouse. I should be disgusted with myself, but I'm not. I actually feel happy.

She went into the main room to put the last trims on her mauve blouse before Philip awoke, for she wouldn't let him see her in clashing colors.

Awhile later, Philip called her name from the bedroom. She knew he thought her gone, and was about to answer when she heard him swear.

He came tearing through the curtains, still putting on his robe. But he stopped abruptly when he saw her, the rage on his face turning to surprise.

"Why didn't you answer me?"

"You didn't give me a chance to." Christina laughed heartily as she put down her scissors. "Did you think I'd left you again?"

"I was merely concerned for your safety."

"Well, you needn't fear, I'm quite safe," she replied. She feared she'd burst into laughter again if she had to look at Philip's disgrun-

91

tled expression, so she bent quickly over her sewing.

Philip turned and left the tent. Christina wondered about the concern he'd shown for her. She didn't know whether he was truly worried about her safety or whether he simply didn't want to lose a plaything.

Christina went for a walk to the corral that afternoon. The sun was not too hot, for it was nearly winter. She would have to start making warmer clothing.

The horses were all inside the corral. She looked about, but couldn't see Philip anywhere. Sensing someone behind her, Christina turned abruptly, thinking it was Philip, but was surprised to find Amine looking shyly at her.

"I did not mean to frighten you," Amine said timidly.

"You didn't frighten me. I thought you were Abu."

"Ah, Sheik Abu guards you like a hawk. He is very much in love with you, I think."

"That's ridiculous. He doesn't love me." Christina laughed at the thought. "He only desires me."

"I do not understand," Amine replied, looking puzzled.

"That's all right, I don't understand it, either."

"May I ask you a question?" Amine looked embarrassed, but continued when Christina nodded her head. "Is it true that you eat at the same table with Sheik Abu?"

Christina was surprised.

"Of course I eat with him. Where else would I eat?"

Amine's dark-brown eyes widened. "I did not believe Nura when she told me, but now that you tell me, I must believe."

"What's so shocking about my eating with Abu?" Christina asked curiously.

"It is forbidden for women to eat their meals with men," Amine answered, shaking her head. "It just is not done."

So Philip was breaking a rule by eating with her. But this is ridiculous, Christina thought. I'm not one of them. Their rules don't apply to me. But she didn't want to offend Amine.

"Amine, you must understand that I was brought up differently. In my country, men and women always eat together. So, you see, Abu is just trying to make me feel at home in this land."

"Ah, I understand now," Amine smiled. "That is very thoughtful of Sheik Abu. You are very lucky that he chose you."

Christina wanted to laugh. Lucky! She had been kidnapped and taken against her will! But Christina could see Amine was a romantic, and didn't want to spoil her illusions.

"Abu is a handsome man. Any woman would feel lucky if he chose her," Christina lied. Any woman but herself. "But where are your babies, Amine?" she asked.

"Maidi is watching them. They are her only grandchildren, and she dotes on them. It is hard to make a marriage here, for we do not have many visitors who come to our camp."

"Then how did you and Syed meet?"

"Ah, Syed stole me from my tribe," Amine said proudly.

"Stole you!" Christina exclaimed. Were all these men alike?

"Our tribes used to share pasturelands before they became enemies. I knew Syed when I was just a child, and I have always loved him. When I was old enough to marry, Syed had to steal me. My father would have forbidden the marriage."

"But why did the two tribes become enemies?" Christina asked, her interest growing.

"I do not know, for men do not tell women about such things. I know only that it is Sheik Ali Hejaz of my tribe who holds a grudge against Yasir Alhamar. It has something to do with Rashid's mother, who was the sister of Ali Hejaz."

Just then, Philip rode into camp, a rifle slung across his back and a long sword hanging from his belt.

"I must go now!" Amine gasped when she saw Philip.

"I've enjoyed talking with you, Amine. Please come and visit me in my tent. You will be most welcome, and bring your children."

93

"I will be very happy to," Amine said timidly.

She hurried away to her tent as Philip rode his horse up beside Christina and dismounted.

"Why did Amine leave so quickly?" Philip asked. The yellow flecks in his eyes reflected the sunlight as he stood towering above her.

"I think she's afraid of you," Christina answered, a faint smile crossing her features.

"What?" He looked incredulous. "There's nothing to fear from me."

"But there you're wrong, my lord, for your very presence causes fear," she teased. "Can't you see me shaking asunder?"

Philip gave her a devilish grin.

"You, my sweet, have much to fear," he said, tracing a line down her arm with his finger.

Christina blushed as she understood his meaning. She did have much to fear from him. And the time she feared most was nearing, as the sun had disappeared.

They shared a savory meal prepared by Maidi's skilled hands. Afterward Philip reclined on the couch, reading one of the books that he had brought for Christina, with a goatskin of wine beside him. Christina sat on the couch opposite him cutting out pieces of silk material. She had decided to add long sleeves to the dress she'd designed. The weather was getting colder, and she didn't want to borrow any of Philip's robes to keep her warm.

Perhaps she could make a robe of her own — a rich velvet robe and a *kufiyah* to match. She laughed aloud as she imagined herself dressed like a Bedouin tribesman.

"Something amuses you, my pet?"

"I was just imagining myself in the velvet robe that I plan to make. I've noticed the weather is getting cooler," she answered.

"You're wise to prepare, but I fail to see the humor," Philip remarked, putting his book down on the table.

"Well, it wasn't just the robe that I pictured, but a *kufiyah* to match it. Hardly what the well-dressed Englishwoman is wearing these days."

Philip smiled, his eyes soft and warm. "Would you like me to bring your luggage from Cairo? It could be arranged."

Christina thought for a minute.

"No — my luggage disappearing suddenly would only upset John. I don't want him worrying about me and where I am. I can make do with the material you have given me."

Christina stared blankly at the scissors in her hand. Poor John. She hoped that he would learn to accept her death instead of wondering where she was and what she might be suffering. Rage consumed her as she thought of the man whose desire had torn her life asunder.

"Christina!" Philip shouted, startling her out of her thoughts. "I asked if you wanted your brother to believe you dead?"

"Yes!" she yelled back at him, her body stiff with anger. "My brother and I were very close. John knows how I'd suffer being dominated by a barbarian like you. It would be kinder if he thought me dead until I can return to him."

Philip arose, surprised at her sudden anger.

"And do you suffer here, Tina?" Philip asked quietly. "Do I beat you and force you to slave for me?"

"You keep me prisoner here!" she returned, her dark-blue eyes shooting daggers at him. "You rape me every night! Do you expect me to enjoy being taken against my will?"

"Do you deny it?" Philip inquired softly, his eyes laughing at her.

She lowered her head to avoid Philip's gaze, afraid of his meaning.

"What are you talking about? Deny what?" she asked.

Cupping her chin in his hand, Philip brought her eyes back to his.

"Do you deny that you enjoy my lovemaking? Can you deny that I give you as much pleasure as you give me? Do you suffer so much when I ride between your legs each night, Tina?"

Christina's rage turned to humiliation, and she lowered her eyes meekly in defeat. Did he always have to turn the tables on her? Why did he have to ask her that?

Damn him! He left her no pride, for he knew she couldn't deny it. But she wouldn't give him the satisfaction of admitting the pleasure he gave her.

"I have nothing more to say to you," Christina answered icily. "So if you will excuse me, I would like to retire."

"You haven't answered my question, Tina," Philip replied softly.

"Nor do I intend to," Christina returned haughtily. She stood to walk into the bedroom, but Philip pulled her back to face him.

Christina thrust against his shoulder to push him away from her, and the forgotten scissors she held stabbed into him. She gasped, horrified at what she'd done. He showed none of the pain she knew he felt as he pulled the scissors from his shoulder. The blood gushed forth.

"Philip, I'm sorry. I — I didn't mean to do that," she whispered. "I forgot the scissors were in my hand — you must believe me! I wouldn't try to kill you. I swear it!"

Philip walked over to the cabinet without a word to her. He opened the doors and took out a small bundle. Slowly he walked back to her, took her hand, and pulled her into the bedroom. He gave her no clue what he intended.

But Christina removed his robe and tunic and made him lie down. He eyed her warily as she pressed the robe to his shoulder to stanch the flow of blood.

Racing from the tent, Christina found Maidi. She obtained water and fresh towels from her without question, then ran back to Philip. Her hands were shaking uncontrollably as she cleaned the wound and applied the salve and bandages that she found in the bundle. She was all too aware that he watched her every move as she clumsily wrapped the bandages about his chest and shoulder.

Christina was still deathly afraid of what he was going to do to

96

her. Did he think she had deliberately tried to kill him? Why didn't he say something — anything? Christina didn't look into his eyes for fear of the anger she might see.

When she had finished bandaging his wound, Philip suddenly grabbed her wrists and pulled her down on top of him.

"You must be crazy!" she gasped, struggling to free herself. "You will start the bleeding again."

"Then tell me what I want to hear, Tina," he whispered. "Tell me you enjoy my lovemaking, or I will take you now and prove it on your body again."

His green eyes were glazed from loss of blood, but he had enough determination to carry out his threat.

So this was to be her punishment for hurting him! She must admit that he gave her pleasure. But she would not admit it to him — she couldn't!

The pain she felt in her wrists from his iron grip gave her courage, and she glared at him furiously.

"Damn you, Philip! Why must you hear it from my own lips, when you know the answer already?"

"Tell me!" he demanded harshly.

Christina had never seen him so cruel and merciless before. He gathered her wrists together in one hand and started to pull her skirt up with the other. She realized that if he carried out his threat, he could bleed to death when his wound opened again. Yasir would surely have her killed if he died.

"All right!" she sobbed. "I admit it. I admit everything. Are you satisfied now, damn you?"

She rolled to her side of the bed when he released her, and cried softly into her pillow.

"You give in too easily, my love," Philip laughed weakly. "I wouldn't have made love to you, no matter how enjoyable it would have been. I'd rather enjoy all the sweet nights to come than die in your arms tonight."

"Oh! I hate you, Philip Caxton. Hate you, hate you, hate you!" Christina wailed.

He only laughed, and presently went to sleep.

Damn him — damn him to hell, she thought silently, gritting her teeth so she wouldn't scream it out loud. He could so easily make her break all her firm resolutions. She gave in too quickly, as he'd so laughingly reminded her. She should have let him bleed to death! But what would have become of her then? Did she really want to see him dead?

She'd felt utterly sick to her stomach when she saw the scissors slide into his shoulder and thought she'd killed him. But why? Was it fear for Philip, or for herself? She didn't know, but she promised herself that he wouldn't find her so easy to bluff in the future.

Chapter 13

During the week that followed the accident, Philip rested in the tent most of the time. Christina became resigned to living with him for a while, and decided to make the best of it. She even began to enjoy Philip's company, since he made no demands on her. He talked with her, laughed with her, and even taught her to play cards. She mastered the art of poker playing quite easily, and soon was able to beat him at his own game.

She began to feel at ease in Philip's presence, as if she had known him all her life. He told her about coming to Egypt to look for his father, and about his life with the tribe. He told her how they had roamed from oasis to oasis on the desert in search of pasturage for the flocks, occasionally raiding caravans or other Bedouin tribes. She asked him why he preferred this way of life, but he said only, "My father is here."

Four days after the accident, Philip became irritable from confinement and inactivity. He began snapping at her for the smallest thing, but she paid no attention to his temper. She'd felt the same way when he'd confined her to the tent at first. When his temper flared, she escaped the tent and went to visit Yasir.

Yasir Alhamar welcomed her visits. His old brown eyes lit up and crinkled with his smile whenever she entered his tent. Yasir was so unlike her own father, who had still been a young and vital man when he died. But she knew Yasir wasn't near the age he looked. Egypt's torrid weather and hardships had aged him early.

Philip's father was dying now. He was pale, weaker than when she had first met him, and his attention often wandered.

Christina read to him from the *Arabian Nights*, which he enjoyed.

But Yasir dozed off after an hour or so, or just stared into space as if she weren't even there.

When she mentioned Yasir's weakness to Philip, he said only, "I know." But she could see sorrow in his dark-green eyes. He knew his father didn't have much longer to live.

On the seventh day of Philip's recuperation, Christina was aroused from a sound sleep by Philip's hand caressing her boldly. She drowsily turned and put her arms around his neck, arching her body against his as she welcomed his kiss.

"No!" she shrieked, when she realized she wasn't dreaming. She tried to push him away, but he pinned her arms to her sides.

"Why not?" he demanded brusquely. "My shoulder has healed sufficiently. You gave yourself willingly to me before making an invalid of me last week. Now I've recovered to my satisfaction, and I've a desire for you that needs quenching." He brought his lips hungrily down on hers, taking her breath away as he kissed her long and hard.

"Philip, stop it," Christina implored. "I gave into you once for a reason, but I won't again. Now let me go!" She tried to pull her arms loose, but it was no use. Philip had regained all his strength.

"So — you were only playing games with me on that beautiful night. Well, I won't let you go, my sweet, so fight me if you will. Fight me until you die of pleasure!"

That afternoon, Christina heard angry voices outside. She ran to the entrance of the tent and saw Philip and Rashid arguing heatedly. Three women sat on the ground beside them. Philip suddenly turned from Rashid and strode toward their tent, a dark scowl on his handsome face.

"Get inside, Christina," Philip growled at her when he came into the tent. He headed straight for the cabinet, filled his goblet with wine, and drank it down.

"What's wrong, Philip?" she asked. She wondered what had made him so angry, and hoped that she wasn't the cause. "I notice we have visitors."

"Visitors, ha!" he stormed, pacing back and forth. "Those women aren't visitors. They're slaves Rashid abducted from a slave trader's caravan last night. He plans to take them north tomorrow and sell them."

"Slaves!" Christina gasped, horrified. She ran over to Philip and pulled him around to face her. "You were raised in England. You can't condone the selling of human beings. Tell me you don't!"

"I don't condone it, but that has nothing to do with it."

"You will set them free?" she asked, searching his eyes for assurance. But he only pulled away from her.

"No," he replied curtly. "Damn, I knew this would happen."

If Philip let Rashid sell those women, what was to stop him from selling her? All her hopes vanished once again.

"Why won't you let them go?" she asked quietly.

"Must you always question my motives, woman? The slaves are Rashid's property. He stole them. As I told you once before, I let him keep what he steals. Do not question me again where he is concerned. Do you understand me?"

"I understand this much," she flung at him. "You're a cruel, merciless barbarian. If you ever put your hands on me again, my scissors will hit a more vital spot!"

She ran to Yasir's tent, and hoped Philip wouldn't follow her there. But Rashid shared the tent with his father, and she ran straight into his arms.

"You," she whispered venomously. "You're worse than Philip. You're all a bunch of barbarians."

Rashid released her and stood back pretending not to understand. "What have I done to offend you, Christina?" he said.

"Have you no respect for other human beings?" she snapped, hands planted firmly on her hips. "Why do you have to sell those women?"

"I don't," Rashid said, eyeing her hungrily from head to foot. "The last thing I would wish is to have a beautiful woman angry with me. If you wish me to set those slaves free, I will."

Christina stared at him. So Rashid wasn't the greedy man Philip would have her believe.

"Thank you, Rashid, and I'm sorry. It seems I've misjudged you." She smiled. "Will you take your evening meal with us tonight? I'm afraid I'd rather not be alone with Philip."

"Ah, you are not happy here?" he inquired softly. "All is not well between you and Abu?"

"Why, did you thank it ever was?" she laughed. Perhaps she had found a friend in Rashid.

"That is too bad, Christina," he said. She saw the desire in his dark-brown eyes, but his face was so soft and boyish, she could almost imagine him younger than herself.

That evening, Christina played the gracious hostess attending all Rashid's needs. She entertained him with stories of England and her girlhood.

Rashid couldn't keep his eyes off her, and didn't care that his desire showed so openly. There couldn't be another woman in all the world who could match her beauty, Rashid thought. She was dressed in a pale-green silk skirt and blouse, with a shawl of the same material draped about her creamy white shoulders. She wore her hair gathered loosely at her nape, and the golden curls cascaded down her back. He could almost forget his plans watching her, but he had waited too long for their fulfillment.

Philip watched Christina, too, but for a different reason. He fumed silently while she flirted openly with Rashid. With each glass of wine, Philip thought of a different way he would enjoy killing them both. He had been angry when she left the tent that afternoon, but now he felt able to strangle her pretty neck. He hadn't said a word when she told him Rashid was going to set the women free. Now he waited, rage festering inside, to see just how far she'd provoke him.

Through the meal and afterward, Christina ignored Philip completely. She could tell he was furious, for his eyes were dark and angry as they followed her every move. She wanted him to be as angry as she had been that afternoon. She was getting even in her own way, and thoroughly enjoyed herself.

After Rashid left, Christina sat across from Philip sipping her tea and waiting for him to make the first move. She felt nervous now as he continued to stare silently at her.

"Did you enjoy making me look like a fool tonight, Christina?"

Starting, she glanced at him warily. "Pray tell, how did I make you look the fool?" she inquired innocently.

A shiver ran down her spine when he answered, "Don't you know when you've pushed me too far, woman?"

"I'm afraid you will be pushed even farther before this night is through," she whispered.

When Philip stood up, Christina swiftly grabbed for the scissors she had concealed beneath her skirt. But Philip saw her movement and guessed her game. Before she could get at the scissors, he had both her hands in his. He pulled Christina roughly to her feet, untied her skirt, and threw the scissors across the room.

"Could you really kill me, Tina?" he asked, his face hard. He'd underestimated this woman he had made his own.

"Yes, I could kill you!" she hissed. How humiliating to stand half-naked and helpless before him! "I hate you!"

He stiffened and tightened his grip on her. "I've heard you say that often enough. You've gone too far this time, Christina, and you deserve punishment." Seemingly without emotion, he sat down and pulled her across his lap.

"Philip, no!" she screamed, but he brought his hand down with all his might across her bare buttocks. She screamed with pain, but he brought his huge hand down again, harder this time, leaving another bright red imprint.

"Please, Philip," she cried. "I couldn't kill you. You know that!"

But he paid her no mind and hit her a third time.

"Philip, I swear I'll never try it again!" she cried, the tears running down her cheeks. She was begging him, but she didn't care anymore. "I swear it, Philip. Please stop!"

Philip turned her over gently, and cradled her in his arms. Christina felt like a child sobbing uncontrollably. Nobody, not even her parents, had ever spanked her before. But no matter how humiliating it had been, Philip was right, she had deserved it. She should have known Philip would call her bluff. She wouldn't have stabbed him, she didn't have the courage.

Finally Christina stopped crying and laid her head against Philip's broad chest. She was still trembling when he carried her into the bedroom. She didn't have the will to protest, whatever he planned to do next. He laid her on the bed and removed her blouse and the material she had wrapped around her leg to hold the scissors. He pulled the covers over her shivering body and smoothed the golden hair back from her face. Bending low, he kissed her tenderly on her forehead and left the room, but still she didn't care.

Crossing the room in long strides, Philip went directly to his wine and drained the goblet, trying to wash away the events of the day. He lay down on the couch and contemplated the woman sleeping in his bed.

All evening he had thought how pleasant it would be to make her suffer for flirting with Rashid. He had wanted to make her beg and scream for mercy. But after she gave him a real reason to punish her, he felt ashamed. He felt sick inside for making her cry with pain. But damn it, she had put him in a blinding rage and deserved what she got! Of all the stupid pranks to pull — but now he was the one who was suffering, not her. He had never before hit a woman, and it sure as hell didn't sit well with him. And she had been ready to stab him if he touched her! Damn, that woman was getting under his skin!

Philip wondered what sort of game that pup Rashid was playing now. Philip had asked him either to free the slaves or take them out of camp. But Rashid had refused him, only to turn around and set them free for Christina.

Philip knew Rashid was fascinated by Christina, and he couldn't blame him for that. Christina was so beautiful any man would desire her. Perhaps he was trying to win her affections, where Philip had failed. He would have to keep an eye on Rashid. Christina was his own. And even though she hated him, he would let no one take her from him.

Chapter 14

The day was hot when Christina finally stirred beneath the covers. The room was empty, and she wondered if Philip had bothered to come to bed at all last night. She couldn't blame him, for she had given him new reason to distrust her. He must hate her now, but perhaps that was better. He might even let her go.

Christina rubbed her hand gently across her buttocks, but there was no pain. It was her pride that was bruised. She wondered how Philip would act toward her today, for he had not said a word after spanking her. She hoped he would not punish her further.

Amine came to visit Christina before the midday meal and brought her oldest child with her. Little Syed was about two years old, and Christina laughed as he ran about the room looking for things to get into. But she was embarrassed in the other girl's company, for Christina knew Amine must have heard her screams last night.

Amine smiled at her knowingly. "I would tell you something, Christina, for I know what is bothering you. There is no shame in what Sheik Abu did to you last night. It shows only that he really cares for you, otherwise he would not bother. Nura was filled with jealousy last night, for she knows this, too."

"The whole camp must have heard me," Christina gasped. "I'll never be able to show my face again."

"Most of the camp was asleep. But still, it is nothing to be ashamed of."

"I don't exactly feel proud," Christina said. "But I do know that I deserved punishment last night."

Just then, Philip walked in, startling them both. He walked into the bedroom without a word. Christina hoped he hadn't overheard their conversation.

"I will go now," Amine said, picking up little Syed. "I am sure Sheik Abu wishes to be alone."

"You don't have to go yet, Amine," Christina replied nervously.

"I will come again."

"I've enjoyed our talk," Christina said. She walked Amine to the entrance and squeezed her hand, whispering, "Thank you, Amine. I feel much better now."

Amine returned her smile and scurried away. Christina thought how happy Amine seemed, even though she had been stolen from her family, too.

Christina sensed Philip's presence behind her, but before she could turn around, he put his arms around her and pulled her forcefully against him. He cupped his hands over her breasts, and her knees became weak with his nearness. She fought against the weakness and pleasure that his touch gave her.

"Stop it, Philip. Let go of me this instant!" she demanded, trying desperately to pull his huge hands from her body. But Christina stopped struggling when he tightened his grip.

"You're hurting me," she gasped.

"That's not my intention, Tina," he whispered in her ear. Loosening his hold, he played with her nipples, gently rubbing them between his fingers. They rose tautly beneath the thin silk material of her blouse, demanding satisfaction.

But she couldn't let him continue. She had sworn never to give in again.

"Oh, please stop, Philip," she begged as he moved his smoldering lips down the side of her neck. A burning desire arose within her, making her tremble with its intensity, and suddenly she prayed that he wouldn't let her go.

"Why should I stop? You are mine, Tina, and I will caress you when and where I please."

107

She stiffened at his words. "I am not yours. I belong only to myself!" She pried his hands loose and turned to face him. She stood proudly staring up into his dark-green eyes, her own flashing defiantly.

"There you are wrong, Tina." He held her face between his hands so she couldn't turn away from his penetrating gaze. "I stole you. Therefore you belong to me and only me. You'd feel better about it if you had some affection for me."

"How can you talk of affection, Philip, when you are the cause of my troubles! You know I want to go home, but you keep me prisoner here."

"I want you here, and it's what I want that matters. I only thought that you might be happier if you softened your heart toward me." He released her and started to leave the tent.

"And what of you, Philip?" she asked. "What are your feelings toward me? Do you love me?"

"Love you?" He turned around to face her, and laughed softly. "No, I don't love you. I have never loved a woman, except perhaps my mother. I desire you, and that is enough."

"But that isn't enough! You can quench your desire with any woman — why must it be me?"

"Because no other woman has ever pleased me as much as you have." His eyes roamed her body intimately. "I'm afraid you've spoiled me, Tina," he chuckled, and left the tent.

The afternoon was hot and sticky. There had been no rain since Philip had returned to Egypt, and their water hole was slowly diminishing. But it had to rain soon; it always did this time of year.

Philip was breaking in a three-year-old horse when he saw Christina cross the camp and enter Yasir's tent. Grinning, he thought of that morning when he had visited with his father.

"That girl is kind and gentle, Abu," Yasir had scolded him. "And you ought to treat her right. It hurt my heart to hear her scream last

108

night. If I weren't so weak, I would have stopped you myself!"

Philip's head had been throbbing with a dull ache from the night's drinking, and he had felt irritated by his father's words. He was ready to tell him caustically about Christina's real character, but changed his mind. He could see his father was quite taken with Christina, and that pleased him. Christina would be like a breath of fresh air for Yasir. She could be charming when she tried.

An hour passed before Philip saw her again. He eyed her warily as she slowly approached him, a half-smile gracing her lips. He noticed that her eyes were a soft turquoise. Well, at least she's not angry with me, he thought, remembering the dark blue her eyes had been the last time he talked with her.

"Philip."

She spoke demurely, biting her lower lip, and rested her soft hands on the corral fence. She must want something, he guessed as he dismounted and walked toward her.

"What can I do for you, my sweet?" he asked.

"I was wondering, do you have any horses that haven't been trained yet?"

"Yes, but why do you ask?"

"I wish to ride," she said, looking down demurely.

Philip looked at her doubtfully. "You ask me to trust you on one of my horses after last night?"

"Oh, please, Philip. I can't stand idleness. I'm used to riding every day," she pleaded.

Philip searched her eyes. "How do I know you can handle a horse? I have only your word that you've ridden before."

"You insult me! I've ridden since I was a child, and my stallion at home is two hands taller than any horse you have here."

"Very well, Tina," he laughed, pointing to the horse he had been working. "Will this one do?"

"Oh, yes!" she said brightly. The beautiful Arabian was raven-black and reminded her of Dax, except he wasn't as large. He had a proudly arched neck, a deep chest, and long, slender legs. She couldn't believe he was hers to ride.

"It will take me only a minute to change!" she exclaimed, then ran to the tent.

"You will have to ride without a saddle," he called after her, for they didn't use them here.

"That's all right," she yelled over her shoulder. "I'll manage."

Christina dashed into the bedroom and took out the loose-fitting breeches that she'd just finished making. She was glad that she'd decided to make a robe instead of a dress first.

Throwing her skirt onto the bed, she quickly donned the black silk breeches. She wrapped a black strip of material securely about her head, concealing her golden hair. She slid into the flowing black velvet robe, tied the robe about her waist with a wide sash, then put the black velvet *kufiyah* on her head, binding it around with a heavy black cord.

When she thought of what Philip would think of her riding outfit, she laughed. But she didn't care, for she was gloriously happy.

Philip was surprised when he saw her come out of the tent. She looked like a young boy until she came closer and he could see her voluptuous curves enhanced by the soft velvet.

"I'm ready." She turned to the horse, nuzzled his nose, and whispered in his ear. "We're going to be fine friends, my black beauty, and I'll love you as if you were my own. Does he have a name?" she asked Philip as he lifted her onto the blanketed back of the horse and handed her the reins.

"No."

"I shall call you Raven," she said gleefully, leaning over so the horse could hear her. "And we'll ride the wind freely, like the raven."

Philip mounted Victory, and they slowly walked down the hillside. He marveled at how gentle Raven was with Christina, after the trouble he'd had breaking the horse.

Christina quickly became accustomed to the feel of riding bareback. She managed Raven beautifully as they rode down the winding path.

When they finally reached the bottom of the mountain, Christina urged Raven into a slow canter, then a speeding gallop, leaving Philip behind. She raced across the vast expanse of desert without destination, feeling like a free spirit flying in the wind. Her troubles fled from her as she dreamed she was back in Halstead riding across her estate, but then Philip caught up with her.

He pulled up on her reins. "If you insist on racing me, Tina, perhaps we should wager on who the victor will be."

"But I have nothing to wager," she replied. But she would dearly love to beat him at something for a change.

"Then we'll wager what we want from each other," he suggested, his dark-green eyes piercing hers. "We'll race back to the bottom of the mountain, and if I win, you'll give yourself to me freely from now on."

Christina thought about his wager for a minute. "And if I win, you'll send me back to my brother."

Philip looked at her curiously. She rode the horse well. She might beat him, and he couldn't take that chance.

"You ask too much, Tina."

"So do you, Philip," she returned curtly. Turning her horse, she headed back toward camp.

Smiling, he shook his head as he watched her ride away. She'd known he wouldn't accept her stakes. Well, it had been a good try. He caught up with her, and they rode back silently together.

The clouds came from nowhere, sending down a torrent of rain to wash away the heat. Christina and Philip were soaked through by the time they reached the camp. The men were working furiously to secure the tents so water couldn't seep under them. Someone was sitting in the rain by the fire, fanning smoke out of the shelter that had been erected over it.

Philip dismounted in front of their tent and carried Christina inside. "Get out of those wet clothes and do whatever you have to do now. It will be dark soon, and there will be no fire tonight." He set her down gently and added, "I have to see to the horses' shelter, but I'll be back shortly."

As Philip left, Amine asked to come in. She had brought their dinner and some fresh towels. "You must change quickly, Christina. The rain brings the cold, and you will fall sick if you do not get warm now."

"I was just wondering what to do with these wet clothes," Christina replied, laughing. "I can't very well hang them on a tree to dry."

"Come," Amine said, taking Christina into the bedroom. "Do you have needles that you sew with?"

"Yes."

"Good. I will hang your clothes with them to the inside of the tent. It will take a few days, but eventually they will dry."

While Christina took off her robe, Amine stared in wonder at her breeches. Christina laughed at the shocked look on Amine's face. "I made them for riding. They let me ride swiftly without a skirt flying into my face."

"Ah, but Sheik Abu, he must not like them," Amine giggled as Christina handed her the breeches and then her blouse.

"He hasn't seen them yet, but I suppose he won't like them when he does," Christina said, laughing at the thought of the breeches impeding Philip's eagerness to bed her.

Taking the towel as Amine left to hang her clothes, Christina rubbed her body down vigorously. She was cold from the draft blowing through the tent. Quickly she decided to put on one of Philip's robes, since she had nothing warmer to wear. She unpinned her hair, which was only slightly damp, and was combing out the golden locks when Amine came back into the room.

"I must go now and feed my children."

"Thank you, Amine. I don't know what I'd do without you as a

112

friend," Christina said sincerely.

Amine smiled bashfully at Christina's compliment and scurried from the tent. Christina laid the comb down on her chest and went into the main room to dine before it got so dark she wouldn't be able to see what she was eating.

She ate the mutton stew and rice slowly, pondering Philip's complete change from the night before. She had been surprised and happy when he agreed to let her ride. Raven was such a fine animal. She couldn't wait until tomorrow when she could ride again. But then, Philip hadn't said she could ride every day.

"Do something with these, will you, sweet?"

The first words he spoke made Christina jump and drop her food onto her plate. She hadn't seen Philip come in, and now he stood behind her holding out his wet clothes. He had changed already and was toweling his hair dry with his other hand.

"I didn't see you enter," she said, taking his clothes and going for more needles.

"You won't be able to see me at all, shortly," he called after her. He smiled, thinking of the rest of the night to be spent in his warm bed. Ha, she wouldn't be too happy about that!

Christina hung Philip's clothes alongside her own in the narrow space between the tent and the curtains. She then joined him to finish her meal while he ate his.

"Are the horses all right?" she said. She was worried about Raven.

"The young colts are a bit jittery, but the older horses are used to sudden storms."

"Does it rain like this often?" she asked, starting as a flash of lightning illuminated the tent.

"Only in the mountains," he laughed. "But this storm is worse than usual — it's been a long time in coming. Does thunder frighten you, Tina?" he asked as he finished off the stew. He could barely see her.

"Of course not!" she returned haughtily. She drained a glass of wine she'd poured to warm herself. "There's very little I'm afraid of."

"Good," he replied heartily, stretching his arms wide. "I suggest we go to bed, then, since there's no longer any light to see by."

"If you don't mind, I'll stay here awhile." She reached for the bag of wine, but her hand was intercepted by his.

"Ah, but I do mind."

He yanked her to her feet and pulled her resisting body behind him toward the bedroom. But Christina had gained courage from the wine. She sank her teeth into his hand, freed herself, and dashed frantically behind the curtains.

"Damn it, woman! Is there no end to your trickery?" she heard him call out in a rage. But she knew he couldn't see her.

Just then, lightning again crashed through the sky and silhouetted Christina's small frame against the curtains. The next thing she knew, she was lying flat on her back with Philip's weight pressing her deeply into the soft rugs.

He laughed cruelly as he roughly yanked her robe apart, not bothering to untie it. His lips seared hers painfully, silencing her screams as he entered her viciously. Her mind was beyond reason as her body accepted his like a wild animal, and the pain turned to violent waves of ecstatic pleasure.

"I'm sorry, Tina," he said later. "But you never cease to amaze me with the lengths you will go to avoid lovemaking. You crave it as much as I do!"

"I do not!" she cried, pushing him off her and running into the bedroom. She threw herself on the bed and let the tears flow freely.

She felt his weight on the bed, and turned to face him in the darkness of the room. "Philip, I want to go home. I want to go back to my brother," she pleaded between sobs.

"No," he replied curtly. "And I don't want to hear any more about it."

She cried her heart out into the pillow, but Philip was immune to her crying, and eventually they both fell asleep.

Chapter 15

A month passed swiftly by, and then another. Though it was winter, the days were warm, with soft eastern breezes, but the nights were extremely cold. Christina resented the fact that she needed Philip's body for warmth during the long, cold nights. She awakened each morning to find herself curled up next to Philip or him molded against her back.

The weather worked against Christina, for the close contact of their bodies seeking warmth aroused Philip's desire. If he woke first, there was no possible escape for her.

Philip enjoyed their morning romps because he didn't have to chase Christina around the tent and put up with her fighting and kicking. In the mornings, he pinned her down before she awoke fully and knew what was happening. Then he took his time with her, and only had to suffer a few weak protests before she abandoned herself to his caresses.

Philip spent his days hunting, at which he was skillful. He rarely missed his target and often brought welcome meat home to his people.

Christina's days were full, and she had fallen into a routine. She spent her mornings in the tent either sewing or reading. Amine came often to visit. Christina loved children and enjoyed playing with Amine's, especially the baby.

As Christina watched the children play together, she would sometimes wonder what would happen it she were to become pregnant. She would love to have a child of her own, but she didn't want Philip's child. She hated him too much.

And how would Philip react? Would he send her away if she lost her figure and could no longer satisfy him? He'd said he hadn't brought her here to bear children. Perhaps he didn't like children. But if she were to give him a son, would he keep the baby? Would he send her away without her child? Such questions were pointless, however, so she didn't ponder them long.

After the noon meal, Christina went to visit Yasir each day. His health was much improved. He could concentrate longer and talked more to her, his fondest subject being Philip. Once he started talking about his son there was no stopping him. He told her about Philip as a child growing up in the desert. He told her how he taught Philip to walk and talk.

"Abu's first sentence was half-Arabic and half-English," Yasir said. "He didn't know the difference!"

Christina felt a bit sorry for Rashid. She could tell that all of Yasir's love went to Philip. Perhaps Philip also felt sorry for Rashid, and so always gave him his own way.

After visiting Yasir, she went riding. She looked forward to it every day. If Philip was away, she went with Ahmad or Saadi, and sometimes even Rashid when he was in camp, which wasn't often.

As Christina rode through the desert on Raven's back, she made believe she was safe and secure in Halstead without a care in the world. No Philip, no troubles, nothing to make her wish for past happiness. Only Dax beneath her and Tommy or John beside her racing across grassy fields, cool winds caressing her face. But the arid breath of the desert always shattered her dreams and reminded her of reality.

Christina prayed desperately that Philip would soon tire of her. But his desire for her seemed insatiable. She spent her evenings devising ways of avoiding the inevitable, but she quickly ran out of ideas, and nothing seemed to work. She was waspish and nagging. She feigned sleepiness and headaches. But he always saw through her schemes.

Baiting him into anger only made him take her viciously. She wore her breeches to bed one night, but she was sorry afterward, for they ended up on the floor torn to pieces. Her only respite came when he was exhausted, but he usually made up for it the next morning.

Christina hadn't seen Philip all day. Rashid had dined with them last night and had presented her with a beautiful handcarved looking glass. She'd kissed him lightly on the cheek in appreciation of the gift. Philip had been sullen and taciturn the rest of the evening.

She wondered why he'd acted that way, as she walked quickly toward the corral where Saadi was waiting to ride with her. In her haste, she didn't see Nura leaving the fire, and collided with her, knocking her down.

"I'm sorry," Christina gasped, extending her hand. "Here, let me help you."

"Do not touch me," Nura hissed, her voice filled with hate as she stood up. "You wicked woman! You have cast a spell on Abu to make him want you. But I will break the spell. Abu does not love you. Soon he will cast you out and marry me. You are not wanted here. Why do you stay?"

Christina was speechless. She had to escape the hate she saw in Nura's eyes. She hadn't known jealousy could cause such hatred. She ran to the horses where Saadi stood with shock on his kindly brown face from his sister's words. He started to speak to Christina, but she swiftly mounted Raven by herself and rode recklessly out of camp.

Saadi mounted and tried desperately to catch up with her. He knew Sheik Abu would skin him alive if he let anything happen to his woman. She was riding down the hill so fast, she could easily take a fall from her horse and hurt herself. It would be Nura's fault for upsetting her, but Saadi would have to take the blame.

Ah, that Nura! He would make her pay for this. He must make her understand that the sheik was happy with his foreign woman, even though he hadn't married her yet. Nura must give up her false hopes.

Christina's vision blurred with tears. She wasn't crying over Nura's words, for she didn't care whether Philip loved her or not. She was crying because Nura hated her, and it wasn't her fault. Christina would gladly give Philip to Nura. She would leave if she could. She hadn't asked to be kidnapped!

Christina stopped Raven at the bottom of the hill to wipe her eyes before galloping on. She was going to ride as far as Raven would take her into the desert, and she didn't care what happened to her.

Suddenly she noticed two men on horseback in the distance. They were standing motionless at the base of the mountains. She considered riding to them, until the tallest man came toward her. She thought the man must be either Philip or Rashid, because he was too tall to be anyone else. She couldn't tell which it was, for he was still too far away and his *kufiyah* covered his features.

If it were Philip, she could not escape him. She heard Saadi coming up behind her, and turned to look into his worried eyes.

"I wish to apologize for my sister," Saadi managed to say as he caught his breath. "She had no right to say what she did to you, and I will punish her for it."

"It's all right, Saadi. I don't want you to punish Nura because of me. I understand how she feels."

Glancing to where she had seen the two men, Christina saw that they had both disappeared. She continued her ride with Saadi as usual, and returned to camp before dusk.

When Christina entered the tent, she found Philip waiting to take her to bathe. He seemed in good spirits, and whacked her bottom as she passed him to get the towels and soap. She didn't ask him if he were one of the men she had seen on the desert. He had made it quite clear before that he didn't like her questioning him.

In the late hours of the following morning, Christina was mending the hem on one of her skirts when Amine came into the tent very slowly. She stood before Christina wringing her hands.

A terrible pain crept into Christina's heart. She realized something awful must have happened, but she didn't know why she felt so sick inside.

"What is it, Amine?" she gasped. "Has something happened to Abu?"

"No," Amine answered, a tear sliding down her cheek. "It is his father — shiek Yasir Alhamar is dead."

"But that can't be!" Christina cried, jumping to her feet. "Yasir was fine yesterday, and he's been so much better these last months. I — I don't believe it!"

Christina ran from the tent, oblivious of Amine's calls. But she knew, even before she entered Yasir's tent to find it empty, that it was true. He really was dead. She cried then, the tears flowing unchecked as she stared down at the empty sheepskins on the floor that had been his bed only yesterday. She went down on her knees and touched the soft sheepskin. She had come to care for Yasir, and now he was gone.

She felt Amine's arms go around her and help her to her feet.

"Come, Christina, it is not good to stay here." Amine led her back to her tent and sat with her on the couch, holding her closely for comfort. She remained silent until Christina's tears were spent. "Sheik Yasir died in his sleep during the night. Rashid discovered him early this morning, and he and Sheik Abu took him to the desert to bury."

"But why wasn't I told sooner?" Christina asked.

"It was a private thing between two sons and their father. Sheik Abu did not want you to be disturbed."

"Where is Abu now?" Christina asked, knowing how he must feel. She remembered the agony she had felt when she lost both her parents. Strange as it seemed, she wanted to comfort Philip, to put her arms around him and share his sorrow.

"When Rashid returned to camp, he said Abu rode off into the desert, and then — then Rashid left, too."

Christina waited patiently for Philip to return. She tried to keep busy so she wouldn't think of Yasir, but it was impossible. She kept seeing his face as it lit up whenever she entered his tent. She kept hearing his voice as he talked fondly about Philip.

The moon floated high over the mountains and cast a soft gray light that filtered gently through the juniper trees surrounding the camp. Philip stood dejectedly by the fire, warming his exhausted limbs.

It had taken him most of the day riding wildly across the desert to come to terms with Yasir's death. He thought now that it was better to have come at last. Yasir had always lived a vigorous life, and the months after his illness had turned him into an invalid chafing at his confinement.

Philip wished he had been allowed more time with Yasir, but was grateful for the years he'd had. He had many fond memories to carry with him through the years to come, for he and Yasir had been closer than most fathers and sons; they had been good friends and shared much together.

After feeding and rubbing down Victory, Philip quickly made his way across the sleeping camp to his tent. He was physically and mentally exhausted and was eager to feel Christina close beside him.

Philip went directly to their bedroom, but found it empty. A number of emotions crossed his features — misery, anger, regret, as he wondered why she would choose this of all times to escape him.

Damn, how much more will I suffer before this day ends, he thought. Turning swiftly, he started to run from the tent, wondering how much time Christina had gained. A soft voice halted him before he reached the entrance.

"Philip, is that you?"

Feeling as if a heavy weight had been lifted from his chest, Philip walked slowly over to the couch. Christina was leaning on one elbow, her feet curled under a heavy sheepskin cover. She was gazing up at him with a worried look on her beautiful face.

He sat down beside her and saw that her eyes were red from crying. She put her hand gently on his and spoke softly.

"I'm sorry, Philip."

"I'm all right now, Tina. I will grieve for a while, but the worst has passed and I must continue to live my life."

As he searched Christina's eyes, he realized that she was grieving, too. He hadn't known she cared so much for Yasir. Philip took her in his arms and held her gently against him as she started crying again.

In the days that followed, the camp was in a strange kind of mourning. All the gay shouts and loud talking had disappeared.

Amine tried in her own way to lift Christina's spirits. Christina was grateful to have a friend she could talk to. If it weren't for Amine and her children, she would really be lonely.

Christina couldn't seem to bring Philip out of the mood he had fallen into. She chatted away about nothing in particular whenever he was about, but he just sat and stared into space as if she weren't there. He answered her questions and greeted her, but that was all. She remembered she had been in the same state after her parents died, but John had helped her through it. She didn't know how to help Philip.

At night when they went to bed, Philip held her in his arms, nothing more. It began to get on her nerves. She constantly wondered when he would take her again. She wasn't pleased with the present arrangement, she told herself, because she wasn't used to the way Philip was acting.

She tried to think of ways to pull him out of his depression, but couldn't. Besides, hadn't she wanted to see him suffer? It was what she'd once wanted, but not anymore. It hurt her to see Philip unhappy, and she didn't know why.

Chapter 16

It had been five days since Yasir died, and the tension was wearing Christina down. Philip was off hunting somewhere, and she had no idea when he would be coming back. She'd chosen to stay in her tent these last days, but now she just couldn't stand it anymore.

She left the tent, searched out Ahmad, and asked him to make Raven ready for her. Then she quickly donned her robe and breeches, and by the time she reached the corral, Ahmad was ready to go.

"It is good that you resume your activities," he said with a big smile as he helped her mount.

"Yes, it is," Christina returned. But not all activities, she added to herself, thinking of the quiet nights she'd been granted lately.

They rode down the mountainside slowly, but when they reached the bottom, Christina urged Raven into a fast gallop. Ahmad was accustomed to the way she rode and managed to stay beside her.

They had been riding for at least half an hour and were far into the desert when Christina spied four men on horseback coming swiftly toward them. They had come from nowhere, it seemed, and were soon upon them.

Christina slowed Raven and turned to see Ahmad raising his rifle. But before he had time to pull the trigger, a shot rang through the air, and Christina felt sick as Ahmad fell slowly from his horse, blood oozing from his chest.

"Oh, God — no!" she screamed, but Ahmad lay motionless on the hot sand.

Immediately Christina turned Raven and whipped him into a gallop. She wanted to go to Ahmad, but she had to think of herself now. She could hear her pursuers closing in behind her. An arm went around her waist, yanked her from her horse, and threw her across another one. She struggled fiercely and was rewarded when she fell off backward onto the hard sand.

The man who had grabbed her got off his horse and slowly approached Christina. He had an angry, ferocious look on his bearded face.

Christina's heart beat painfully as she scrambled to her feet and started to run, but before she had got ten feet away, the man had swung her around and slapped her brutally across her face, knocking her down. He lifted her up halfway by the front of her robe and hit her two more times, then dropped her as if she were dirt. She was crying hysterically as she turned over on the sand so he couldn't hit her any more.

Vaguely, Christina could hear voices quarreling, but they sounded so far away. She felt dazed, and for a moment she didn't even know where she was or why she was crying. It all came back to her painfully when she cautiously raised her head and saw Ahmad's lifeless body lying some distance away from her.

Oh, God, why did they have to kill him? she thought miserably. A few yards away from her three of the men still sat on horseback, one of them talking harshly to the man who had beaten her.

Amair Abdalla dismounted and walked over to the woman lying on the sand. He felt pity when he turned her over and saw her face, already discolored and swelling. He had been told this woman was a beauty, but now her face was dirty from the sand, with clear streaks running down her cheeks from her tears.

That bastard Cassim! It had happened so fast that Amair had been unable to stop him. They were in a hurry, or he would punish the beast now. Cassim had always been a cruel man. His wife had nearly died twice from his cruelty and beatings.

Sheik Ali Hejaz would not take kindly to the beating of this woman. Christina Wakefield was important to Sheik Ali in more ways than one, and he had given strict orders that she was not to be harmed.

Cassim would be taken care of when they returned to camp — and he knew it. But now they must hurry. The plan did not call for a confrontation on Sheik Abu's home ground, and Amair didn't want to have a run-in with the big man. It would mean sure death.

Moments had passed since the young man had turned Christina over. He had been staring at her face, and she could see the pity in his brown eyes. What was going to happen now? Perhaps they wouldn't hurt her any more — not now, anyway. Christina instinctively cringed away from the man when he bent down to pick her up. He carried her to the horses, put her on his small Arabian, and got on behind her. The other three men were mounted and waiting, and they all rode off at a gallop.

Christina closed her eyes when they passed Ahmad's body. Poor Ahmad. He was only a little older than she, and now his life was finished. The four men left Raven and Ahmad's horse behind. If they were thieves, why didn't they take the horses, too?

Who were they? They couldn't have known she was a woman, not the way she was dressed, so why hadn't they shot her also? The men couldn't be here to rescue her, for nobody had known she was here. Besides, if they meant to take her back to her brother, they wouldn't beat her. It just didn't make any sense.

These men must be from the neighboring tribe that Philip had warned her about. Would they all use her, then sell her into slavery? Philip would never be able to find her!

Philip, where are you? You've got to find me! But what could she be thinking! Hadn't she wanted to leave Philip?

At least my new master will never have the power to make me weak with his touch the way Philip does. No other man will be able to arouse my desire like Philip. Suddenly she realized what she'd just said in her thoughts.

I love him! I loved him all this time and didn't even know it!

Christina, you're a fool, a stupid little fool. You fought Philip all these months and prayed to be sent home, when all the time you loved him. You may never see him again, and Philip still thinks you hate him.

But what if he doesn't come? What if he's glad I'm gone and off his hands? Can I blame him after the way I've acted toward him? Oh, no, he's got to come for me, he's got to save me so I can tell him how much I love him. And he's got to find me soon, before it's too late!

When Yasir died and I wanted to comfort Philip, I should have known then that I loved him. It has taken a nightmare to make me see the truth, and now it may be too late. Oh, God, give me another chance!

It was getting dark now, and they were still riding hard, as if the devil himself were chasing them. Again it didn't make any sense. If these four men were from the neighboring tribe Philip had talked about, they should have gone into the mountains and reached their camp already.

She must be wrong. They had been riding along the base of the mountains, but now, as the moon came out to light the way, they turned and headed into the desert. Where were they taking her? And what would happen to her when they got there?

Christina remembered the long-ago time when she had asked herself these same questions, only Philip had been her abductor then. She really had hated him those first weeks after he brought her to his camp. He had taken her away from all she loved. He had manipulated everyone to bring her to this land. But every young woman leaves behind all that she knows when she marries. It takes time to become accustomed to a new life.

Well, she had become accustomed — too accustomed, in fact. And she felt a fear and emptiness in her heart that she would never see Philip again. It was worse than the pain that she felt in her swollen face with each step of the horse. She closed her eyes to shut out all the misery she felt, and, somehow, fell asleep.

The sound of loud voices brought Christina's eyes open. She was lifted down from the horse. She wondered what had happened until she saw all the new faces about her and felt the soreness in her face. The sun was up and the heat was torrid, bouncing off the sand, forcing her to shade her eyes from the glare in order to see.

Before Christina was taken into a small tent, she glanced about the encampment. They were at a desert oasis. Two huge palm trees towered over six small tents, and she could see goats, sheep, and camels grazing on a stretch of grass behind them.

Inside the tent, it took Christina a moment to become accustomed to the darkness. She saw an old man sitting alone on a pillow behind a low table covered with bowls of food.

The old man hadn't even glanced in her direction yet. He was still eating his meal, so Christina looked about the tent. A few pillows were scattered about, and she saw a large chest in one corner, but there were no chairs to sit on or rugs to cover the sand.

When Christina looked back at the old man, he was dipping his fingers into a small bowl of water, as she had done many times after finishing a meal with Philip. He looked up at her then, and his brown eyes widened in anger at the sight of her bruised face. She jumped when his fist slammed down on the table, making all the bowls clatter.

He was dressed in a colorful robe and *kufiyah,* and she noticed that his feet were bare beneath the table. When he stood up, he appeared to be no taller than herself, but when he spoke, he commanded authority.

He spoke harshly to the young man with Christina, and she surmised he must be the sheik of this tribe. Heated words passed between them that Christina couldn't understand, and then the young man led her behind a curtain in the corner of the tent.

The small space was barely big enough for her to lie down. There was a sheepskin on the sand, and Christina was deposited there, then left alone.

A few minutes later, an old woman opened the curtains and brought in a tray with a large bowl of food and a glass of wine. The woman set the tray down on the sand, handed Christina a wet towel, pointing to her face, and left Christina alone again.

She washed her face with the towel, but couldn't remove all of the dirt around her painfully swollen eyes. The food was greasy, but was luckily soft, for it also hurt her to chew. The wine tasted wonderful, but she felt strangely tired after she finished drinking it. Christina fought to stay awake so she could be prepared for what would happen next, but she couldn't manage to keep her eyes open or think coherently, and presently she fell into a sound sleep.

When Amair Abdalla left the woman in Sheik Ali Hejaz's tent, he stopped long enough to tell Cassim that Sheik Ali wished to see him, then he went directly to his father's tent. He did not feel sorry for Cassim, for whatever befell him was of his own doing. Sheik Ali was angrier than Amair had expected, and Cassim would probably die for his deed.

"Amair, did everything go well?" his father, Cogia Abdalla asked when Amair walked into the tent that they shared.

"Yes, father, all went as planned," Amair replied distastefully. He sat down on the sheepskin that was his bed, and grabbed the goatskin of wine beside it. "But I will tell you this — I do not care for what I was ordered to do. That woman has done nothing, and she should not be made the pawn for revenge. Already she has suffered, for Cassim beat her before I could stop him."

"What! That no-good —"

"Don't you see, father?" Amair cut in. "None of this should have happened in the first place. Cassim shot the man Christina Wakefield was riding with. I pray that he is found before he dies, for he is Ahmad, the brother of Amine's husband. If Ahmad dies, then Syed will hate us and we will never be able to see my sister, Amine, again."

"I should have known this plan would come to no good." Cogia hung his head dejectedly. "I should never have agreed to let you take part in it. I only want this hatred to come to an end so I can see my daughter again. Amine must have children now, and I have never seen them. I might never see my grandchildren!"

"But even so, father, you should never have agreed to this plan. Sheik Abu had nothing to do with what happened all those years ago. He was across the seas then. I do not think he should be made the target for Sheik Ali's revenge now that Sheik Yasir is dead."

"I know, my son, but what can we do now? Perhaps Sheik Abu will not come," Cogia said. He looked out of the open tent. In the center of the camp three little boys were playing with a baby lamb. Cogia ached with wanting to see his own daughter and her children.

"He will come," Amair replied. "And if he brings the men of his tribe, there will be much useless bloodshed for something that happened twenty-five years ago. And not one man who will die had anything to do with it."

And Philip did come, less than an hour later. He came alone and cursed himself for doing so when he realized the danger he was up against.

Philip had returned to his camp and was told that Christina had gone riding with Ahmad. He was glad she'd decided to resume her daily rides, and realized it was time to break out of his own depression. His father was dead, but he still had Christina.

Thoughts of Christina went through Philip's mind as he paced the tent waiting for her to return. But when the sun went down and there was still no sign of her, a sickening dread came over him. He ran from the tent and, seeing Syed by the corral, told him to follow.

Philip broke out in a sweat as they galloped down the hillside, Syed desperately trying to keep up with him. After riding some distance in the direction Christina usually took, Philip saw two horses standing close to each other. The color drained from his face when he came closer and saw a body lying on the sand.

He jumped from his horse and ran to Ahmad. The wound was in the lower part of Ahmad's chest; he had lost a lot of blood but was still alive. Syed arrived, and they forced some water down Ahmad's throat. He finally opened his eyes. He looked from Philip to Syed and tried to sit up but was too weak from loss of blood.

"Can you talk, Ahmad?" Philip asked. "Can you tell me what happened?"

Ahmad looked at Philip through glared eyes. "There were four desert men riding toward us at a fast speed. I — I raised my rifle to fire, but they shot me. That is all I can remember." Ahmad strained to look about, and when he saw Christina's horse he sank back onto the sand. "They have taken her?"

"It looks that way," Philip replied. His body was tense, ready to do battle. He looked to the older brother. "Syed, you take Ahmad back to camp. Maidi will know what to do for him. I don't know how long I will be, but do not follow. I will find Christina, and the man who shot your brother will die."

"Allah be with you," Syed replied as Philip mounted his horse.

The tracks from the kidnappers' four horses could still be seen, since there had been no wind to cover them with sand. Philip followed the tracks with a speed Victory had never reached before. He kept seeing Christina's frightened face, and he prayed that he could find her in time, before the men raped and sold her.

He should never have let her ride on the desert. If he had limited her to the camp, she would be there now. And he wouldn't be fearing for her life. Please, God, let him find her in time!

Philip had a sick feeling in his heart as he tried to imagine what his life would be without Christina. He pictured the empty bed that he had shared with her, the empty tent that he had always been eager to enter, her beautiful, soft body that could tempt him so easily. How could another woman ever take Christina's place? He couldn't bear the thought of never seeing her again.

He must love her if he felt this way!

Philip had never believed he would fall in love. What a fool he had been! But what if he couldn't find Christina? Worse, what if she didn't want to be found? Well, he would find her or die trying, and he would force her to go back with him. He would rather live with her hate than live without her. Perhaps someday she would grow to love him in return.

Philip thanked heaven for the full moon that gave him enough light to follow the tracks. The hours passed by slowly, filled with his tortured thoughts, and the sun was high before Philip spotted the camp of a desert tribe in the distance. The tracks he followed led directly to the camp. It won't be long now, Christina, he thought. I will find you and take you home.

Philip slowed his horse and entered the encampment. Several men came forward as he halted Victory in the center of the camp.

"I am looking for four men and a woman," Philip said in Arabic. "They came through here, did they not?"

"You have come to the right place, Abu Alhamar. You will dismount and come with me."

Philip turned to see the man who spoke. A rifle was pointed at his back, leaving him little choice. "How do you know who I am?"

"You have been expected. Come with me."

Philip dismounted, and the man prodded him with the rifle toward a tent entrance. More armed men walked behind him, ready for his slightest move. How the devil do they know who I am? Philip wondered.

An old man at the far end of the tent stood up and looked Philip over. "It did not take you long to come, Sheik Abu. I have waited a long time for this moment."

"What the hell is this all about?" Philip demanded. "How do you know who I am? I've never laid eyes on you before?"

"You have seen me before, but you would not remember. Perhaps you have heard of me? I am Ali Hejaz, sheik of this tribe and uncle to Rashid, your half-brother. Do you know me now?"

"I have heard your name before, but that's all. Why were you expecting me?"

"Ah, I see your father kept the truth from you. Now I must tell you the whole story, so you will understand why I am going to kill you to avenge my sister's death."

"You must be crazy," Philip laughed. "I've done nothing to you. Why do you want me dead?"

"I am not crazy, Abu Alhamar." Ali Hejaz spoke calmly, relishing his moment of triumph. "You will soon learn why you must die. I knew you would fall into my trap, because I have your woman."

"Where is she?" Philip exploded. "If you've hurt her . . . !"

"All in good time, Abu," Ali Hejaz interrupted. "You may see her later, for the last time. Do not fear for her, for she will not be harmed in my camp. I am grateful to Christina Wakefield for bringing you to my vengeance. Later, I will return her to her brother for the reward."

"How did you know about her?" Philip asked.

"You have so many questions! You see, Rashid visits me from time to time. He mentioned you were back from England, and that you were keeping a foreign woman as your mistress. It seems I have rescued Christina Wakefield from her abductor!" Ali paused. When he spoke again, his voice was filled with anger. "I also recently learned of Yasir's death. I was cheated out of killing him myself, so you, his beloved son, will take his place!"

"What do you claim my father did?" Philip asked.

Ali Hejaz poured two glasses of wine and offered one to Philip. He declined, and Ali smiled. "It will be your last — I suggest you drink it. It is not poisoned, I assure you. I have a slower, crueler death planned for you."

"Get on with your explanations, Hejaz. I wish to see Christina," Philip replied. He took the wine and toasted the old man mockingly.

"I see you do not take me seriously yet. Ah, but you will when your slow death begins. However, you deserve to know why you are

131

going to die." Ali paused and drank from the glass he was holding.

"A very long time ago, your father and I were close friends. I would have done anything for Yasir. I also knew your mother, and I was with Yasir when you were born. I rejoiced for your father in those days. He had two fine sons and a woman he loved more than life itself. I remember holding you on my knee when you were only three years old and telling you stories. Can you remember that?"

"No."

"I didn't think you would. Those were happy days — until your mother left. She was a good woman, but she destroyed Yasir. He was never the same again. His wife gone, his two sons gone, Yasir felt he had nothing to live for. I suffered with him for three years, for I loved Yasir as a brother. I hoped he would forget your mother, and find happiness again. I had a sister named Margiana, a beautiful girl who adored Yasir. So I offered Margiana to Yasir in marriage."

"But my mother and father were still married. How could he marry your sister?" Philip interrupted.

"Your mother had gone and was not coming back. It was the same as if she were dead. Yasir was free to marry again. He could make a new life and sire sons he could watch grow to manhood. So Yasir agreed to marry my sister. I was called away just then, and asked Margiana not to marry until my return. But she refused to wait.

"I was wounded while away and was bedridden for months. It took me almost two years to find my sister and Yasir's tribe. Rashid, my sister's son, was a year old then.

"And so the years passed, and I thought all was well with my sister. Yasir was still unhappy. He did not love Rashid as he had you. However, when I visited my sister she acted as though she were happy.

"Several years ago, my sister came to me and finally told me the truth about her so-called marriage. Yasir refused to marry her at the last minute. But on the night they were to have been married, he got drunk and raped her. When she discovered months later that she was with child, she begged Yasir to marry her. But he still refused. He couldn't forget your mother. Margiana felt ashamed because she was not married, so she lied to me and let me think she was happy. Yasir never took her again, but he let her and Rashid live with his tribe. She loved him, and he treated her like dirt.

"After my sister told me the truth, she killed herself. It was as if Yasir had plunged the knife into her. He killed my sister, and on that day I swore revenge. I waited, but Yasir knew of my sworn hatred and never ventured from his camp alone. He never forgot I was waiting for him, and I waited too long. Yasir died a happy man, without suffering the way my sister suffered."

"But all that has nothing to do with me. Why do you want me dead?" Philip asked. He believed the story. Yasir had lived with the memory of his first and only wife until the day he died. He probably never knew that Margiana loved him and was suffering because of it.

"You will take Yasir's place," said Ali Hejaz. "You, his beloved son, who were everything to him, as my sister was to me. You, who gave Yasir pleasure in his last years when he should have had none. You, the son of the woman who was to blame for my sister's death. You, who are just like your father in every way, taking women without marriage and making them suffer.

"You shall die, and I will be avenged at long last." Ali laughed, a short, satanic laugh. "Ah, but revenge is sweet. If only Yasir were here to see your death, I would be the happiest of men. I will even grant you a last wish if it is reasonable."

"You are too kind," said Philip sarcastically. "I would like to see Christina Wakefield now."

"Ah yes, the woman. I did say that you could see her, did I not? But first I must warn you, I am afraid she met with a slight accident before she came here."

"An accident? Where is she!" Philip demanded.

Ali Hejaz motioned to one of the men behind Philip. The man

133

lifted a curtain at the back of the tent.

Philip saw Christina huddled on the floor. "Oh, my God!" he gasped. He bent down to touch her, but she didn't move.

"I thought it best to drug her for a few days until the swelling goes down," Ali said from behind him.

Philip stood up and turned very slowly to face the old man. The muscles in his cheeks twitched with the violent rage consuming him.

"Who did this?" he said quietly, emotions held tautly in check. "Who did this to her?"

"It should not have happened. The man who beat her has always been cruel to women. When she ran from him he went wild and beat her before my men could stop him. He will die, of course. I gave strict orders not to harm the woman, and he disobeyed me. I have not yet decided how he will die, but he will."

"Give him to me," Philip said grimly.

"What?"

"Give the man who did this to me. You have granted me one request. I want the man who beat her."

Ali looked at Philip incredulously, then his old eyes widened. "Of course! It is right that you have the honor. I have no doubt you will win, but it will be a fair fight. You will fight with knives, immediately, in the center of the camp. After Cassim dies, you shall die a slower death."

Philip followed the old man from the tent. He could think only of killing the man who had dared hurt Christina.

"Bring Cassim out and tell him what is expected," Ali ordered.

Ali took his own knife from his belt and handed it to Philip. "When the fight is over, you will throw down the knife and offer no resistance. If you do not, Christina Wakefield will never be returned to her brother, but will be sold into slavery. Do you understand?"

Philip nodded and took the knife. He stuck it into his waistband, removed his robe and tunic, then grasped the knife in his right hand. Cassim was brought out of a nearby tent, fear showing clearly on his face. He was dragged forward to stand before Philip.

"I will not fight this man!" Cassim screamed. "If I must die, then shoot me!"

"Stand up and fight like a man. Or I will have your heart torn from your living body!" Ali shouted.

Philip felt no pity for the man cowering before him. All he could see was Christina's swollen face. "Prepare to die, woman-beater."

Cassim was released and fell back a few feet, then lunged forward. But Philip was ready for him. He stepped aside, and his knife caught Cassim in the right arm, below the shoulder. They circled each other warily, arms outstretched. Cassim jabbed forward again, intending to stab Philip in the chest. But Philip moved like lightning striking its unsuspecting victim. He cut downward on Cassim's extended arm, slicing it to the bone. Cassim dropped his knife to the ground, staring dumbfounded at the wound. Philip backhanded him across the face, knocking him down.

He gave Cassim time to retrieve his knife, then attacked again. Cassim was obviously no knife-fighter and his fear made him careless and an easy victim for Philip's skill.

Philip knew many tricks he had learned from his father, but he had no need of tricks now. Philip's knife struck Cassim again and again until he was covered with his own blood. Philip finally tired of the game and cut his throat, Cassim fell forward onto the sand.

Philip felt disgusted. He wouldn't have believed that he had such violence in him. How could he kill a man so mercilessly? The man would have died anyway, and he deserved to suffer for hurting Christina, but Philip felt sick for executing him. He threw the knife down beside Cassim's body and walked over to Ali Hejaz.

"You do not look pleased, Abu, Perhaps you will feel better knowing that Cassim also shot your tribesman."

"There's no way to feel better after killing a man," Philip replied.

"When you have waited many years to kill a man, as I have, revenge can be pleasurable," said Ali. "You will go with my men

135

now. Remember that you hold Christina Wakefield's future in your hands. Also, I have ordered my men to shoot if you try to escape. A wound in an arm or a leg will only make your death more agonizing."

The men seized Philip and led him behind Ali Hejaz's tent. Four stakes stood embedded in the sand, with ropes attached to each. He knew then how he was going to die.

He gave no resistance. The men spread-eagled him on his back and tied his arms and legs to the stakes. Philip heard one man whisper, "Forgive me," then he left. The other man walked to the shade of Ali's tent and sat down to guard Philip.

Guard against what? Philip wanted to know. He could not escape. It was late afternoon, but the sun would beat down for at least two more hours. He felt a slight hunger, but that was the least of his worries.

Not much damage would be done today, but tomorrow his suffering would begin. Would he be able to stand it? Could he will himself to die?

He would force himself to stay awake this night, that was the only way. The two nights and days he had gone without rest would enable him to sleep tomorrow, and perhaps he would die quickly in the hot sun without ever waking.

An hour passed, and Philip was already fighting to stay awake. A shadow loomed over him, and he opened his eyes to see Ali Hejaz.

"I think it is ironic that you should die this way, don't you? You wanted to live under our sun and make Yasir happy, so it is only fitting that you die under our sun. It is not a pleasant way to die. Your tongue will swell. But I do not want you to choke to death too soon. You will be given enough water to prevent that. You will suffer long, as the sun bakes you alive. And if you thought of staying awake this night and sleeping through your suffering tomorrow, I will have to disappoint you. I drugged your wine slightly, and you will sleep tonight." Ali laughed as he put an end to Philip's only hope. "You look surprised, Abu. But, as you see, I have thought of everything.

136

Yes, you will be awake tomorrow when the sun rises. Have a pleasant night, Abu. It will be your last." With that, he left Philip to his thoughts.

Philip pulled against the ropes with all his strength, but there was no hope for escape. He slept.

137

Chapter 17

Yes, you will be awake tomorrow, when the sun rises. Have a pleasant death, Abu. It will be your last." With that, he left Philip to his thoughts.

Philip pulled against the ropes once again, but there was no hope for escape. He slept.

The pain in his eyes brought Philip awake. When he opened them, he stared directly into the late morning sun and was blinded for a minute. He wondered for a moment why he had slept outside, until he tried to rise and felt the pain in his shoulders.

So — the sun was already doing its work, he thought when he looked down at his burned chest and arms. At least Hejaz had been wrong about one thing — he had not been awake to see the sun rise. Philip lay perfectly still.

The sun was directly above him now. Philip's tongue felt foreign in his mouth, like a piece of dry cloth. The sweat baked from his body hurt him as it rolled over burned skin. How long could he last? He forced himself to think of pleasant things and lost himself in thoughts of Christina.

Philip heard a voice calling him from a distance, pulling him out of his unconsciousness as it became louder. He opened his eyes with an effort to see Ali Hejaz standing beside him. He tried to speak, but his mouth was too dry and his lips were cracked and blistered.

"So — you are still alive. You must have a strong desire to live." Ali turned to the guard standing beside him. "Give him a few drops of water, but no more."

The guard dribbled a few drops of water into Philip's mouth, and Ali said, "Tomorrow morning should finish you off. If you still live, I will have one of my men kill you, because we must break camp tomorrow and move on. The water here is running low. I would take you with me and stake you out again, but your tribesmen will come searching for you soon. You will die tomorrow, one way or the other. Pleasant dreams, Abu."

138

The sun went down, but Philip was still on fire. The water he had been given had only teased his senses. He thought of Christina lying only a few feet away from him in Hejaz's tent. At least she was sleeping through this nightmare. But she might enjoy seeing him roasted alive. After all, she hated him. Well, soon she would be back with her brother, as she'd always wanted.

The moon was high when Philip sensed a presence beside him. "The camp is finally asleep, but we must be quiet to give no alarm," the man whispered as he bent down beside Philip. "I am Amair Abdalla, brother to Amine who lives in your camp. I beg you to forgive my father and me for our part in this. My father is an old man and only wished to see an end to our sheik's hatred and to see his daughter once again. He realizes now it was wrong to capture your woman. She did not deserve to suffer, nor did you. I will rub a salve onto your skin now. You must not cry out."

Philip's body jerked when the cooling grease touched his skin. He fought back screams as the man worked the salve into his chest and face.

"I would have set you free last night, only you were too heavily drugged. The salve will draw some of the pain after a while," Amair said. He wiped the grease from his hands.

He cut the ropes, pulled Philip to his feet, and handed him a canteen of water. Philip drank sparingly.

"I have your horse waiting in the shadows," said Amair. "The woman is still drugged and will not be able to ride by herself. I will get her presently. Can you talk?"

Philip drank more of the water and was able to whisper hoarsely, "What will happen —"

"My father will meet with the elders in the morning, before Sheik Ali awakes. They will stop Ali from seeking you again, and they will protect me from him. I pray you understand that I was ordered to take the woman. I did not like doing so, but I had no choice. Can you forgive me?"

139

"You are welcome in my camp," Philip returned.

"I will get your woman now. You have five hours before the sun rises. You should be able to wear your robe by then."

Amair went to the side of the tent and slit it with his knife. He crawled inside and a moment later emerged with Christina in his arms. He put her down beside Philip and went to get the horse.

Amair helped Philip onto Victory, then set Christina in front of him. "Will you be able to ride?"

"I'll have to," Philip said.

Amair walked the horse silently out of the sleeping camp. "I wish you a long and fruitful life, Sheik Abu. Allah be with you."

"Farewell, my friend. I owe you my life," Philip whispered. He urged Victory into a canter and headed toward home.

Philip felt excruciating pain with every movement of the horse, but the salve began to help after a while. Oddly enough, he could not hate Ali Hejaz. He pitied the man for living with his own hatred for so many years.

Philip thanked God he was still alive. He would heal soon, and he had Christina back. Yes, he had everything to be thankful for.

If only Christina would grow to love him, he would be the happiest man alive. But he couldn't push her. If he declared his love now, she would only laugh. No, he must win her love slowly. He would be patient now that she was with him again.

Christina's mind slowly cleared, and she realized that she was on a moving horse.

It was daylight. She could see the horse's neck and the desert before her. She remembered a desert camp, a meal, and drinking some wine, but nothing more. How did she get on this horse? Where was she being taken now?

She had to escape. She had to get back to Philip. Christina threw her leg over the horse's neck and fell forward onto the sand. The man groaned when she pushed against him, but she didn't care. She

140

scrambled to her feet and started to run.

"Christina!"

Christina stopped. She couldn't believe it. Philip had come for her and was taking her home. She screamed his name and swung around.

"Oh, my God!" She gasped when she saw his blistered face.

"That's exactly what I said when I first saw you, but I don't want to explain now. Please get back on the horse, Tina, I'm anxious to get home."

"But Philip, your face is —"

"I can imagine what I must look like," Philip interrupted her. "But have you seen your own face yet? Neither of us is quite — ah — recognizable, but we will heal. Come on, Tina."

Christina managed to mount in front of Philip without any help. She was confused and worried about his condition. How had he been burned so badly? At least they were together, and she thanked God for it.

An hour later, they rode into camp and were greeted by an assortment of surprised and shocked faces. Christina and Philip were helped down from the horse. Amine rushed forward crying and embraced Christina tenderly.

"I thought you were dead — we all did. And when Sheik Abu did not return, we thought that he had been killed trying to save you. But your face — oh, Christina, does it hurt? How did this happen?" Amine asked. She clasped Christina's hands tightly. "And Sheik Abu — he is burned so badly."

"I was beaten by an Arab from some desert tribe, and then I was taken to their camp. But I don't know why. That is all I can remember. I don't even know how Philip rescued me, or how he got so burned." She turned to see Syed helping Philip into their tent. She looked back at her friend. "Amine, I am so sorry about Ahmad."

"Ahmad will be all right, but I must help Maidi look after Sheik Abu."

"Ahmad is alive!" Christina exclaimed happily.

141

"Yes, he will be well in a few days. A rib stopped the bullet, and his wound is healing nicely. I must get Maidi now."

"Of course. We'll talk later," Christina said. She went into the tent.

Syed was taking Philip's robe off when she came into the bedroom. She stopped short when she saw his burns.

"Oh, Philip. Your chest, too?" she winced.

"I'm afraid so, Tina. But don't fret so. It's not as bad as it looks. A week or so, and the pain will be gone and the peeling will begin. I do not intend to remain two colors forever."

"Oh, Philip! How can you jest about it?" She came forward and viewed his chest and arms closely. She frowned at the sight of the horrible, dark-red skin. "Does it hurt badly? How did this happen?" she demanded.

"Settle down, my sweet. This is nothing for you to get angry about. I am the injured party." Philip moaned as he lay down on the bed very slowly.

"But how could this happen, Philip?" Christina asked again, completely perplexed.

"It's a long story, Tina, and my throat is still too parched to tell you now. I am tired, sore, and hungry as a wolf. Why don't you see about getting us some food?"

"Oh, damn you!" she stormed, and stalked from the tent.

Amine was by the fire, filling two bowls with a delicious-smelling stew. Christina was furious as she walked over to her.

"He's impossible! He won't answer any of my questions. He just asks for food!" Christina raged.

"Sheik Abu must surely be in great pain, Christina. He does not want you to know how badly he hurts."

"You're right. He is suffering, and I am thinking only of myself. It has taken this nightmare to make me realize how much I love him."

"It is obvious he cares for you," Amine said. "Have patience, Christina. He will tell you what happened when he has rested. Now you both need food, so come."

142

"You're right. I feel as if I haven't eaten for days."

"You have been gone three days and nights."

"Three days! But how can that be?" said Christina "How could I be missing for so long?"

"Sheik Abu will be able to explain. We are all anxious to learn what has happened. But come now, you must eat."

Christina couldn't argue, and followed Amine back into the tent. Amine took Philip's food into the bedroom where Maidi was still ministering to him, and then left.

I feel so ashamed, Christina thought as she wolfed down the stew. Philip must be in extreme pain, and I have to go and jump on him, demanding answers when he is in no condition to give them. I have to forget about it and just think about making him well again. He will tell me everything when he is ready — or will he? He doesn't like to answer questions. Well, he will have to answer these questions. They concern me, too!

Christina had forgotten all about her own injuries. Her eyes and cheeks were still swollen and sore, but it didn't bother her to eat or talk.

Her robe was a mess — completely covered with dirt. She felt so sticky, but how could she bathe when Philip was bedridden? It was too dangerous to go alone. When she finished eating, Syed came into the tent carrying a bucket of water in each hand.

"Sheik Abu ordered the water for you. He said you would have to wash this way for a while," Syed said quickly as he put the buckets down.

He was obviously embarrassed, and Christina wanted to laugh, but didn't. "Thank you, Syed. You are very kind."

Maidi came out of the bedroom, and finally Christina was left alone in the tent with Philip. She decided to wash in the bedroom. Someone might walk into the tent and find her without any clothes on, but she also wanted to be near Philip. She went to the cabinet for towels and soap, then carried the buckets into the other room.

"Philip, are you asleep?" she asked.

"No."

"I wanted to bathe in here where it's more private, but if it will disturb you, I can leave."

"Of course not. It was my intention that you should wash in here. In fact, I have been looking forward to it."

"Oh, you!" she retorted angrily. But when she saw the grease caked so thickly all over the upper half of his body, she started laughing.

"What the devil is so amusing?" he demanded.

"I'm sorry," she giggled. "But you look so ridiculous. Have you seen what you look like yet?"

"No I haven't — have you?"

"What is that supposed to mean?" she asked.

"I suggest you view your own face before you laugh at mine."

Christina picked up her looking glass and gasped at her own reflection. "Oh, God — that's not me! I look so horrible! I'd love to horsewhip the bastard who hit me!"

"Damn, Tina. Must you swear so much? I hardly think it's lady-like."

"Ladylike! Look at my face, Philip. Is this swollen and bruised face the face of a lady? Ladies are not supposed to be beaten, but I was."

"Now that I think of it, besides not speaking like a lady, you hardly look like one in that robe and breeches," Philip chuckled.

"You go too far now, Philip. Before insulting my appearance, why don't you view your own?" she replied haughtily, tossing him her looking glass. "Now tell me which of us looks the worst."

"Touché, my sweet. I give you this round gladly. Why don't you wash up so we can stop this ridiculous banter and get some rest?"

"Whatever you say, master. But as long as I no longer look like a lady, I see no reason why I should act like one." She untied her robe and let it drop to the floor. Slowly the rest of her clothes followed.

144

"Now what the hell was that remark supposed to mean?" Philip asked.

"Oh — nothing," she teased, then she began to scrub her body from head to foot. She knew that Philip was watching her. And, surprisingly, it didn't bother her in the least. She had been shy about undressing in front of Philip before, but now she enjoyed what the sight of her body could do to him.

"Christina, perhaps you'd better wash in the other room."

He sounded annoyed, and she could guess the reason. "But why, Philip?" she returned innocently. "I'm almost finished, and you can always close your eyes if you can't stand to look at me."

She heard him groan, and suddenly she was angry with herself for teasing him. A month, even a week ago, she would have enjoyed having Philip at her mercy. But now she just wanted him to get well. She wanted to feel his arms around her again.

After drying herself, Christina let her hair down and gave it a few quick strokes before coming to the bed.

"Christina, wait. I think it might be best if I slept on the couch for a few days — until this blasted pain goes away."

She looked hurt for a moment, but then her expression changed to one of determination.

"You will do no such thing. If anyone is going to sleep on the couch, it will be me. There's no point in your moving after you're already comfortable." She went to his chest and took out one of his robes to sleep in.

"Christina, I will not have you sleeping out there alone!"

"You're in no condition to argue with me." She slipped the robe on and tied it about her waist, then began rolling up the long sleeves. "Now relax and get a good night's rest. I'll see you in the morning."

"Will you?"

She turned and looked at him tenderly. "Is that what's bothering you — that I will run away during the night? Shame on you, Philip. It would hardly be fair of me if I escaped now, while you're

145

incapacitated. Besides, I don't trust your damn desert. I give you my word that I'll be here in the morning."

"Is your word any good?"

"Oh, you're impossible! You'll just have to wait until tomorrow to find the answer to that. Now, good night."

With that, she left the bedroom and curled up on the lonely couch. Well, at least it was comfortable. Damn, she didn't want to sleep here, she wanted to sleep in the bed with Philip. But he was right, of course. She might hurt him during the night, and she didn't want that. She wanted him to get well as soon as possible.

Everything was changed now that she knew she loved Philip. She could no longer fight him or deny him anything. But how could she explain her change of attitude without telling him of her love? Perhaps he would believe her grateful for her rescue. Yes, he might believe that. Then again, he might not even wonder.

But after she gave in, what if he tired of her because he'd won the game? No — Philip wasn't like that. He must care something for her or he wouldn't have come to rescue her. Christina couldn't stand it if he sent her away now. She didn't even care that they weren't married. She only wanted to stay with Philip.

Perhaps they would have children. That would bind them together. A child — a son! That would solve everything, for Philip couldn't send away the mother of his son. Life would be so wonderful!

Chapter 18

It seemed to Christina that she had been running for an eternity. The miles flew by, she reached no destination. All she could see was sand — everywhere she looked, just sand and a monstrous sun beating down on her. But behind her was death, and she had to escape. Her legs ached terribly, and they felt apart from her body. Her chest hurt with every gasp, but death still chased her. She had to run faster — she had to get away! She heard death call her name. She looked back, and fear engulfed her, for he was getting closer. The sweat of fear broke out on her body. He called her name again and again, but she kept running, praying for some miracle to save her. The man's voice was getting louder as he kept calling her name. She looked back again. Dear God, he was right behind her, his hands reaching out, and then she saw his face. He was that horrible man who'd beaten her, and now he was going to kill her. Philip! Where are you!

"Christina!"

She sat up suddenly, her eyes wide open and frantic. But she relaxed when she saw the familiar surroundings of the tent.

A dream, she laughed — a stupid dream. She wiped the perspiration from her forehead. Damn, but it's going to be hot today.

"You stupid fool. You should have known better than to trust her."

Christina wondered whom Philip was talking to. She quickly got up and walked to the bedroom. When she opened the curtains she saw Philip sitting on the side of the bed, trying with great difficulty to put his pants on.

"What the devil do you think you are doing, Philip? You shouldn't be sitting up yet," Christina scolded him. She glanced about the room, but saw no one. "And whom were you talking to just now?"

Philip stared at her with surprise written all over his face, then it changed to anger. "Where the hell have you been?"

"What?"

"Where have you been, damn it? I have been calling you for the last ten minutes. Where were you?" he stormed.

"So — you were talking to yourself just now. Well, you're a stupid fool if you can't find a little trust in your heart for me. I was on the couch sleeping. I told you I wouldn't leave, and my word is just as good as yours is."

"Then why didn't you answer me?"

"I was having a nightmare, Philip. I dreamed I was being chased through the desert by that man who beat me. The dream was so intense — I thought he was calling my name. When I finally woke up, all I heard was you mumbling to yourself."

"All right, I'm sorry I jumped to the wrong conclusion." Philip eased himself off the bed and tried to fasten his pants.

"Philip, you shouldn't be up," she said quickly when she saw the pain on his face.

"I intend to stay in bed, Tina, but it's too damn hot in this tent for that heavy cover. And for modesty's sake, I would like something on."

Christina came to him and fastened his trousers, then helped him to lie back down on the bed. "Can I get you some food, Philip?"

"That's why I called you in the first place. I'm famished."

Christina started to leave the room, then turned back. "After I feed you, will you tell me how you were burned?"

"I will tell you one thing now. There's no need to have any more nightmares about that man — he's dead."

"Dead!" she gasped. "But how?"

"I killed him."

"Philip! Why did you have to kill him? Because of me?"

"I thought you wanted him dead!"

"I would have seen him horsewhipped, not murdered." She felt

148

sick to her stomach that he would kill a man for her.

"The man also shot Ahmad, and I promised Syed he would pay. I'm not happy now with my deed, but the man would have died anyway for disobeying orders. He was awaiting execution when I arrived at that camp. At least I gave him a fair fight, Tina — we were both armed."

"But why did *you* have to do it?"

"Damn it, Tina! I was filled with rage when I saw how he'd hurt you. And when I found out he was the same man who'd shot Ahmad — I had to do it. The man would have died anyway and without a chance. Besides, I was already told I was to die a slower death, so if the man had won, he would have saved me from that."

"What do you mean, you were supposed to die? Is that how you were burned — you were to be roasted alive?"

"Yes."

"But why?"

"As I said last night, Tina, it's a long story. Could I please have some food first?"

She nodded without saying any more, and left the room. But she didn't have to leave the tent, for there was a large tray of food awaiting her on the table. That Amine, Christina smiled, she's always one step ahead of me. Christina brought the food into the bedroom and insisted on feeding Philip herself. She knew it hurt him to move his arms.

She ate also and waited until he was satisfied before saying anything more. There were so many questions to be answered. Why would anybody want to kill Philip? And how could she have forgotten a whole day?

When they were through eating, Christina took the tray out, then came back and hurriedly donned a skirt and blouse. Philip watched her without saying anything. When she finished, she sat down on the bed beside him.

"Are you ready now?" she asked.

149

Philip told her the whole story. She was angry at first — when she learned that she had been used to bring Philip to his death. But then she felt sorry for Hejaz, who had lived all those years filled with hate. Perhaps it was better that she had been drugged through everything. She couldn't have borne seeing Philip suffer.

When he told her how he'd escaped, she thanked God that Amair had had the courage to help him. She knew Philip hadn't mentioned the anguish and pain he must have suffered beneath the burning sun. The only thing was, she couldn't thank Philip for rescuing her. That would be admitting she'd rather stay with him, because her captors would have sent her back to John. And she just couldn't tell him she loved him, when he didn't love her.

Christina looked at Philip with great tenderness. He had suffered so much for coming to rescue her. She saw new hope — maybe he did love her! "Philip, why did you come after me?" she asked.

"You're mine, Tina. Nobody takes what is mine."

Christina stiffened. She got off the bed and walked slowly from the room. So that was all she was to him. She was property to be used until he tired of her, but nobody could take her away. She'd been a fool. What had she expected him to say — that he had come after her because he loved her? That he couldn't bear to lose her?

But then she halted. She had no right to be angry at his answer. She was expecting too much. At least Philip had said she was his, and that was what she wanted to be. She only needed time — time to make him love her, time to give him a child to bind them together.

Christina needed something to do to take her mind off Philip. She went over to the cabinet and took out one of the books he had given her, then she settled down on her temporary bed and began to read.

After a few moments, Rashid walked into the tent. When he saw Christina, his mouth fell open in surprise. Christina was equally surprised, for Rashid didn't usually just walk into their tent, not after Philip had warned him against it.

150

"What — what are you doing here?" Rashid asked after an unusually long silence.

"I live here — where else would I be?" she laughed.

"But you were. . . . How did you get here?"

"What's the matter with you, Rashid? Has no one told you what happened? I was abducted and Philip was nearly killed by your uncle, but he escaped and brought me back."

"Is he here?"

"Of course he's here. You're acting very oddly, Rashid. Don't you feel well?"

"Rashid!" Philip called from the bedroom.

"There, you see?" Christina said, for she had a funny feeling that Rashid didn't believe her. "You had better go in, for he can't come out."

"What is the matter with him?"

"He is badly burned, so it's better for him to stay in bed for a while," Christina returned.

Rashid hesitated a moment and then walked into the bedroom. Christina followed and sat down on the bed beside Philip.

"Where have you been, Rashid?" Philip asked calmly.

"Why — I have been searching the desert for Christina. I came back the night she was taken, and Syed told me what had happened."

"And didn't Christina just tell you what happened?"

"She mentioned my uncle."

"Tell me something, Rashid. Didn't you know of the hatred your uncle had for our father?"

"Yes, but my uncle is an old man. I did not think he would try to do something about it," Rashid answered, a bit nervously.

"When you told Ali Hejaz that our father had died, he then directed his hate to me!"

"I did not know that," Rashid whispered.

"As a result of your loose tongue, Christina was used to lure me to your uncle's camp. She was beaten by one of his tribesmen, and your uncle almost succeeded in killing me." Philip paused and regarded Rashid intently. "In the future, Rashid, I would be grateful if you'd refrain from mentioning my name or anything that concerns me to your uncle — or anyone else, for that matter. If anything should happen again to disrupt my life as a result of you, I won't take it kindly. Is that clear?"

"Yes," Rashid answered nervously.

"Then you may go. I need rest."

Christina watched as Rashid left the room, then she turned to look at Philip. "Don't you think you were a bit hard on him? It wasn't really his fault."

"Must you always defend Rashid? The blame could fall on many — Amair, who set me free, but abducted you in the first place; Amair's father, who agreed to the abduction; Hejaz, for his hate; and Rashid, for innocently giving out information about me. Let the blame fall where it will as long as nothing like this ever happens again. Will you not agree to that, Tina?"

"Yes," Christina smiled meekly.

"Good, let's talk of it no more. Now, would you kindly bring me two full skins of wine? After I fall into a drunken stupor, you can do me the service of removing this damn grease."

"But you need that to take away the pain."

"I can think of a few things I need, but this grease isn't one of them. The pain isn't as bad as it was, but the grease is driving me mad."

"Oh, well, I could remove it now if you'd like," she ventured innocently.

"No! I will take the wine first. The pain has lessened, but it has not disappeared."

"Yes, master, whatever you say," she teased, and quickly left the room. Well, at least his disposition is getting better, she thought.

152

Chapter 19

Ten days had passed since Philip brought Christina back to camp. Ten days of pain, complaints, and frustration. Ten miserable nights in his lonely bed. The pain was completely gone now, leaving only dark-brown skin that would start to peel in a few days. Hopefully, he would look like his old self soon. And tonight — tonight he would lure Christina back to his bed. Tonight he would have her again after waiting too long.

Philip felt like a child waiting for Christmas Eve. Christmas was actually only a few days away. But he would have his present tonight, and the anticipation was hard to bear. He could have taken Christina this morning, but he wanted it to be just right, so she could have no possible excuses.

Philip had resumed his regular routine today, including taking Christina to bathe. Seeing her in the pool had been an extreme test of his willpower! But now, evening had come.

Christina was curled up on the couch across from Philip. She was sewing a small robe for little Syed and was almost finished, but her mind kept wandering. She wondered what the matter with Philip was. He was well now, but she was still sleeping on the couch. An unwanted thought kept coming back to her — what if he didn't want her anymore?

Well, she would soon know one way or the other, for tonight she was determined to sleep in his bed.

"Philip, I'm going to bed," she said.

She got up from the couch and went into the bedroom as she had done these last ten nights — to take off her clothes and put on one of Philip's robes to sleep in. But tonight she wasn't going to wear his robe and she wasn't going back into the other room.

As Christina removed her blouse and laid it on top of her clothes chest, she felt a draft as the curtains opened. But she didn't turn around. She started unbraiding her hair. She did it slowly, for her fingers were shaking nervously.

This was the moment she had waited for. She knew Philip was in the room with her, but she didn't know what he was going to do. He could just get into bed — asking nothing of her — or he could come to her. Oh, God, let him come!

Suddenly Christina felt his presence behind her. She slowly turned to face him, her eyes soft and loving, his filled with intense yearning.

"Christina."

She came to Philip and put her arms around his neck, pulling his lips down to hers. His arms crushed her against him. As he lowered her onto the bed, she wondered if she would ever be this happy again.

After making love, Christina lay with her head on Philip's shoulder. With her finger she traced little circles in the curls on his chest. She was assured of one thing now — Philip still wanted her. And as long he wanted her, he wouldn't send her away.

She was too elated to sleep, and she found it surprising that she felt no guilt after having given herself so willingly to Philip. But why should she feel guilty about giving herself to him? She loved him, and it was only natural to want to make him happy. She wanted to give herself completely to the one she loved. And it was only an added bonus that when she gave herself to Philip, he in turn gave her the greatest pleasure in the world.

What was marriage, anyway? It was just a signed contract for civilization to see. Well, she wasn't exactly living in civilization, and it was what she felt that mattered. To hell with the civilized world! It was not here to condemn her, and she didn't plan on returning to it.

But she must think of John.

"Philip, are you awake?"

"How can I sleep with your fingers teasing me?" he replied jokingly.

Christina sat up in the bed and faced him. "Philip, could I write to my brother to let him know I'm all right?"

"Would that make you happy?" he asked.

"Yes."

"Then write to him. I will have Saadi deliver your letter, only don't tell your brother where you are, my sweet. I don't think I'd care to have the whole British Army charging up this mountain."

"Oh, Philip, thank you!" she cried and leaned over and kissed him tenderly.

But Philip circled his arms about her and wouldn't let her go. "If I'd known what results it would produce, I'd have let you write your brother sooner," he chuckled. He rolled over with Christina in his arms, and all their thoughts disappeared.

The following morning, Christina awoke knowing that something was urgently important. Then she remembered she was going to write to John this morning. Excited, she started to get up. Then she felt Philip's hand resting lazily between her breasts, and a different excitement consumed her.

Philip still slept, and there was nothing important enough to make her leave his side. Christina wondered fleetingly if she should wake him, but then his eyes opened slowly and he smiled at her.

"I'd have thought that you'd be writing your letter already," he said sleepily as his hand moved slightly, cupping a soft, rounded breast.

"You were sleeping so peacefully that I didn't want to disturb you," she lied. "Are you hungry?"

"Only for you, my sweet." He smiled and brought his lips down to her other breast, sending fire coursing through her body.

155

"I wouldn't want to deny nourishment to a hungry man," she whispered, and wrapped her arms about him as he mounted her.

Later, Amine called for entrance just as Christina and Philip came out of the bedroom. When she entered with the morning meal and saw the contentment on Christina's face, she was very happy for her friend.

"It is going to be a nice day, I think," Amine remarked cheerfully as she set the tray of food down on the table.

"Yes, it's a beautiful day," Christina sighed contentedly as she sat down on the couch. She blushed deeply when she saw Philip looking at her quizzically, for she had not been outside the tent yet and would have no idea what kind of day it was. "Ah — how is little Syed?" she blurted out, trying to hide her embarrassment.

"He is fine," Amine smiled knowingly. "He follows his father everywhere now, and Syed is happy to take him along."

"I'm glad," Christina replied, gaining back her composure. "That's the way it should be. Oh — I'm almost finished with little Syed's robe. I'll bring it to you later."

"You are so kind, Christina." Amine smiled timidly. She had never before had a friend like Christina, who was so good to her and generous with her time. She loved her dearly and would do anything for her. "I will see you later."

Philip regarded Christina all through breakfast, making her nervous and embarrassed. When they finished eating, he finally spoke to her.

"I used to write to Paul before I went back to England, so everything that you'll need to write your letter is in my chest. I'll go and tell Saadi what he must do, and be back later."

As soon as Philip left the tent, Christina rushed into the bedroom. She was filled with happiness to be able to let John know that she was all right. She found the box containing writing supplies and went back into the main room. She sat down and after a few minutes started the letter.

156

To My Beloved Brother,

Forgive me, John, for not writing to you before now, but it didn't occur to me to do so until just recently. Let me begin by telling you I am perfectly well in both body and spirit, and that I am truly happy.

You probably thought me dead, since three months have passed. I am so sorry if I have caused you anguish, but that is what I wanted you to think. At first I didn't know what was to become of me, so it was better that you did not know I was alive. But now everything has changed.

Do not think badly of me when I tell you that I am living with a man. I don't wish to tell you his name, for that doesn't matter. What does matter is that I love him and I want to stay with him. We are not married, but that doesn't matter, either. As long as I know that he wants me, I will be happy.

This man that I love is the same man who took me from you, and at first I hated him. But being with him from day to day slowly turned that hate into love. I didn't even know it had happened until two weeks ago when he was almost lost to me. But since then I have learned that I want to stay with him forever. I don't know if he loves me or not, but as time passes, I pray that he will.

Perhaps in the future he will marry me, but even if he doesn't, I will stay with him until he no longer wants me. I would tell you where I am, but he doesn't wish it. I know in my heart that someday I will see you again, John. Until I do, please don't worry about me. I am happy here, and I do not want for anything.

John, I pray you, don't judge me harshly, for I cannot help what I feel in my heart for this man. I would do anything for him. Please understand this and forgive me if I have caused you pain. You know that I wouldn't do so intentionally. He wanted me, and so he took me. As he says, it is the

way of this land, and now I love him and want him more
than anything. Understand this for my sake.

I love you,
Crissy

Christina leaned back and sealed the letter. She was satisfied with
what she had written, but she couldn't let Philip see the letter. She
started to leave the tent to find Saadi, when Philip came in.

"If you're finished with your letter, my sweet, I'll give it to Saadi.
He's waiting outside."

"No," she said a bit too quickly. "I'll give it to him."

Philip looked at her critically. "You haven't told your brother
where you are, have you?"

"Philip, you asked me not to, so I didn't. I give you my word. If
you will not trust me now, then you never will."

"All right. You may give the letter to Saadi," he said, and opened
the entrance cover for her.

Saadi was waiting on his horse. Christina handed him the letter
and whispered, "Go with God."

He smiled down at her sheepishly, his eyes filled with admiration,
then he kneed his horse and started down the hill. Christina stood
and watched him until he was out of sight. Then she turned to Philip,
who was standing beside her, and placed her hand nervously on his
arm.

"Thank you again, Philip. I feel much better now that John will
know I'm all right."

"Doesn't that warrant another kiss, my sweet?"

"Indeed it does," she returned. And she put her arms around his
neck, pulling him down to her lips.

158

Chapter 20

Christina was curled up on the couch absentmindedly staring at the chipped glass cup in her hands that contained her morning tea. She was trying desperately to remember what Philip had told her this morning before he left. It had been so early, and she had been so tired from the night before, that she hadn't come fully awake to listen to him.

He had said something about going to sign a treaty with Sheik Yamaid Alhabbal to ensure that the two tribes would not conflict over the water they shared. He would be making arrangements for a meeting of the tribes to celebrate their renewed friendship. He would be gone for the entire day and possibly the night as well.

It all seemed so vague that Christina wondered if she could possibly have dreamed the whole thing. But if it had been a dream, where was Philip? He had not been in bed when she finally awoke. And Amine told her later that she had seen him talking to Rashid very early by the corral and that Philip had then ridden out of camp.

Suddenly Christina felt very lonely. Philip had never been away from her for a whole day before, except that time when she was stolen from him. It was still early morning, and she missed him already. What the devil was she going to do with herself today?

Perhaps there was a book in the collection Philip had given her that she had missed reading. She went to the cabinet where she kept her books and started rummaging through them. But before she had a chance to look them over, Rashid called from outside asking to enter.

Christina straightened up and smoothed her skirt before he entered. She started to smile, glad that she had someone to talk to for a while, but stopped when she saw the grave expression on Rashid's face.

"What is it, Rashid? What has happened?" she asked hurriedly.

"I have something for you, Christina. It is from Abu."

She ran to Rashid and quickly took the piece of paper he held out to her. But she was afraid to open it. Why did Rashid look so nervous, and why had Philip left her a note? But she was being silly. This was probably some kind of surprise or perhaps an apology for leaving her so quickly this morning while she was still half-asleep.

Christina walked over to the couch and sat down, still holding the note clutched in both hands. Slowly she opened it and began to read.

Christina,

I have asked Rashid to take you back to your brother. I did not think it would happen, but the fires have died and there is no point in going on. I am setting you free, which is what you have always wanted. I wish you to be gone before I return. It will be better that way.

Philip

Christina shook her head slowly, staring at the note in disbelief. No — this wasn't true! It was some kind of cruel joke. But why did she feel so sick inside? She wasn't even aware of the tears that had come to her eyes, but she felt a choking lump swelling in her throat and a tightening in her chest. Her hands felt cold and clammy as she crumpled the piece of paper and squeezed it tightly in one hand.

"Dear God, why — why would he do this to me now?" she whispered hoarsely.

The tears flowed freely down her cheeks, and her nails dug deeply into her palm as she squeezed the piece of paper that had shattered her life. But she felt nothing but the anguish that consumed her.

Rashid stood before her and rested his hand gently on her shoulder.

"Christina, we must leave now."

"What?"

Christina looked up at him as if she didn't even know who he was. But life returned to her, and she suddenly felt angry at Philip. How could he so callously dispose of her?

"No!" she said quickly, her voice filled with emotion. "I am not leaving. I will not be cast aside like an old shirt, I'll stay here and face him. Let him tell me himself that he wants me to go. I'll not make it easy for him."

Rashid looked at her in surprise. "But I thought you wanted to go back to your brother. You told me yourself that things were not well between you and Abu."

"But that was a long time ago. Everything has changed since then. Rashid, I love him."

"You did not tell him of this?"

"No," she whispered. "How could I tell him when I didn't know how he felt? But now I do know."

"I am sorry, Christina. But you cannot stay here. He ordered me to take you away before he returns."

"Well, I won't go. Let him tell me to my face he doesn't want me."

Rashid looked desperate. "Christina, we must go! I did not wish to tell you this, but you have force me. Abu does not desire you any longer. He wants you out of the way so he can marry Nura when he returns."

"Did he tell you this?"

"Yes," Rashid said quietly, with his eyes downcast.

"When?"

"This morning — before he left. But he has spoken of it before. It was always expected that he would marry Nura. Now we must go. I will help you get your things."

There was no point in staying to be tortured further. Christina went to the bedroom and opened the curtains. She wanted to have one last look at the room where she had spent so many happy nights. Why did she have to feel this way — why had she fallen in love with

161

Philip? If she had continued to hate him, she would be happy at this moment. Instead, she felt as if her life had ended.

Then she remembered that she couldn't ride through the desert as she was dressed now. She walked to the chest that contained all her clothes, took out her black velvet robe and *kufiyah,* and donned them quickly.

She would take nothing with her except the clothes she wore — not even the ruby-studded comb in her hair. She remembered how surprised she had been when Philip gave it to her for Christmas. She tossed it on the bed, for she wanted nothing that would remind her of him. But when she saw the looking glass that Rashid had given her, Christina thought of Amine. She picked it up and left the bedroom.

"Christina, we must get your things."

She turned to face Rashid.

"I will take nothing that Philip has given me. I just want to say good-bye to Amine — and give her this," Christina said, holding up the mirror. "I don't want anything that will remind me of this place. But Amine has been a good friend to me, and I'd like to give her something. You understand, don't you?"

"Yes."

After looking once more around the main room, she left it quickly. Christina stopped in front of Amine's tent and called her. A few moments later, Amine came outside, and Christina started crying again.

"What is wrong?" Amine asked as she rushed to her friend's side.

Christina took Amine's hand and placed the looking glass in it.

"I want to give this to you. Remember that I love you as a sister. I am leaving, and I came to say good-bye."

"Where do you go? You will be back soon?" Amine asked, but she had already guessed that she would never see her friend again.

"I'm going back to my brother, and I won't be coming back. I'll

162

miss you, Amine. You have been a true friend."

"But why, Christina?"

"It doesn't matter. I just can't stay here any longer. Tell Syed and his brothers good-bye, and tell them I wish them well. Kiss little Syed and the baby for me. I would cry too much if I kissed them myself." She smiled weakly at Amine and then put her arms around her. "I will think of you often. Good-bye."

Christina ran to the corral where Rashid had the horses ready. He helped her mount Raven, and they rode out of camp together. When they were a little way down the hillside, Christina stopped and looked back at the camp. Through tear-filled eyes she saw Amine standing at the top of the hill, waving her hand with the mirror in it.

With a last glance behind her, Christina dug her heels into Raven's sides and urged him into a suicidal pace. Rashid called out behind her, but she didn't stop. She wanted to die. She felt she had nothing left to live for. If she died on Philip's mountain, he might feel guilty for the rest of his life. But why should she let him know she couldn't live without him? It wasn't his fault that he no longer wanted her. And she did still love him. She hoped he'd be happy with Nura if that was what he wanted.

Christina slowed Raven to a steady pace. She'd think of some other way to end her life. But she'd wait so Philip wouldn't find out about it. She thought of Margiana and how she had killed herself because of Yasir. Christina truly understood now the anguish and suffering a woman could feel.

The heat of the desert closed in, but Christina was oblivious to it. Her mind was so full with misery that she felt nothing. She couldn't understand why this was happening to her.

Night approached and passed, and the sun came again, but Christina could find no peace.

Questions tormented her. She raked her mind to find the answers, but there were none. Why — why didn't he want her anymore? She was still the same person she had been four months ago. Her

163

appearance was the same — only her feelings had changed. Why had Philip done this to her?

Was it because she had given in to him? Had he cast her aside because there was no longer a challenge? But that wouldn't be fair — besides, that couldn't be the reason, or he would have sent her away a month ago.

And what about this last month? It had been so beautiful — so wonderful and perfect in every way. Philip had seemed happy and content, just as she was. He had spent more time with her. He had taken her riding each day. He had spoken to her about his past, had opened up and given more of himself to her. So why was she here now? Why had Philip changed? Why? Why?

The questions would not let her sleep. She lay awake during the heat of the day while they rested, and thought, and thought, but could find no peace. She took the bread and water that Rashid offered and ate mechanically, but her mind kept working — turning everything over and over — trying desperately to find a solution. Dusk always came again, and they rode on.

Chapter 21

Damn, but it's going to be another sticky day, John Wakefield thought irritably as he sat at his desk sorting out the morning's correspondence. It was winter. It wasn't as hot as when he'd first come to this horrible land, but the days had been warm and humid this last week without rain. The bloody weather was getting under his skin.

At least he could look forward to seeing Kareen Hendricks tonight. Sweet, lovely Kareen. John thanked his lucky stars he had let William Dawson drag him to the Opera House last week, otherwise he wouldn't have met Kareen.

A cold chill swept over John when he thought of the hell he had lived through during his first three months in Egypt. But everything had changed when he received Crissy's letter — including his luck.

The pounding on John's door broke into his wandering thoughts.

"What is it?" John snapped.

The door opened, and Sergeant Towneson walked into the sweat-box that was John's office. He was a portly man about twice John's age, with curly red hair and a bushy moustache of the same bright red.

"There's an Arab outside who wishes to see you, Lieutenant. He said it's a matter of importance," Sergeant Towneson said.

"Isn't that what they all say, Sergeant? I understand we're here to keep the peace, but isn't there someone else these people can go to with their petty quarrels?"

"There ought to be, sir. These darn people don't realize that we're here basically to keep Frenchy out. Should I send this one in?"

"I suppose so, Sergeant. Damn — I'll be glad when I can get out of this country."

"My sentiments exactly, sir," Sergeant Towneson said, and left to summon the Arab.

A moment later, John heard the door quietly close, and looked up to see an unusually tall Arab striding toward his desk. The young man was the tallest Arab that John had ever seen, even taller than his own six feet.

"You are John Wakefield?" the young man asked as he stood proudly in front of John's desk.

"Lieutenant Wakefield," John corrected him. "May I ask your name?"

"My name does not matter. I have come for the reward you have promised for the return of your sister."

Not another one, John thought miserably. How many more of these money-grabbing opportunists and thieves was he going to have to put up with? He had lost count of the many people who had come to him hoping to gain the reward with false information. Most of them backed down when John told them he must verify their information first. He had gone on many wild hunts through the city and desert, all of them fruitless.

Even though he had received Crissy's letter from a young Arab who'd just handed it to him and run off, he still had not given up looking for her. He wanted to believe that she was happy where she was, but he had to find out for certain. After all, it could have been a lie. She could have been forced to write that letter. He would dearly love to get his hands on the man who had abducted Crissy, and who kept her as his mistress instead of marrying her. John would force the cad to marry her!

"Do you not want your sister back?"

"I'm sorry," John said. "I was lost in thought. Do you know where my sister is?"

"Yes."

"And you can take me to her?"

"Yes."

This man was different. He didn't hesitate with his answers as the others had. John saw a glimmer of hope.

"How do I know you're telling me the truth? I've been tricked many times."

"May I ask you a question?"

"Of course."

"How do I know you will give me the money after I take you to your sister?"

"A good question," John said grimly. He unlocked the bottom drawer of his desk and lifted out a small, heavy sack. "I've had this money ready and waiting ever since Christina was abducted. You may count it if you wish, but the total sum I promised is here, and it's yours if you're telling the truth. The money doesn't matter to me. I just want Christina back." John paused a moment, studying this young man. "Tell me — how do you know where my sister is?"

"She has been living in my camp."

John stood up so fast that his chair fell over behind him. "Are you the man who took her?"

"No," the young man replied simply, not wavering under the stormy blue eyes that glared at him.

John calmed down when he saw that he would not have to do battle.

"How far is it to your camp?"

"We will not have to travel to my camp."

"Well, then —"

"Your sister is outside."

"Outside!"

"We have traveled many days. She is asleep on her horse. You can see her from your window."

John rushed to the window overlooking the street. After a moment, he turned back to the Arab with anger showing on his tanned face.

"You lied! There's no one out there except an Arab boy leaning over a horse. What did you expect to gain by this trick?"

"Ah — you English are so skeptical. Did you expect your sister to be dressed as was her custom? She has been living with my people and has dressed as they do. If you will go outside, you will see the truth of my words," the Arab replied, then turned on his heel and left the room.

It was too simple to be a trick, John thought. All he had to do was walk outside and see for himself. Why was he still standing here? John picked up the sack of money and followed the Arab outside. It had to be true.

Outside in the sun-baked street, John ran to the two horses tethered in front of the building. He stopped beside the silky black Arabian with the dusty, black-robed figure on its back. If this was another trick, he was afraid he might tear the young Arab standing beside him limb from limb.

If this was Crissy, all he had to do was lift the black *kufiyah* covering her face, and find out. It was that simple.

Just then the horse moved, and the sleeping figure slowly started to fall. John caught her in his arms. As he did so, the *kufiyah* fell back to reveal a dirty, tear-streaked face that he would have recognized anywhere.

"Crissy! Oh, God — Crissy!"

Christina opened her eyes for a moment and whispered John's name, then sagged against him, her head nestling against his shoulder.

"As I said, she has gone two days and nights without rest. All she needs is sleep."

John turned to look at the young man who had brought his sister back to him.

"I owe you an apology for doubting you. I am eternally grateful for what you have done. If you will take the money from my hand, it's yours."

"I am more than happy that I could do this service for you, I will go now, but when Christina wakes, tell her I wish her well."

168

He took the reins of the black horse, mounted his own, and rode off down the street.

John looked down at Christina sleeping peacefully in his arms. Thank God, he thought. Please help me make it up to Christina for what she has suffered.

John carried Christina inside. He sat down in the chair across from Sergeant Towneson's desk, still holding Christina tenderly.

"Lieutenant! Did she faint in the street? You had better set her down, sir. The dust on her robe is dirtying your uniform."

"Stop your babbling, Sergeant. I will do no such thing. But I will tell you what you are going to do. First, have my carriage brought around to the front. Then you can inform Colonel Bigley I'm leaving for the day."

"Leaving? But what if the colonel asks why?"

"Tell him I've found my sister and I'm taking her to my quarters. Do you think you can manage that, Sergeant?"

"Yes, sir. But you don't mean to say that this girl here is your sister?" The sergeant was sorry he'd asked when he saw the cold glint in Lieutenant Wakefield's eyes.

"You will have my carriage brought around at once, Sergeant. That's an order!"

It was nearing noon when John reached home. He managed to get the door to his apartment open without disturbing Christina, but as he headed for the spare bedroom, Mrs. Greene, his housekeeper, stopped him.

"What on earth are you doing home in the middle of the day, John Wakefield? And what have you there?" she asked disapprovingly.

"This is my sister."

"Your sister?" Mrs. Greene was shocked. "You mean this is the little girl you've been searching for high and low? Well, why didn't you say so? Don't just stand there, take your sister into the bedroom."

"That was where I was going until you stopped me, Mrs. Greene,"

John said. He walked into the room that contained all of Christina's possessions, and laid her gently on the bed.

"Is she hurt — how did you find her?"

"She just needs to sleep, that's all," John said. He looked down lovingly at Christina. "Perhaps you could take off her outer robe so she will be more comfortable, but try not to wake her."

"Well, if you don't want her to waken, you'd better help me."

John noticed a crumpled piece of paper squeezed tightly in Christina's hand. He managed to pry it loose, and tossed it on the small bedside table. Then together they removed Christina's robe and slippers. Christina opened her eyes once, but closed them again and continued to sleep.

Mrs. Greene and John left the room, and he quietly closed the door. He went straight to the liquor cabinet in the drawing room, poured a stiff glass of whiskey, and sank down into his favorite stuffed chair.

"What would you like me to do with this, sir — throw it away?" Mrs. Greene asked, holding up Christina's dirt-stained robe.

John looked up at the matronly Mrs. Greene standing in the doorway. "Just put it aside for now. The decision is Christina's."

John wanted to get Christina back to England as soon as possible. Egypt had caused them both nothing but suffering, but now that Crissy was back, they would be happy again.

Why, he wondered, had Christina left the man she claimed she loved? She'd written she would stay with him until he no longer wanted her. Was that it? The bastard had abducted her, used her, and then discarded her to collect the reward money. Crissy had said she loved him. How she must be suffering!

Draining the last of his whiskey, John got up and crossed through the small dining room and into the equally small kitchen. He found Mrs. Greene standing over the stove.

"I'm going to leave for about an hour, Mrs. Greene," he said. "My sister shouldn't wake up. But if she does, tell her I had to break an appointment but will be back shortly. And give her anything she wants."

"But what about your lunch?"

"I'll eat when I get back," John said, picking up an apple from the bowl of fruit on the counter. "I won't be long."

It was a short distance to Major Hendricks's quarters, and John hoped to find Kareen at home, for he wanted to break their evening's engagement personally.

Kareen was a year younger than he, and was visiting her uncle, Major Hendricks, for a short while. Her home was in England, and her mother was part Spanish. But he knew nothing more about her, except that she attracted him greatly.

Kareen looked Spanish, with her silky black hair and black eyes. Her body was slim, yet perfectly rounded in all the right places. John had looked forward to this evening, but now he had to call it off. He hoped Kareen would understand.

John knocked on the door to Major Hendricks's modest apartment. After a few moments, it opened to reveal a young girl smiling cheerfully at him. John was shocked, for this girl looked only sixteen or seventeen, and yet. . . .

"Kareen?"

The young girl laughed at John's confusion.

"It happens all the time, Lieutenant. I'm Kareen's sister, Estelle. Won't you come in?"

"I didn't know she had a sister," John said as he stepped into the hallway. "You look so much alike."

"I know — like twins. But Kareen is five years older than I am. My father always says that Kareen and I are the exact images of our mother when she was young. Our mother is still a beautiful woman, so it's nice knowing what we will look like in the future." She laughed sweetly, giving John a beguiling smile. "Forgive me. Everybody says I talk too much. Did you wish to see Kareen, Lieutenant — ?"

171

"John Wakefield," he volunteered with a short bow. "And yes, I would like to speak with her if it's possible."

"I think it could be arranged. She's in her room resting. It's this hot weather. We're not used to it yet — it certainly can wear a body out. So you're John Wakefield," she said, looking him over from head to foot. "Kareen sure has talked a lot about you, and I can see that she wasn't exaggerating, either."

"You certainly are outspoken, Miss Estelle."

"Well, I believe a body ought to say what they think."

"That can get you into trouble sometimes," John said lightly.

"Yes, I know. But I like to shock people. I can't say I shocked you, though. You must be used to compliments from the ladies," she went on mischievously.

"Not exactly. I'm used to giving them — not receiving them." John laughed.

"Spoken like a true gentleman. But you've let me ramble on again. If you will wait in the drawing room, I'll go and tell Kareen you're here."

"Thank you, and it has been a delight meeting you, Miss Estelle."

"I can definitely say the same about you, Lieutenant Wakefield. But we'll meet again, I'm sure," she added, and disappeared down the hallway.

After a few minutes, Kareen appeared in the doorway looking as beautiful as he last remembered.

"I thought my sister was playing a joke on me when she said you were here," she said. "She does that occasionally. But why are you here so early, Lieutenant Wakefield?"

"Kareen — I know this is only our second meeting, but won't you please call me John?" he asked, putting all his boyish charm into his request.

"All right, John," she smiled. "But what brings you here?"

"I don't exactly know how to tell you this," John said, turning away from her inquiring eyes. He walked over to the open window and stood looking out, his hands clasped behind his back. "You've been here only a month, Kareen, but you know about my sister's disappearance?"

"Yes, my uncle told me about it when I mentioned I'd met you," she replied.

"Christina was kidnapped right from her room the very first night we were in Cairo. Christina and I were very close. I searched everywhere for her and practically went out of my mind with worry. But she was returned to me today — this morning."

"John — that's wonderful! I'm so happy for you. Is she all right?"

He turned to face her, and could see that she was really pleased for him.

"She's fine, but I haven't had a chance to talk with her yet. She rode for nearly a week and is sleeping now. I wanted to tell you first so you'd understand why I can't escort you to the opera tonight, I have to be there when Crissy wakes up."

"Of course I understand, and I thank you for explaining it to me. Can I do anything to help?"

"It's kind of you to ask, Kareen. Perhaps in a few days you could call on her. I don't know how easily she will adjust to being home again. I only pray that she will be able to forget her terrible experiences."

"I'm sure she will be all right in time, John," Kareen replied.

"I hope so."

Christina had been asleep for twelve hours. It was nearly midnight, and John continued to pace the drawing room impatiently. There were so many things he had to know. He didn't want to pounce on her the minute she awoke, but he had to have some answers. Would Crissy be the same person, or had these last four months changed her?

John went to her door and opened it quietly. But Crissy was still curled on her side, her head resting on one hand. He walked into the room slowly and stood beside the bed gazing down at her as he had done so many times this evening.

She hadn't lost any weight and looked healthy, though dirty. She wore a skirt and blouse in the style of the desert people. But it was made of fine green velvet with spangled lace adorning the edges. She looked like an Arab princess.

She had said in her letter that she wanted for nothing. The man must have taken good care of her. And that just made it more puzzling, because John wondered how any man, once having her, could let her go. Christina had such unusual beauty. Something about her was different — stunning and yet indescribable — something that set her apart from all other women who were called beautiful.

Suddenly Christina opened her eyes and blinked a few times, obviously wondering where she was.

"It's all right, Crissy," John said. He sat down on the side of the bed. "You are home now."

She looked at him, her eyes filling with tears, and the next moment she was clinging to him as if her life depended on it.

"John! Oh, Johnny — hold me. Tell me it was just a dream — that it never happened," she sobbed.

"I'm sorry, Crissy, but I can't tell you that — I wish I could," he said, holding her tightly against him. "But it will be all right — you'll see."

He let her cry herself out without saying more. When she was finished, he held her away from him and pushed back her hair from her wet cheeks.

"Feel better now?"

"Not really." She smiled weakly.

"Why don't you wash your face while I get you something to eat, and then we can talk."

"What I'd really like is to soak in a hot bath for hours. I've had nothing but cold baths for the last four months."

"That will have to wait until later. We've got to talk first."

"Oh, John, I don't want to talk about it — I just want to forget."

"I understand that, Crissy. But there are things I have to know. It would be better if we talked now, and then we can both forget it."

"Very well, I suppose you're right." She got off the bed and looked about the room. "Give me a minute to —"

She stopped abruptly when she saw the crumpled piece of paper that John had thrown on the table earlier.

"How did that get here?" Her voice held a note of anger.

"What's the matter with you, Crissy? I took it out of your hand before putting you to bed."

"But I thought I had thrown —" She turned quickly to face him, frowning. "Did you read it?"

"No. Why are you so upset?"

"It's my dismissal, you might say," she said lightly, only her eyes were stormy. "But it doesn't matter. How about that food?"

After supper, John poured two glasses of sherry and brought one to Christina in the dining room. He sat across from her with his legs sprawled beneath the table, and studied her face.

"Do you still love him?" John asked.

"No — I hate him now!" she said quickly, staring down at the glass she held before her.

"But only a month ago —"

She looked up at him, her eyes flashing dangerously. "That was before I found out what a cruel and selfish man he is."

"Is that why you left him?"

"Left him? He sent me away! He left me that note saying that he no longer desired me and he wanted me gone before he returned. He couldn't even tell me in person."

"Is that why you hate him now — because he sent you away?"

"Yes! He cared nothing for me or for my feelings. I thought I loved him, and hoped he would come to love me. But now I know how foolish I was. He didn't even care that I might be carrying his child!"

"Oh, God, Crissy — then he raped you!"

175

"Raped? No — he never actually raped me. I was sure I made it clear to you, John, in the letter I sent you. I thought you would understand that I gave myself to him. That's why I asked your forgiveness."

"I guess I haven't been able to accept it. I didn't want to believe it. But Crissy, if he didn't rape you — you can't mean that you gave in to him from the beginning?"

"I fought him!" she cried indignantly, trying to defend herself. "I fought him with all the strength I had."

"Then he did rape you?"

Christina hung her head in shame. "No, John, he never had to rape me. He had patience — he took his time and slowly brought my body to life. Please understand this, John — I hated him, but at the same time I wanted him. He stirred fires in me that I never knew existed. He made me a woman."

She started crying again. John felt miserable for blaming her for something that she couldn't help. But why did she defend the bastard?

John leaned across the table and lifted her face to look into her soft blue eyes.

"It's all right. It wasn't your fault. It was the same thing as if he'd raped you."

"I fought him, but it was the same way every time. I tried to escape, but he threatened to find me and beat me if I did it again. I was deathly afraid of him at first, but as time passed, I feared him less. I even stabbed him once, and yet he did nothing. And then another tribe stole me, and he almost died getting me back. I realized then that I was in love with him. I didn't fight him after that, John. I couldn't fight the man I loved. If you can't forgive me for that, I'm sorry."

"I forgive you, Crissy. There are no rules in love. But you said you hate him now. Why do you keep defending him?"

"I'm not defending him!"

"Then tell me his name so I can track him down. He deserves

176

punishment for what he did to you."

"His people called him Abu."

"And his last name?"

"Oh, John — it doesn't matter. I don't want to see him punished."

"Damn it, Crissy!" John yelled, slamming his fist down on the table. "He used you and then sent you back to me for the reward."

"Reward?"

"Yes. The man who brought you here asked for the money, so I gave it to him."

Christina slumped back in her chair, a slight grin on her lips.

"I might have known Rashid would do that. He takes money wherever he can find it. Abu will probably never know Rashid took the reward. And that's not why Phi— why Abu sent me back. He is sheik of his tribe, he has no need of money. He even turned down a sack full of jewels once."

"You started to call him something else," John said, raising one eyebrow.

"Well — he has another name, but it's not important." She stood up and finished the last of her sherry. "Can we forget about it now, John? I want to put him from my mind forever."

"Can you do that, Crissy?" He looked at her skeptically. "You still love him, don't you?"

"No!" she wailed, but then she bit her lip and the tears welled in her eyes again. "Oh, God — yes! I can't help it. Why did he have to do this to me, John? I love him so — I want to die!"

John held her close, feeling her pain. He couldn't stand to see her hurting like this — tearing her heart out over a man who didn't deserve her love.

"It will take time, Crissy, but you will forget him. You'll find a new love — someone who will give you the kind of life you deserve."

Chapter 22

Two months had passed since Philip sent her away. Christina tried desperately to put him out of her mind. But she thought about him constantly. She prayed each day that he would change his mind and come for her. But he didn't come. She couldn't sleep. She lay awake every night wanting him, craving his hands on her, missing his body next to hers in bed.

Christina had seen no one since returning, except Kareen. She liked Kareen instantly the first time that John brought her to their small rooms. Kareen asked no questions of her, and soon they became good friends. Christina knew Kareen was in love with John, and she was glad John loved her in return. They spent many days together, and finally Christina confided everything to Kareen — everything except Philip's real name.

She hid her unhappiness from John, but when she was alone she spent her time remembering and crying in her room. She neither went out nor received visitors, using the excuse that she didn't feel well, which was actually the truth. It was much hotter in the city than it had been in the mountains. She suffered in the stifling humidity and the bad ventilation of the small apartment. She often felt dizzy and sick.

Christina knew she had to start living again, so she finally consented to receive the officers' wives for tea.

At first they chatted politely about the weather, the opera, and the servant problem. But then the five middle-aged women started gossiping about people Christina didn't know — and didn't care to know. She mechanically turned them off with thoughts of Philip, but her attention returned when she heard her name spoken.

"As I was saying, Miss Wakefield, my husband was one of the

178

men who helped search for you," the heavyset woman said.

"So did my James," another woman chimed in.

"We were all so worried when you couldn't be found. We thought surely you must be dead after so long," added another woman, biting into a delicate little cake.

"And then you showed up perfectly safe and unharmed. It was like a miracle."

"Tell us, Miss Wakefield, how did you manage to escape?" the heavyset woman asked pointedly.

Christina stood and moved away to stand facing the mantel. These women only wanted to worm information out of her so they could retell it all over the city and criticize her.

"I would rather not discuss it if you don't mind," Christina said calmly, facing them again.

"But dear, we're all your friends. You can tell us."

"I would have killed myself if it had been me," one of the ladies remarked distastefully.

"So would I," replied another.

"I am sure you two value your lives cheaply. For myself, I prefer to go on living," Christina remarked coldly. "You call yourselves friends — you're nothing but a bunch of gossips. I have no intention of telling you anything. I want all of you to leave this house immediately!"

"Well! Listen to Miss High and Mighty. We came here to offer our sympathy, and you act as if you're proud of what happened to you — of being a dirty Arab's captive. Why — you're nothing but a —"

"Get out of here — all of you!" Christina screamed.

"We're going! But let me tell you this, Miss Wakefield. You're used goods now! No decent man will ever consider marrying you after you've laid down with a filthy Arab. Mark my words!"

Christina didn't tell John about the incident when he came

179

home. But he already knew.

"They made you cry, didn't they, Crissy?" he said softly, taking her face in his hands. "You must not take it to heart. They're just a bunch of jealous biddies."

"But what they said was true, John. No decent man will ever marry me now. I'm dirty!"

"That's ridiculous, and I don't want to hear you talk like that again," he scolded her. "You underestimate your beauty, Crissy. Any man would give his right arm to be married to you. Hasn't William Dawson been here to see you a dozen times? If you'd just get out and start living again, you'd find yourself swamped with proposals! Why don't you come to the opera with Kareen and me tonight?"

"I don't want to intrude upon your evening with Kareen." Christina sighed heavily, her shoulders slumping forward. "I'll read a book perhaps and retire early."

"Crissy — I can't stand what you are doing to yourself," John said. "More times than not, when I come home your eyes are just as red as they are now. You've tried to hide it, but I know you still cry for that man. He's not worth your tears! Lord, I would kill him if I could lay my hands on him!"

"Don't say that, John!" she said wildly. She grabbed his arms, her fingers digging into them with uncommon strength. "Don't *ever* say that again! He's made me suffer, yes, but it's my load to carry. He's not entirely to blame, for he never knew I loved him. He thought he was giving me what I wanted — freedom. Swear to me you'll never harm him!"

"Calm yourself, Crissy," John said, shocked by her outburst. "I'll probably never run into the man."

Christina's voice was urgent, and tears stood in her eyes. "But you might meet him someday. I must have your word that you won't hurt him!"

John hesitated, looking into his sister's pleading face. He would never meet this Abu, so there was no harm in giving Crissy his word

180

as long as it made her happy. Then an idea came to him.

"I'll give you my word on one condition — that you stop torturing yourself over that man. Get out and meet new people. And you can start by coming to the opera with me tonight!"

A sudden calmness came into Christina's face. She relaxed and let go of John's arms.

"All right, John, if that's what it takes to secure your word. But I still think you'd enjoy yourself more if I weren't along."

"Let me be the judge of that." He glanced at the clock on the mantel. "You have less than an hour to make yourself ready." He grinned when he saw her dismay. It was very little time to dress for her first night out in six months. "I will have Mrs. Greene heat water for your bath."

Christina rushed into her bedroom. She picked out one of her London gowns. It was dark-gold satin with shimmering golden braid laced through the skirt and bodice. She chose her sapphires to match her eyes. She felt timid at facing society so soon. But she put her fears aside while Mrs. Greene chatted cheerfully about the opera and how good it was that Christina would finally see it.

True to John's word, less than an hour later they were in the carriage and on the way to pick up Kareen. Christina waited in the carriage while John went up the few steps and rapped loudly on the door of the whitewashed house.

A moment later, Kareen came down the steps on John's arm. She wore a deep-red velvet gown that was stunning with her silky black hair braided into a thick chignon.

Christina gasped when she saw Kareen's large Spanish comb with rubies running across the top. In her mind she saw Philip's quick smile as he presented her with a comb much like it. "It was purchased honestly, my sweet. I had Syed sell one of the horses last month and bring back the best comb he could find," Philip had said, and she had been pleased with the gift. She wished she had kept it now and hadn't been so hasty in leaving everything behind that would have

181

reminded her of Philip. There was no possibility of her ever forgetting him, and some of the items she'd left carried fond memories. Well, at least she still had that horrible note and the Arab clothes she'd been wearing the day she got it.

"Christina— you look as though you're a million miles away. Are you all right?" It was Kareen who spoke, her face filled with concern.

"I'm sorry — I was just lost in thought," Christina answered.

Kareen smiled warmly. "I'm so glad that you agreed to come with us. I just know you'll enjoy the opera."

They arrived shortly thereafter, and John escorted them into the old Opera House. As they entered, the many men and women standing about turned to stare openly at Christina and whisper remarks to their companions. The women gave her contemptuous glances and then turned away. But the men grinned lasciviously and raped her body with their eyes. A few young men, who obviously knew John and Kareen, ventured forward to meet Christina. They paid her lavish compliments, but their eyes roved over her body boldly, and she replied tartly to their flattery.

"Miss Wakefield!"

Christina turned abruptly to see William Dawson coming toward her with a huge smile. He was exactly as she remembered him — tanned and athletic-looking. She remembered his exciting stories, and she wished she had received him when he called so many times.

"It's been so long," he said, taking her hand and drawing it to his lips. "And you're still so beautiful. I hope you have recovered completely from your illness?"

"Yes. I was ah — persuaded to join the living world again," she said. "It's good to see you again, Mr. Dawson."

"William," he corrected her. "We're such old friends, Christina. You injure me by calling me anything but William. Have you an escort?"

182

"Well — I came with John and Kareen."

"Shame on you, John, for keeping the two most beautiful women in Cairo all to yourself."

"Well, I guess I am a bit selfish when it comes to these two," John laughed.

William Dawson's soft gray eyes rested on Christina. He still held her hand in both of his.

"You'd make me the happiest man in Cairo if you'd allow me to sit with you during the performance, and perhaps take you home afterward. With your brother's permission, of course."

"Well, I —" Christina looked to John for help, but he sent her a warning look to remind her of the promise she'd made. She smiled weakly. "I would be delighted to accept your offer, William. It seems I have my very own escort now — doesn't it, Kareen?"

Kareen nodded with sympathetic eyes. "Yes, and a charming one, at that."

She knew Christina wasn't ready for this. She still carried a broken heart so openly. Kareen wondered how John had managed to talk Christina into coming tonight. It was good for Christina to get out, but she wasn't ready yet to trade polite quips with an escort.

On the way home, Christina listened absentmindedly to William's story of some adventure in the wilds of Texas. She couldn't recall anything about the opera, except impressions of brightly colored costumes and loud music. Her thoughts had wandered every time she'd glanced at the comb in Kareen's hair. Couldn't she forget Philip even for a little while?

"We're here, Christina."

She was glad she'd agreed to let William bring her home. John would want to be alone with Kareen for a while, and she'd have been in the way.

"Would you like to come in for a glass of sherry, William?" she said, feeling guilty about the many times she'd refused to see him.

"I was hoping you'd ask me just that."

Inside, Christina went directly to the liquor cabinet, but William came up behind her and pinned her there with one hand on either side. He poured two sherries, then stepped back to hand her one.

"I'd like to toast this moment. How I've dreamed of it," he murmured. His eyes caressed the bosom revealed by her low-cut gown.

"I hardly think it worth toasting, William," she said nervously.

Christina moved away and sat down in John's favorite chair for what little protection it offered. She suddenly remembered that Mrs. Greene was visiting friends and would probably stay the night.

"You're wrong, Christina," William said, taking her hand and pulling her to her feet. "Tonight will be a night to remember for both of us."

Suddenly he pulled her into his arms. His lips found hers and bruised them in a demanding kiss. Christina felt shocked and repelled. How had she let herself into this situation? She pulled her mouth away, but he still embraced her, pressing her body against his.

"William, please — let go of me." She tried to speak calmly. But she knew she was alone with him, and fought a rising panic.

"What's wrong, Christina?" He held her at arm's length, running his gray eyes boldly over her body. "There's no need to act the coy virgin with me."

"You're too bold, William Dawson," Christina replied coldly, jerking out of his grasp. "You have no right to take such liberties with me."

"I haven't begun to take the liberties I intend taking."

William reached for Christina, but she ran to put the big chair between them.

"I must ask you to leave," she said curtly.

"Is that any way to act, baby doll? I'll take good care of you. I'm not a rich man, but I can certainly afford a mistress. After a while, if you're a good little girl, I might even marry you."

"You must be crazy!"

He laughed. She could see the lustful desire in his face. He shoved the chair aside and moved forward with his arms outstretched. Christina turned to run, but it was too late. William grabbed her around the waist and jerked her back against him.

His wicked laughter infuriated her. His hands explored her breasts and belly while she struggled to get free.

"Do you like it rough? Is that what you're used to, baby doll? One more man isn't going to matter after all those stinking desert outlaws you've spread your legs for. Tell me — how many were there? And which one sired the bastard you're carrying? I'm sure the little fellow won't mind if I sample his mama's goods."

Christina froze at his last words. She stood perfectly still. Not even a breath escaped her, and the words kept ringing in her ears. *Bastard you're carrying — bastard.* A baby!

"So you've decided to be reasonable. Well, you'll enjoy having a man after all the scum you're used to."

Suddenly Christina burst out laughing. It had been a long time since she'd heard the sound of her own laughter. William swung her around roughly and shook her by the shoulders.

"What the hell's so funny?" he demanded. But she laughed hysterically, tears running down her cheeks.

And then they both heard the sound of John's carriage pulling to a halt in front of the building.

"You bitch!" William whispered furiously, pushing her from him.

"Yes," she replied gaily. "I certainly can be a bitch when the situation warrants it."

"I'm not through with you yet — there will be another time," he said coldly.

"Oh — I doubt that, William."

John walked into the room, his eyes going first to Christina's amused face, then to William's scowling expression. He wondered

185

briefly what had happened, but refrained from asking.

"Still here, William? Well, it's early — care to join me in a drink?"

"Well, I —"

"Oh, go ahead, William," Christina cut in playfully. She hoped he was squirming. "I'm going to retire, anyway. It's been a most unusual evening. Not quite enjoyable, but informative. 'Night, John."

She turned and went to her room. She closed the door, leaned against it, and could still hear the men in the drawing room.

"What did she mean by that last remark?" John asked.

"I have no idea."

Christina pushed herself away from the door and twirled around and around, just as she used to do when she was a little girl. Her skirt floating around her and pins flying from her hair, she continued twirling until she reached her bed. She fell backward onto it, giggling in sheer delight. She felt her belly with both hands, searching for proof of William's words.

There was only the slightest little bulge — no proof at all. Had William only presumed her pregnant because she'd lived four months with a man?

Christina jumped off the bed and quickly lit the lamp. She ran to the windows overlooking the street and snatched the curtains closed. Then she tore off her gown and chemise and stood perfectly naked before the full-length mirror in the corner.

She examined her body, but could see no change. Turning sideways, Christina pushed her stomach out as far as it would go, which wasn't much, and then sucked it in. There was her proof. Her stomach wouldn't go in as far as it used to. But she frowned, for that could just be added pounds instead of a baby. After all, her appetite had increased this last month. She had to think this out.

She blew out the light and crawled into bed, pulling only a light cover over her unclad body. It was funny. Now that she could wear a nightdress again, she no longer wanted to. She was used to sleeping with Philip and having no clothes between them.

But if she were carrying Philip's child, there had to be other signs. It hit her like an explosion. All the signs were there, but she had put them aside with excuses. The dizziness, the nausea, she had blamed on the weather. She had missed her monthly time twice, but had reasoned it was because she was so unhappy. She had missed her time before, when her parents died.

She had made excuses because she was afraid to let the idea of being pregnant even enter her mind. But now she was overjoyed to have something to live for. She would have a baby — a baby that would remind her of Philip forever. Nobody could take that away from her.

But how far along was she? She was late right now for the third month, so there were only six months to go. Six beautiful, joy-filled months until she gave birth to Philip's son. She knew she would have a boy, and he would look just like his father.

With that happy thought, Christina turned on her side to sleep, a smile on her lips and her hands gently cradling her stomach.

Chapter 23

"John, can I talk to you before you leave?" Christina asked. She was sitting at the dining-room table sipping her third cup of tea that morning.

"Can it wait until later, Crissy? I have to get these papers to the colonel this morning before he calls the staff meeting," John replied.

"It can't wait. There's something I have to tell you now. I waited up for you last night, but you came home too late."

"All right," John sighed. He sat down across from her and poured a cup of the steaming tea. "What is so important?"

"When I was at the marketplace yesterday afternoon, I learned there's a ship sailing for England in four days. I plan to be on it."

"But why, Crissy? I realize you want to get away from this land as soon as possible, but can't you wait another five months so we can return together?"

"I can't wait."

"Of course you can. There's no reason to leave now. Why, you've been downright happy this last month: no more tears, no more sad faces. Ever since you started going out, you've changed completely. You love going down to the marketplace. You've been going out, meeting new people, and enjoying yourself, so why can't you stay with me for just five more months?"

"There's a very good reason why I have to leave now. If I stayed here five more months, I'd have to stay even longer. I can't take my" — she paused — "my baby across the sea right after he's born."

John looked at her as if she'd struck him. Christina turned away from his shocked expression, but felt greatly relieved that she'd finally told him.

"A baby," he whispered, shaking his head. "You're going to have a baby."

"Yes, John — in five months' time," Christina said proudly.

"Why didn't you tell me sooner?"

"I didn't even know myself until last month, and even then there was still some doubt in my mind."

"How could you not know about something like that?" John asked.

"I was too upset, John — too caught up with the tortures of my mind to know what was happening to my body."

"Is that why you've been so happy this last month — because of the baby?"

"Oh, yes! It's given me a reason for living again!"

"Then you intend to keep the baby, and raise it yourself?"

"Of course! How can you even ask such a thing? This baby is mine. He was conceived in love. I will never give him up!"

"It all boils down to that — that man! You want this child because it's *his* child. Are you going to leave without telling him about the baby? Perhaps he'd marry you now," John said angrily.

"If I thought he would marry me, I'd go to him immediately. But there's no chance. He has married Nura by now. He doesn't want this child, but I do. And I want to give birth at home in England. I must leave soon, and it might as well be four days from now."

"Have you thought what people will say? You're not married, Crissy. Your child will be a bastard."

"I know. I have thought about it often, but it can't be helped. At least he will be a wealthy bastard," she said. "But if gossip bothers you, I won't stay at home. I can always live elsewhere with my baby."

"Crissy, I didn't mean it like that. You know I'll stand by you, no matter what you decide. I was only thinking of your feelings. After all, you were pretty upset about the nasty remarks of those officers' wives."

"But I felt unwanted and miserable then. It made me feel worse to hear that no man would ever want me. But now I'm happy. I can't be hurt anymore by what people say about me. I don't care if I never marry. I only want my baby — and my memories."

"If you're happy, that's all that matters," John said. He tried to accept the fact that Christina would be an unwed mother. He knew she was strong, and he wanted to believe nothing else could hurt her.

"Your child won't have a father, but he'll have an uncle. I'll help you raise him, Crissy."

"Thank you, John!" Christina cried. She came over and stood behind his chair, wrapping her arms about his neck. "You're so good to me, John, and I love you so."

"Well, I still don't like the idea of you sailing all by yourself. It's not right."

"You're such a worrier. I'm sure nobody will bother me in my condition. As you can see, my baby is showing already," she said, turning sideways to show him. "And by the time I reach London — why, I'll be as big as an ox. I'll take lots of material and yarn with me, and spend the whole voyage in my cabin making baby clothes. And when the ship docks in London, I'll hire a coach to take me straight to Wakefield Manor. So you see, there's nothing to worry about."

"Well, at least let me write to Howard Yeats. He can meet your ship and escort you home."

"There's no time for that, John. My ship is the first one leaving. Your letter would arrive with me. And anyway, Howard and Kathren would probably insist I stay with them, and I don't want to. I want to get home as soon as possible. I want to have time to turn that small guestroom next to mine into a nursery. I'll have to put up new wallpaper, and a door to connect my room to the nursery, and —"

"Wait a minute, Crissy," he interrupted her. "You're going much too fast. What's the matter with our old nursery? It was good enough for us."

"John, do you know how far that old nursery is from my room? I intend to take care of my baby all by myself. I'll be his mother, his

190

nanny, and his nursemaid. It's not as if I had a husband to devote half my time to. All I will have is my baby — all of my time will go to him."

"You certainly have thought this all out," John said. He was amazed how adept Christina had become at managing her own life. "Well, If you want your baby next to your room, that's where he'll go. But Johnsy won't be happy that you want to care for him all by yourself."

"Johnsy will understand once she knows the whole story. And I'll still need her help," Christina replied.

"Do you plan on telling Tommy everything, too?" John asked.

Christina hadn't given a thought to Tommy.

"No — not everything, only what's necessary."

"You know he's going to be hurt. Tommy wanted to marry you."

"Yes. But I never loved him that way. Tommy will get over it. Perhaps he's already found somebody else."

John looked at her doubtfully. Tommy had cornered him before he and Crissy had gone to London. He had declared his love for Crissy and said he could never be happy with anyone else.

"You don't really believe Tommy has found someone else, do you, Crissy? The boy loves you, and I think I can safely say that he'll still want to marry you, despite the baby."

"But I never felt that way about Tommy. I doubt I would have married him even if I'd never met Abu. He's the only man I'll ever love. He is lost to me, but I have his child and that's all that matters. I don't want to hurt Tommy, but I can't marry him."

"Well, perhaps you'll feel differently about it later. But right now, I am more than late, little sister. There's going to be hell to pay at the colonel's office. I just hope he'll understand and give me leave to take you to Alexandria," John replied.

"I'm sure he will, John. If he doesn't, then I'll just have to talk with Mrs. Bigley."

"The colonel won't like you two women ganging up on him," John laughed. He stood up and kissed Christina tenderly on the cheek. "I'll try to come home early tonight, and we can talk more then."

As soon as John left, Christina went to her bedroom to decide what she'd need to buy for her trip home. She rummaged through her wardrobe. All her clothes would fit in her two chests, but she'd have to buy another chest for the baby clothes she intended to make. And then she suddenly realized that all her tight-waisted clothes would be useless in a few weeks.

Christina laughed at herself for forgetting something so important. Now she'd have to buy yards and yards of material to make clothes for herself as well as the baby, and she would have to purchase two more chests.

"You certainly are going to be busy on this voyage, Christina!" she said aloud.

Chapter 24

A warm, fresh breeze brushed against Christina's face and played with her loose-fitting dress as she stood on deck holding onto the railing of the ship. She looked down at her protruding belly and smiled when she felt her baby's forceful kick. His kicking and thrashing had become noticeable during the last month, and Christina loved every minute of it.

She'd been standing on deck for over an hour now. Her feet hurt terribly, but she wasn't about to go back to her stuffy cabin — not with the shores of England before her.

The voyage had gone by so quickly and she had kept herself so busy that it seemed only yesterday that she'd said good-bye to John. She had cried a little and reminded him that in five months he, too, would be boarding a ship for home. She'd kissed and hugged Kareen, who had come with John to see her off.

"You take good care of yourself and the baby," Kareen had said, then she, too, had started crying.

And now it was a clear, beautiful early summer morning in England. The passengers all crowded against the rail, happy that their journey was finally over.

Christina patted her belly and whispered softly, so no one else would hear, "We'll be home soon, little Philip very soon."

Christina had no trouble finding a coach to take her to Wakefield Manor. They traveled slowly, stopping at a cozy inn overnight to pamper Christina's condition. But she didn't mind. She watched the beautiful English landscape hungrily as they left London and drove toward Halstead.

It had been so long since she had seen such lush countryside. They passed majestic forests and open fields filled with wild flowers of every color. They passed farms surrounded by rich crops, and small, charming villages. This was rural England. How she loved it!

Late the next evening, the coach finally pulled to a halt before beautiful Wakefield Manor. Lighted sconces beside the large double doors cast welcoming light into the driveway. Christina threw open the door of the coach, not wanting to wait another second.

"Hold on there, madam!" the driver yelled, jumping down from his high seat. He came to the door and helped Christina down. "You must think of the wee one."

"I'm sorry. It's been so long since I've been home! Besides, I'm quite used to getting down by myself."

"Maybe so, but —"

The big double doors swung open, and Dicky Johnson stepped outside.

"Who be you come to call this late at night?" he asked warily. Christina lifted her head to the light, and Dicky squinted his eyes disbelievingly. "Is that you, Miss Crissy? Is that really you?"

She laughed and embraced the small man.

"It's me, Dicky — home at last."

"Oh — it's so good to have you back, Miss Crissy. And Master John, has he come home, too?"

"No, he won't be coming home for a few months. But I wanted to come back early — to have my baby here."

"Baby! Aye, you did feel a bit heavy under that cape."

"Who is it, Dicky?" Johnsy called from the doorway.

"It's Miss Christina. She's come home sooner than expected. And all by herself, I might add," he said disapprovingly.

"My baby!" Johnsy cried. She ran down the steps and caught Christina in her arms. Then she stood back, surprise written on her face. "My baby's gonna 'ave a baby of 'er own. Oh, Lord, I've waited

194

for this day. But why didn't you write to your old nanny and let 'er know?"

"And would you have been able to read my letter?" Christina teased.

"No, but I would 'ave found someone who could. Now you come inside, love. You've got some explainin' to do, and you can do it over a nice cup of tea," Johnsy said, then looked to Dicky over her shoulder. "You bring Miss Christina's baggage in an' give that driver something to eat before 'e goes on 'is way."

Inside the brightly lit hallway, Christina was swamped with glad greetings from the rest of the household servants. Johnsy soon sent them scurrying with a host of orders to bring tea, prepare food, heat bath water, and unpack baggage.

Christina stood back and laughed. "You haven't changed a bit, Johnsy. Perhaps a few more gray hairs, but otherwise the same."

"Aye — it's 'cause of you I've added gray 'airs — what with you gallivantin' off to that 'eathen land with your brother. I was fit to be tied when Master John sent word to 'ave the rest of your things shipped over there. An' then I don't 'ear a word from either of you. It's been nigh over a year," Johnsy complained.

"I'm sorry I didn't write, Johnsy. But you'll understand why after I explain things to you."

"Well, I 'ope you've good reason for worryin' your old nanny. But look at me makin' you stand 'ere in the 'all — an you in your condition. You come in 'ere an' sit yourself down," Johnsy said gruffly, leading her into the drawing room.

After she took her cape and bonnet, Johnsy's wide brown eyes went straight to Christina's belly.

"What could 'ave possessed Master Johnny to let you travel by yourself? And where is your new 'usband — don't tell me 'e 'ad to stay in that 'eathen land, too?" Johnsy asked, sitting beside Christina on the gold-brocade couch.

Christina leaned back and sighed heavily. "John agreed that I

195

should come home to have the baby. Otherwise, we would have had to stay in Egypt until the baby was old enough to travel. As for my husband — I don't have one. I was never —"

"Oh, my poor baby! Your child not even born yet, an' you're already a widow."

"No, Johnsy — you didn't let me finish. I don't have a husband because I was never married."

"Not married? Oh, Lord!" Johnsy started crying. "Oh, my baby! You've a bastard growin' in you — oh, 'ow you must be sufferin'. 'Ow could Master John let this 'appen to you?" she wailed. "Oh — the blackguard who did this to you — may a thousand devils —"

"No!" Christina screamed. "Don't ever say anything against him — ever! I love the father of my baby, I always will. And I will raise and love my baby. I don't care that he'll be a bastard!"

"But Miss Crissy — I don't understand. Why didn't you marry? Is the man dead?"

Christina knew it would be a long time before she could go to bed this night. She shifted her weight and then proceeded to tell Johnsy the whole story, including everything that she hadn't told John. She began with her first sight of Philip at the ball in London, and ended with her first awareness of the baby and her plans to come home.

Johnsy cried and held Christina in her arms.

"Oh, baby — you 'ave suffered so. If only I could 'ave been there to 'elp you through it. An' I still say that Philip Caxton is a blackguard — to turn you away like 'e did."

"No, Johnsy — Philip had his reasons. They were selfish ones, but I don't blame him anymore. I just hope he's happy with Nura, for I'm happy with my baby," Christina replied.

"Aye, 'appy you may be, but still sad for 'avin' loved a man an' then losin' 'im in such a short time. I'm sorry, love — truly I am. But now I must get you to bed. You're near to fallin' asleep where you sit. I should be ashamed of myself for keepin' you up till the wee 'ours of the mornin'. But you can sleep as late as you want tomorrow, love. I'll keep the servants away from your room."

Upstairs in Christina's room, Johnsy helped her out of her traveling dress and into a loose-fitting nightdress. The large tub of water sitting in front of the blue marble fire place had turned cold a long time ago, but she was too tired for a bath, anyway.

Christina surveyed her old room while Johnsy put away the rest of her things. She loved this room and had chosen it for herself because she liked the dark blues that dominated its decor.

Oh, but it was good to be home again with the things and people she had grown up with and loved!

Christina got into bed and covered herself. She was already asleep when Johnsy kissed her on the forehead and quietly left the room.

Chapter 25

The bright, clear day was blocked out by the heavy blue velvet curtains covering the windows in Christina's room. A door slammed shut somewhere in the house. Her reddened eyes fluttered open momentarily, but she was much too sleepy to think of crawling out of the soft comfort of her bed. She turned over and lost herself in peaceful sleep once again.

But a few moments later, the sound of angry voices brought Christina's eyes wide open.

"Where is she, damn it?"

Christina raised herself slowly to her elbows.

"Now you can't go in there, Master Tommy. I told you she's sleepin'."

Christina recognized Johnsy's disapproving voice just outside her room.

"Good Lord, woman — it's the middle of the day! Either you go in there and wake her — or I will." It was Tommy Huntington.

"You will do no such thing. My baby is tired. She came 'ome very late last night, an' she needs 'er sleep."

"And that's another matter. Why the hell wasn't I informed that Christina was home? I had to hear it from my servants this morning."

"Now calm yourself, Master Tommy. We didn't know Miss Christina was comin' 'ome until she arrived. I would 'ave sent word to you as soon as she woke up. Now you get yourself out of 'ere. I'll send someone over after Miss Crissy wakes."

"That won't be necessary. I'm not leaving. I'll wait downstairs, but she damn well better wake up soon or I'm coming back up here."

After Tommy stormed downstairs, Christina's door opened quietly and Johnsy poked her head around it. When she saw Christina sitting up, she came into the room.

"Ah, baby — I'm sorry 'e woke you. Master Tommy can sure be 'eadstrong when 'e wants to."

"That's all right, Johnsy. I guess it's time I got up, anyway," Christina replied. "I'll take a bath now, then go down and face him."

"Aye, 'e's gonna be pretty upset when 'e sees your condition. Well, I'll tell Master Tommy 'e can see you in the dining room shortly. You can tell 'im what you 'ave to over breakfast — you an' that baby need your nourishment."

About an hour later, Christina slowly descended the curved staircase and went straight to the dining room. She stopped in the doorway when she saw Tommy seated at the long table with his back to her. She quietly walked into the room.

"It's good to see you again, Tommy."

"Christina, why didn't you —" He stood up and faced her, but he stopped short when he saw her enlarged belly.

A small, choked sound escaped his throat, Christina turned away and sat down on the other side of the table. One of the kitchenmaids brought in a large platter of food, and Christina, as if nothing were wrong, filled her plate with bacon and eggs and two delicious cherry tarts.

"Won't you join me, Tommy? I hate to eat alone, and this food smells too good to waste," she said without looking at him, busying herself buttering a piece of toast.

"How — how can you act as if nothing has happened? Christina, how could you do this to me? You know I love you. I wanted to marry you. I've been waiting patiently here for you and counting the days until your return. From the looks of you, you married as soon as you got to that damn country! How could you? How could you marry another man so soon?"

"I'm not married, Tommy — I never was," she said calmly. "Now do sit down. You're making me lose my appetite."

"But you're pregnant!" he exclaimed.

"Yes," she laughed. "Very much so."

"But I don't understand." And then he gasped. "Oh, I'm sorry, Christina! If John hasn't killed the man, I'll find him and see justice done!"

"Oh, stop it, Tommy! I was not married, and I was not raped. I was abducted and held captive for four months. I fell in love with the man who kidnapped me. He doesn't know I carry his child, and he will never know. But understand this, Tommy. I will keep my child, and raise him and give him all my love. I am happy, so don't feel sorry for me.

"You asked me to marry you a long time ago, but I never said I would, Tommy. And now, of course, it is out of the question. I'm sorry if I have hurt you, but I would still like us to be friends if — if you can forgive me."

"Forgive you! I loved you, and you gave yourself to another man. I wanted you for my wife, and you're going to bear another man's child. You ask my forgiveness? Oh, Lord!" He slammed his fist down on the table and stormed from the room.

"Tommy, don't go like this!" she called after him, but he was already gone.

Johnsy came into the room, her brow wrinkled with concern. "I waited until I 'eard 'im leave. Did 'e take it badly?"

"Yes, I'm afraid I've hurt him terribly," Christina sighed. "I didn't ask for any of this to happen to me."

"I know, love. It's not your fault, so don't be blamin' yourself. It's that Philip Caxton's fault. But Master Tommy will get over it. You and 'e 'ave 'ad many a disagreement before, and you always made up afterward."

"But that was when we were children. I don't think Tommy will ever forgive me for this."

"Nonsense! 'E just needs time to get used to the situation. You mark my word — 'e'll be back. But you finish your meal now. Would

200

you like it warmed up a bit?"

"No. I've lost my taste for food right now," Christina replied, and got up from her chair.

"You sit yourself right back down there. You've no longer just yourself to think of. Your baby needs food whether you do or not. You want 'im 'ealthy an' strong, don't you?"

"All right, Johnsy, you win."

After Christina finished the cold meal, she went straight out to the stables. As soon as she walked through the open doors, Deke, the stable master, came running to greet her.

"I knew you'd be coming here before the day was out. It's good to have you back, Miss Christina."

"It's good to be back, Deke. But where is he?"

"Now who might you be referring to?"

"Come on, Deke!"

"Might you be referring to that big black stallion in the last stall?"

"That I might," Christina laughed gaily and rushed to the end stall.

When she saw the big black horse, she threw her arms around his neck and hugged him tightly, gaining a snort in response.

"Oh, Dax — I've missed you so!"

"Aye, and he's missed you, too. Hasn't been ridden since you left, Miss Christina, although we've kept him busy. He's sired four fine colts, with another one on the way. But I can see he'll still have to wait for that ride," Deke said bashfully.

"Yes, but not for very long," Christina replied. "Bring him out, Deke, and put him in the corral. I'd like to see him move."

"Aye, he'll do that, all right. He'll strut and prance and put on a fine show."

After Christina left Dax, she walked through the woods in back of the stables until she came to the small pond where she and Tommy used to swim. It was a peaceful place, shaded by a tall oak whose limbs reached halfway over the water.

She sat down and leaned against the old tree recalling a similar pond in the mountains. Philip probably took Nura there now.

Christina returned to the house late. The sun had already disappeared, and the sky was a soft purple and steadily growing darker. Christina stepped into the lighted hallway. It had become a bit chilly, and she rubbed her bare arms briskly as she headed for the drawing room.

The room was in darkness when she entered. Only the soft light from the hallway allowed her to see her way to the fireplace. She took one of the long matches from the mantel and lit the fire, then stood back as it gained strength. Gradually the warmth touched her, and she moved away to light the many lamps throughout the room. She had taken only two steps when she saw a figure standing in the shadows by the open window. She gasped in sheer fright when the figure moved toward her, but her fear turned to anger when she saw who it was.

"You scared the wits out of me, Tommy Huntington! What the devil are you doing in here in the dark?" she said angrily.

"I was waiting for you, but I didn't mean to scare you," he replied meekly. He usually backed down when confronted by Christina's anger.

"Why didn't you speak out when I entered the room?"

"I wanted to watch you without being observed."

"What on earth for?"

"Even in your present condition you — you're still the most beautiful girl in England."

"Why, thank you, Tommy. But you know I don't like being spied upon, and I didn't expect to see you again today. Are you here for some special reason? If not, I'm tired and I plan just to have my dinner and then go to bed."

"Then why come in here and light the fire?"

"You can be very exasperating! I'm going to eat in here, if you must know. I don't like having my meals in that big dining room all by myself."

Just then, one of the downstairs maids came into the room, but stopped when she saw Christina.

"I was just going to light the lamps, miss."

"Well, go ahead. Then have Mrs. Ryan prepare my dinner, please."

"Mind if I join you?" Tommy said.

Christina arched an eyebrow, surprised at his request. Perhaps he was willing to remain friends.

"Molly, have two dinners prepared, and you may serve them in here. And let Johnsy know I'm back, please, so she doesn't fret."

After the maid left, Christina moved to the couch, and Tommy sat down beside her.

"Christina, I have something to say, and I want you to hear me out before you answer."

She took a better look at him and noticed that he had matured during the past year. He had grown taller, and his face was less boyish. He'd even grown a moustache, and his voice sounded deeper.

"All right, Tommy. Go ahead — I'm listening."

"I've spent the whole afternoon overcoming the shock of your loving another man. I — I have come to the conclusion that I still love you. It doesn't matter that you will bear someone else's child. I still want to marry you. I will accept your child and raise him as if he were my own. Soon you will forget this other man. You will learn to love me — I know you will! And I won't ask you for an answer now. I want you to think about it for a while." He paused, and took her hand. "I can make you happy, Christina. You'd never regret becoming my wife."

"I'm sorry that you still feel this way about me," said Christina. "I hoped we could still be friends. But I can't marry you, Tommy. And I'll never change my mind. The love I have for the father of my child is too great. Although I will never see him again, I can't forget him."

"Damn it! Christina — you can't live with a memory. He's far

203

away, but I am here. Can't you find room in your heart for another love?"

"Not that kind of love."

"What about your child? I'd give him a name. He wouldn't have to go through life a bastard."

"The news of my pregnancy has probably traveled all through Halstead already. My child would be called a bastard even if I did marry you. Only his true father can right that wrong."

"But still, Crissy — the child will need a father. I'd love him — if only because he's yours. You must think of the child."

Christina moved away from him and stood by the fire. She hated to hurt Tommy.

"Tommy, I've already told you —"

"Don't, Christina — don't say it." He stood behind her and clutched her shoulders. "For God's sake — think about it! You're all I've ever dreamed about, ever wanted. You can't destroy my hopes so easily. I love you, Crissy — I can't help it!"

He turned and left the room without giving her a chance to answer him. A few minutes later, Molly brought in two meals, but had to take one back.

Christina ate at the gold-and-white marble-topped table before the couch, facing three empty chairs.

She felt stuffy and fat, lonely and miserable. Damn, why did Tommy have to make her feel so guilty? She didn't want to marry him, because she just couldn't bear living with another man after Philip. Why did Tommy have to love her? She was not going to marry him, or anyone else.

Pushing herself from the couch, Christina left the room and started up the stairs. She'd thought she could have her baby in peace at home, but she might as well have stayed in Cairo.

Chapter 26

In the slow-moving months that followed, Christina busied herself preparing a nursery for Philip's son. She chose furniture, and decided on a light-blue-and-gold pattern for the drapes and easy chairs, and a light-blue carpet! A doorway was cut to connect her room with the baby's room.

The nursery was ready. All the little clothes that Christina had made were put away. And she was bored with nothing to do.

She couldn't ride, she couldn't help around the house. All she could do was read and take her walks. Her heaviness was becoming impossible to bear, and she wondered if she would ever be slim again. She turned her full-length mirror to the wall; she was so sick of looking at her rounded shape.

Tommy made her life miserable. He came to see her every day, and every day it was the same thing. He just wouldn't give up.

She told him over and over again that she wouldn't marry him, but he never listened. He always had new reasons why she should marry him, and closed his ears when she said she would not. She was getting sick of it.

It was late in the afternoon of a September's day when Christina finally made a decision. She went from room to room in search of Johnsy, and found her in the nursery dusting the furniture where there was no dust. Christina walked in and stood beside the cradle. She flicked the colorful clowns and toy soldiers hanging above the little bed, making them dance merrily in the air.

"Johnsy, I've got to get away from here," she said suddenly.

"Whatever are you talkin' about, love?"

"I just can't stay here any longer. Tommy is driving me crazy. It's

205

the same thing over and over again, every time he comes here. I can't stand it anymore."

"I won't allow 'im to see you, that's all. I'll tell 'im 'e's not welcome 'ere."

"You know he won't stand for that, and it would just give me more to worry about. I'm always nervous, waiting for him to show up."

"Aye, that's not good for the baby."

"I know, that's why I have to leave here. I'll go to London and rent a room at a hotel. I'll find a doctor to call when the time comes. But I've made up my mind. I'm going."

"You'll do no such thing. You'll not go to London — to a place filled with people who 'ave no time for anyone but themselves — an' you all by yourself," Johnsy replied, shaking her finger at Christina.

"But I've got to — I'll be all right."

"You didn't let me finish, love. I agree you should get away from Master Tommy. But not to London. You can go to my sister who works over in Benfleet. She's the cook on a large estate belongin' to a family of the same name as that man you love."

"Caxton?"

"Aye, but that Philip Caxton couldn't be no gentleman, not with what 'e done."

"Well, Philip's only family is his brother, and he lives in London."

"Aye, so you can go and 'ave your baby there, at Victory, I think Mavis said it was called. An' you'll 'ave people there who will take care of you."

"But what will the owner have to say about my staying in his home?" Christina asked.

"Mavis says the master's never there — always gallivantin' across the seas. All those servants 'ave that big 'ouse all to themselves, with nothin' to do but keep it fit."

"But you've mentioned Mavis before. I thought she lived in Dover."

206

"She did, until seven months ago. The old cook at Victory passed away, an' Mavis just 'appened to 'ear of the openin'. The master pays 'is servants 'andsomely. 'E's a very rich man. Mavis said it was 'er porridge that won 'er the position. There was so many applied, she was lucky to get it. I'll send 'er a message tonight to let 'er know you're comin'. Then you can pack and leave tomorrow. I'd like to go with you, love, but this 'ouse would be in 'avoc if I left."

"I know, but I'm sure I'll be fine with your sister to look after me."

"Aye, an' they 'ave a kind'earted 'ousekeeper there, too. I won't worry with you in good 'ands."

Christina didn't tell Tommy she was leaving when he came to call that night. She left that for Johnsy to do after her departure.

After a journey of three days, Christina arrived at the vast estate known as Victory in the late afternoon. They had driven for the last half-hour over the Caxton land. Christina realized that it was at least twice the size of Wakefield. The sprawling three-story brownstone mansion covered with moss and ivy was magnificent.

Christina grasped the knocker, a large iron "C," on the towering double doors and let it fall twice. She felt nervous about coming to people she didn't know, and thought it ironic that she should come to the home of a man named Caxton to have her baby, sired by a man named Caxton.

The door opened then, and a small, chubby woman peered out and smiled warmly. She had black hair streaked heavily with gray and knotted at the back of her head, and soft gray eyes.

"You must be Christina Wakefield. Come in — come in. I'm Johnsy's sister, Mavis. I can't tell you how glad we are that you've come here to have your baby," she said cheerfully, ushering Christina into a mammoth hall that towered at least two stories high. "When the messenger come this morning bringing the news that you were

207

on your way, why, it put this old house to life again."

"I don't want to be any trouble," Christina said.

"Nonsense, child! What trouble could you be? There's nothing but idle hands in this house, what with the master always gone. You are truly welcome here, and you can stay as long as you like — the longer the better."

"Thank you," Christina returned.

The great hall, dimly lit, was lined with ancient tapestries depicting battle scenes and landscapes. Two curving staircases lay at the end of the hall, with heavy, intricately carved double doors between them. Chairs, couches, and marble statues stood against both walls.

Christina was awed. "I've never seen such a huge hall. It's beautiful."

"Yes, the whole house is the same — big and lonely. It needs a family living in it, but I don't think I'll live long enough to see that happen. The master seems not to want to marry and have children."

"Oh — he's young, then?" Christina was surprised. She'd pictured him as old and feeble.

"So I'm told, and irresponsible as well. He prefers living abroad to running his estate. But come, you must be exhausted after traveling across the countryside in your condition. I'll take you to your room, and you can rest before dinner," Mavis said, leading Christina up the stairs. "You know, Miss Christina, your baby will be the first to be born here in two generations. The housekeeper, Emma, told me Lady Anjanet was the last, and she was an only child."

"Then Mr. Caxton was not born here?" Christina asked.

"No, he was born across the sea. Lady Anjanet traveled a great deal when she was young," Mavis replied.

A feeling of uneasiness began to creep over Christina, but she shook it off.

"I will put you in the east wing — it catches the morning sun," Mavis said. They reached the second floor and started down the long corridor. It, too, was hung with beautiful tapestries.

Christina stopped when she came to the first door. It stood open, and the blue interior reminded her of her own room. She was amazed at the size and beauty of the room. The carpet and drapes were dark-blue velvet, and the furniture and coverlet on the massive bed were a lighter blue. There was a huge black-marble fireplace.

"Could I stay in this room?" Christina asked impulsively. "Blue is my favorite color."

"Of course you can, child. I am sure Mr. Caxton won't mind. He is never home."

"Oh — I didn't know this was his room. I couldn't possibly —"

"That's all right, child. The room needs to be lived in. It hasn't been occupied for well over a year now. I'll have your baggage brought in here."

"But aren't his things — his belongs in this room?"

"Yes, but the room was made for two people to live in. There is plenty of empty space for you."

After dinner, Mavis gave Christina a tour of the downstairs. The kindly housekeeper, Emmaline Lawrence, joined them. The servants' quarters, a large library, and a schoolroom were on the third floor. The west wing's second floor was never used, but downstairs a large ballroom covered the entire back of the house. Christina saw the kitchen, a large banquet room, and a smaller dining room on one side of the house. And on the other side was the master's study and the drawing room.

The drawing room was beautifully done in green and white, with many portraits adorning the walls. Christina was drawn to the largest of them, hanging above the fireplace. She stood before it looking into a pair of sea-green eyes flecked with gold. It was the portrait of a lovely woman, her coal-black hair flowing over bare shoulders. Christina's earlier uneasiness returned, powerfully.

"That is Lady Anjanet," Emma informed Christina. "She was so beautiful. Her grandmother was Spanish — that's where she got her black hair, but her eyes are from her father's side of the family."

"She looks so sad," Christina whispered.

"Yes, that portrait was painted after she came back to England with her two sons. She was never happy again, but she never told anyone the reason."

"You mentioned two sons?"

"Yes, Mr. Caxton has a younger brother who lives in London."

Christina felt a wave of dizziness, and collapsed into the nearest chair.

"Are you all right, Miss Christina? You look pale," Mavis exclaimed.

"I don't know — I — I just felt a bit faint. Would you mind telling me Mr. Caxton's first name," she asked. But she already knew the answer.

"I thought I had," said Emma. "His name is Philip. Philip Caxton, Esquire."

"And his brother's name is Paul?" Christina asked weakly.

"Why, yes — but how did you know? Are you acquainted with Mr. Philip?"

"Acquainted!" Christina laughed hysterically. "I'm going to have his baby."

Mavis gasped.

"But why didn't you tell me?" Emma asked, a shocked expression on her face.

"I think it's wonderful!" Mavis blurted.

"But you don't understand. I didn't know this was his home. Mavis, you never told Johnsy Mr. Caxton's first name, and Philip never told me he had an estate in this part of the country. I can't stay here now — he wouldn't like it."

"Nonsense," Emma smiled. "What better place for Mr. Philip's baby to be born than in his own home?"

"But Philip didn't want me. He doesn't want this child."

"I can't believe that, Miss Christina — you're too lovely," said

210

Mavis. "Mr. Caxton cannot be that much of a fool. Did you tell him about the child?"

"I — I knew he didn't want this child, so I saw no point in telling him of it."

"If you didn't tell him, then you can't be sure of his feelings," Emma said reasonably. "No, you will stay here as planned. You cannot deny me the chance to see Philip Caxton's child."

"But —"

"Now I don't want to hear another word about your leaving. But I would love to hear how you and Mr. Caxton met!"

"I want to hear the whole story!" said Mavis.

Christina looked up at the portrait of Lady Anjanet. How like her Philip was!

A few weeks later, Christina's pains started. She felt the first slight cramps while taking her morning stroll in the vast floral gardens behind the house.

Emma immediately put Christina to bed, set water to boil, and summoned Mavis, who was experienced at delivering babies. She remained at Christina's side and assured her that everything was going well. The hours passed by slowly, and Christina fought back screams as her pains came faster.

She labored fourteen long hours. With a final great effort, she pushed her baby into the world, and was rewarded by his lusty wail.

Christina was exhausted, but she smiled contentedly. "I want to hold my son," she whispered weakly to Emma, who was standing beside her bed looking just as worn-out as Christina.

"As soon as Mavis finishes washing him, child, you can have him. But how did you know he was a boy?"

"What else would Philip Caxton sire?"

211

Chapter 27

It was midday in late September, and the slow-moving ceiling fans did nothing to alleviate the stuffiness in the small hotel dining room. Philip had arrived in Cairo only yesterday. This morning he'd managed to find a decently fitting suit, and had ordered everything else he would need for his journey home. Now he sat with a glass of cognac waiting for his meal, his mind a blank. He didn't want to think about his last eight months of living hell.

"Philip Caxton, isn't it? Imagine running into you. What brings you to Cairo?"

Philip looked up from his drink to see John Wakefield standing before him.

"I had some business to take care of," Philip replied. He wondered if John knew that his business was with John's sister. "But it's finished now, and I will be returning to England at the end of the month. Won't you join me for lunch?" Philip asked out of courtesy.

"Well, I'm expecting someone for lunch, but I'll have a drink with you while I wait."

"Is it your sister who's meeting you here?" Philip asked, hoping the answer would be no. He had no wish to see her again — ever.

"Christina went back to England about five months ago. She couldn't stand Egypt. Can't say I care for it, either. The only good thing about my stay here was meeting my wife. We were married only last month, and we'll be sailing for home soon, probably on the same ship as you."

"I guess congratulations are in order. At least your trip here wasn't a total loss — as mine was," Philip said bitterly. He would be glad to be gone from Egypt and the recent memories it held for him.

212

John Wakefield stood up and waved toward the entrance, and Philip saw two lovely women coming toward the table. John kissed the older of the two on the cheek and introduced Philip to his wife and her sister.

"Mr. Caxton is an acquaintance from London. It seems that we will be traveling back to England together," John informed the ladies.

"I can't tell you how glad I am to meet you, Mr. Caxton!" Estelle Hendricks gushed. "I just know the journey is going to be much more pleasant with you along. You're not married, are you, Mr. Caxton?"

"Estelle!" Kareen exclaimed. "That is none of your business!" Then she turned to Philip, a slight smile on her rosy lips. "I must apologize for my sister, Mr. Caxton. She's too outspoken for her own good."

Philip was amused by the young girl's boldness. "That's quite all right, Mrs. Wakefield. It's refreshing to hear someone speak her mind."

That night as Philip lay on the small hotel bed, he cursed his luck for running into John Wakefield. The meeting had brought Christina back to his mind vividly. He had hoped to forget her, but it was impossible. Every night, her image haunted him: her beautiful slender body lying beneath his; her hair when the light would touch it; her soft blue-green eyes and alluring smile. Just the thought of her had the power to arouse him. He still wanted her, even though he would never have her again.

At first, Philip had been determined to stay in Egypt. He couldn't go back to England and chance running into Christina. But everywhere he looked, he saw her. In the tent, at the pond, in the desert — everywhere. He just couldn't get her out of his mind as long as he stayed in Egypt.

Philip had been ready to return to England four months ago. But then Amine's brother, Amair, had come to visit the camp, and had told Philip the truth about Christina's abduction. Rashid had planned

213

the whole thing. He had wanted Philip dead so that he could become sheik himself.

Rashid had never returned to camp after taking Christina back to her brother. If he had, Philip would have killed him. Philip had searched four months for Rashid, but he'd disappeared.

The day before his ship sailed, with nothing better to do, Philip went down to the marketplace to stroll by the many open stands and small shops. The streets were crowded with bartering Arabs and Egyptians. Everywhere Philip looked were camels packed heavily with trade goods.

The fragrant odor of perfumes filled the air and reminded Philip of the first time he had walked through this marketplace, some fourteen years ago. He had been only twenty years old, and Egypt had been a strange and terrifying land. He had come to find his father, but had no idea how to go about it. He had known only his father's name and that he was the sheik of a desert tribe.

Philip had spent weeks walking through the dusty streets and asking people if they knew of Yasir Alhamar. Finally he had realized that he was getting nowhere. His father was a desert man, so Philip had hired a guide to take him into the desert. With two camels laden with supplies, they had set off into the scorching sand.

In the grueling months that followed, Philip had become acquainted with the hardships of living in the desert. The burning sun had beaten down on him during the day; the freezing cold had forced him to curl up next to his camel for warmth at night.

They had ridden for days without seeing another human being. When they had come upon Bedouins, either they hadn't known Yasir or they had had no idea where he could be found.

And then, when Philip was ready to give up the search, he had ridden into his father's camp. He would never forget that day and the look on his father's face when he had said who he was.

Philip had been happy in Egypt, but couldn't stand it anymore. He

214

could not forget Christina as long as he stayed. Since there seemed to be no hope of finding Rashid, he had finally decided to leave.

He would go back to England, inform Paul of their father's death, then sell his estate. He might go to America. He wanted to go somewhere far away from Christina Wakefield.

Chapter 28

Christina stayed at Victory for a month after her lying-in, and became well acquainted with little Philip Junior. She'd named him properly, for he was the image of his father — the same green eyes, the same black hair, the same strong features. He was a beautiful baby — healthy, and with an appetite that wouldn't stop. He was her joy, and her life.

But she had stayed there long enough, and it was time that she went home. Johnsy would be eager to see Philip Junior, and Christina hoped she could now cope with Tommy.

She turned to look at her baby, who was lying in the middle of Philip's big bed and watching her quietly. She smiled at him, put the rest of her things into the last chest, and closed it securely. She had heard the coach pull up to the front of the house a few minutes ago, so she went to the door and asked one of the maids to have the driver come for her baggage.

After the maid left, Christina put on her bonnet and cape and looked longingly about the room. It would be the last time she would ever see anything that belonged to Philip. She suddenly felt sad at leaving his home. She walked around the room, softly running her hand over the furniture, knowing that he had once touched it.

"And who might you be, madam?"

Christina turned quickly at the sound of the strange voice, and gasped when she saw Paul Caxton standing in the doorway.

"'What on earth are you doing here?" he asked. But then he saw the green-eyed baby in the middle of the bed. "I'll be damned! He said he'd do it. He said he'd have you, but I thought you'd never marry him!" Paul laughed aloud, turning to look at Christina again, who was still too surprised to find words. "'Where is that brother of mine? Congratulations are in order.''

"Your brother is not here, Mr. Caxton, and I did not marry him. Now if you will excuse me, I was just leaving," she replied coldly, and crossed to the bed to pick up her baby.

"But you have his child. You mean that scoundrel wouldn't marry you?"

"Your brother kidnapped me and held me captive for four months. He didn't want to marry me. I gave birth to the son Philip doesn't want, but I want him and I will raise him myself. Now if you will excuse me, I'm leaving." She walked past him and down the stairs.

Paul stood watching her, wondering what the hell was going on. He couldn't believe Philip didn't want his own son. And why hadn't he married Christina Wakefield? Had his brother gone daft?

It was obvious he wouldn't get any answers from Christina. He would have to write to Philip.

Christina had been back at Wakefield Manor for a week when she received a letter from John. He told her that Kareen had agreed to marry him and that he would soon bring his new wife home.

Christina was overjoyed. She had grown to love Kareen and was truly happy that she would be her sister-in-law. She thought they might be home in time for Christmas. What a joyful holiday it would be!

Johnsy and Christina busied themselves redecorating her parents' old room for John and his new bride. Christina threw herself into the work, for she needed the exercise to firm her sagging middle. She had been disappointed when she didn't regain her figure immediately and had had to resort to wearing corsets. But she exercised constantly and hoped that she would have her shape back by the time John returned.

The time went by quickly. Christina began riding every day, which benefited both her and Johnsy. It gave Johnsy a chance to play with

Philip Junior, and it let Christina get away from Tommy. He hadn't changed since her trip to Victory. She treated him coldly, but he persisted.

Christina sensed that Tommy hated her child, although he tried to hide it. Every time she left Tommy to tend Philip Junior, he became annoyed. He insisted Johnsy could care for the baby. And it infuriated Tommy that Philip Junior began to cry every time he came near him. Christina kept them apart as much as possible.

And then, two days after Christmas, John brought Kareen home. They arrived early in the morning, and Christina was still sleeping when Johnsy rushed into her room. She had only enough time to slip into her robe before John and Kareen walked in. Christina ran to them and hugged and kissed them both.

"I'm so happy for you, and so glad that you're finally home!" Christina exclaimed, tears of joy welling in her soft blue eyes.

"I'll never leave Wakefield again," John laughed, hugging Christina close to him. "I can assure you of that. But where's that nephew of mine?"

"Right in 'ere, Master John," Johnsy answered proudly, opening the door between the two rooms.

Philip Junior was wide awake, a foot in each hand, when they all gathered around the bassinet.

"Oh, he's beautiful, Christina, absolutely adorable!" Kareen exclaimed. "Can I hold him — would you mind?"

"Of course you may — Philip Junior loves to be cuddled," Christina answered.

"Philip Junior?" John lifted an eyebrow. "I had thought you would name him after our father, or his own father."

"The name just struck my fancy. I couldn't see calling an Englishman Abu."

"Nor could I," John laughed. He grasped Philip Junior's little hand as he lay in Kareen's arms. "He's as strong as an ox. But where did he get those unusual eyes, Crissy? We have no green eyes in our family, and I've never seen an Arab with eyes like that."

"You ask such ludicrous questions, John. How would I know?"

He started to say more, but stopped when he caught Kareen's disapproving look.

"It's time for this little one to be fed. You get yourself out of 'ere, Master John," Johnsy chuckled.

John actually blushed at the thought of his sister's putting the baby to her breast. "Come downstairs when you're through, Crissy. Estelle is with us, and we can all have breakfast together."

Christina was glad to hear that Estelle had come with them. Estelle was a beautiful girl, and perhaps Tommy would be attracted to her.

Awhile later, Christina put Philip Junior down for a nap and joined the others in the dining room.

"It's so good to see you again, Estelle," Christina said, embracing the other girl. "I hope you intend to stay with us. We have more than enough room in this big house."

"For a while, but then I must visit my parents."

"Did you enjoy your journey?" Christina asked.

"Oh — it was the most wonderful time of my life!" Estelle said exuberantly.

"I'm afraid Estelle has fallen hopelessly in love with one of the passengers we sailed with — a friend of John's," Kareen said.

"He's the handsomest man I have ever laid eyes on, and I know he feels the same way about me," Estelle replied happily.

"You take too much for granted, Estelle," said Kareen "Just because he paid you some attention doesn't mean he loves you."

"He does, too!" Estelle cried. "And we'll meet again, even if I have to go to London. I intend to marry Philip Caxton!"

They all jumped at the crash of dishes in the kitchen, and Christina knew that Johnsy had been listening to the conversation. Philip had come back, and he was in London! A wave of jealousy swept over Christina when she thought of Estelle with him on board ship.

Why had he come back? And why had he left Nura? Perhaps he

had tired of her, too, and now Estelle was his new plaything. Was there no end to the women he would captivate?

"Crissy, you remember Philip Caxton, don't you?" John asked, unaware of the emotions she was fighting to control.

"You've met him, Christina?" said Estelle. "Then you must know how I —"

Johnsy came into the room, pale as a ghost, and said, "I'm sorry about the dishes — they slipped. Miss Crissy, could you 'elp me to my room? I don't feel too well."

"Of course, Johnsy," Christina answered gratefully, going to her and pretending to help her out of the room.

When they were out of hearing distance, Johnsy said, "Oh, baby, I'm sorry. You must be miserable. That scoundrel's back in England, and what are you goin' to do?"

"I'm not going to do anything, Johnsy. He won't come here, and I'm not going anywhere that I might run into him. And I am not miserable — I'm angry! That man is despicable. He has to destroy every pretty woman he meets!"

"It sounds to me like you're jealous, love," Johnsy remarked.

"I am *not* jealous," she scoffed. "I'm mad. I didn't blame him for what he did to me, but I should have. He has probably broken Nura's heart, and he'll do the same to Estelle. Estelle doesn't even know he's married!"

"Nor do you, Miss Crissy. You don't know for sure that 'e married that other girl. 'E may 'ave kept her as 'is mistress, as 'e did you."

"He wouldn't dare! Her family wouldn't have allowed it."

"Well, you still don't know for sure."

Tommy came for dinner that night, but he didn't pay any attention to Estelle, nor she to him. After dinner, Christina found a moment alone with John and asked him to help in dealing with Tommy. She explained that Tommy had bothered her ever since her return and she didn't know what to do.

"Can't you talk to him, John? Tell him to stop asking me to marry him?"

"But I don't see why you won't marry him, Crissy. He loves you. He would make you a very good husband. And he would be a father to your child. You can't go on living with memories, and I'm sure, in time, you could learn to love Tommy."

Christina was surprised for a moment. But then she realized her brother might be right. There was no longer any reason why she shouldn't marry Tommy.

Chapter 29

Philip pounded heavily on the single door. It was opened by a dour-looking manservant. "Mr. Caxton, sir, 'tis good to see you again. Mr. Paul will be delighted."

"Where is that brother of mine?" Philip asked, handing over his greatcoat.

"In his study, Mr. Caxton. Shall I announce your arrival?"

"That won't be necessary," Philip replied, and walked down the short hallway until he came to the open door of Paul's study. "I can come another time if you are busy, little brother," Philip said mischievously.

Paul looked up from his papers and rose quickly, bright grin on his handsome features.

"Damn, but it's good to see you again, Philip! When did you get back?" Paul came over and embraced his brother warmly.

"I only just arrived," Philip answered. He sat down in a large leather chair by the window.

"I wrote you a letter not too long ago, but apparently you sailed before it had a chance to reach you. Well, no matter — now that you're here. This calls for a drink," Paul said, walking to the small cabinet where he kept a decanter of brandy and a supply of glasses. "And congratulations are in order."

"I hardly think my coming home merits congratulations," Philip remarked dryly.

"I agree. Your coming home merely calls for a drink, but you deserve congratulations because I've seen your son, and he's a fine, healthy fellow. Looks just like you," Paul said cheerfully, handing Philip a drink.

"What the hell are you talking about, Paul? I have no son!"

"But I — I thought you knew! Isn't that why you came back to England — to find your child?" Paul asked.

"You're talking in riddles, Paul. I've already told you I don't have a son!" Philip returned. He was getting irritated.

"Then you're not going to claim him? You're just going to deny that he exists — pretend it never happened?"

"There is no son to claim — how many times must I say it! Now you had better come up with a good explanation, little brother. You are trying my patience sorely!" Philip stormed.

Paul burst out laughing and sank into a chair across from Philip. "I'll be damned. She didn't tell you, did she? You really don't know?"

"No, she didn't tell me, and who the hell is *she?*"

"Christina Wakefield! Whom else have you lived with this past year?"

Shocked, Philip sank back into his chair.

"She bore a son three months ago at Victory. I naturally assumed you knew about it, since she went to your home to have the baby. I happened to go there and ran into her just as she was leaving to go back to her home. She seemed angry that I had learned about the baby. And she told me what you had done — how you kidnapped her and held her captive four months. How the hell could you do such a thing, Philip?"

"It was the only way I could have her. But why didn't she come back and tell me?" Philip said, more to himself than to Paul.

"She said you didn't want the child — that you didn't want to marry her."

"But I never told her —" he stopped when he remembered that he had told her just that. He'd said he hadn't brought her to his camp to bear his children, and he'd told her in the beginning that he had no intention of marrying her.

"Just because the child looks like me doesn't prove he is mine.

223

Christina could have conceived after she went back to her brother."

"Use your brain, Philip, and calculate the time. You took her when she first arrived in Cairo — in September, did you not?"

"Yes."

"Well, you kept her four months, she left you at the end of January, and she gave birth eight months later, at the end of September. So she had to conceive with you. And besides, Christina as much as told me the child was yours. Her exact words were, 'I gave birth to the son that Philip doesn't want,' and I might add that she intends to keep him and raise him herself."

"I have a son!" Philip exclaimed, slamming his fist down on the arm of the chair, his laughter ringing through the room. "I've got a son, Paul — a son! You say he looks like me?"

"He has your eyes and hair — he's a handsome boy. You couldn't ask for better."

"A son. And she wasn't even going to tell me. I will need one of your horses, Paul. I'll be leaving first thing in the morning."

"You're going to Halstead?"

"Of course! I want my son. Christina will have to marry me now."

"If you didn't know of the child, why did you come back to England?" Paul asked while he refilled their glasses. "Did you come back for Christina?"

"I still want her, but I didn't come back to find her. I came back because there was nothing left for me in Egypt. Yasir is dead."

"I'm sorry, Philip. I never really knew Yasir or thought of him as my father. But I know you loved him. You must have taken it badly."

"I did, but Christina helped me through it."

"I wish I knew what happened between Christina and you," said Paul.

"Perhaps someday I will tell you, little brother, but not now. I'm not really sure what happened, myself."

Philip left at dawn the following morning, and had a chance to think things out while riding through the countryside.

Why hadn't Christina come back and told him when she learned she was carrying his child? Had she been too proud? And what of John? She must not have told her brother, or John would have called him out when they met in Cairo.

Well, John would soon know the truth. Philip wondered how he would take the news, for they had become good friends during their journey back to England. He also wondered how Christina would react when he showed up unexpectedly. She obviously hadn't wanted him to learn of his son. Or had she? Had she gone to Victory so that he would find out?

She was going to keep and raise the child. If she hated him, why keep his son to constantly remind her of him? Perhaps she actually cared for him!

If only he had told her he loved her. If only he hadn't waited to hear her say it first. Well, he would tell her this time, just as soon as he saw her.

Chapter 30

Christina had spent the entire morning trying to avoid Estelle. She couldn't bear the happiness in the girl's eyes, knowing that she loved Philip. Now it was late afternoon, and Kareen and Estelle had gone to Halstead to do some shopping while John went over the estate books in his study.

The house was quiet. Christina reclined in the drawing room trying to read a book so she could stop thinking about Estelle and Philip. But she kept imagining them together, kissing and holding each other. Damn him!

"Christina, I have to talk to you." It was Tommy Huntington.

She stood up and walked over to the fireplace, her red-velvet skirt swaying gently.

"I didn't expect to see you until tonight, Tommy. What's so important that you're here early?" Christina asked. She turned her back to him and busied herself rearranging the figurines on the mantel.

"I talked with John this morning. He agrees we should marry. You can't deny me any longer, Christina. I love you. Will you please marry me?"

Christina sighed heavily. Her answer was going to make everyone happy, everyone but herself. Even Johnsy had been arguing that marriages were made for convenience, not for love, and that it was enough that Master Tommy loved her.

"All right, Tommy, I will marry you. But I can't guarantee to ever —"

She was going to say "love you," but the sound of a deep voice stopped her. She turned deathly pale.

"I have been informed that I have a son, madam. Is this true?"

Tommy grasped Christina's arms violently, but she was too shocked to feel anything. Tommy released her and swung around to face the intruder, leaving her holding the mantel for support. Her legs felt like jelly beneath her.

"Who are you, sir," Tommy demanded, "and what is the meaning of asking my fiancée if you have a son?"

"I am Philip Caxton. Miss Wakefield may be your intended wife, but this matter does not concern you. I am addressing Christina. And I am waiting for an answer."

"How dare you!" Tommy raged. "Christina, do you know this man?"

Christina's mind was in a whirl of confusion. She turned slowly to face Philip, and melted at the sight of him. He hadn't changed — he was still the man she loved. She wanted to run to him. She wanted to throw her arms about his neck and never let go. But the ugly hate in his eyes and the harsh coldness in his voice stopped her.

"Do I have a son, madam?"

Christina stiffened with fear at the menace in his voice. But then her anger grew. How could he ask about her child so coldly?

"No, Mr. Caxton," she said. "*I* have a son — *you* do not!"

"Then let me rephrase my question, Miss Wakefield. Did I sire your son?"

Christina knew there was no way out. Paul must have told him when she gave birth. Philip had calculated for himself and knew she must have conceived by him. Besides, he would need only to look at Philip Junior to know him for his son.

Christina sank into the nearest chair, averting her gaze from the two men awaiting her answer.

"Christina, is this true? Is this man the father of your child?" Tommy choked.

"It's true, Tommy," Christina whispered.

"How *dare* you come here, Mr. Caxton?" Tommy demanded.

227

"I'm here for my son, and I suggest you not interfere!"

"For *your* son!" Christina screamed, springing from her chair. "But you never wanted him. Why do you want him now?"

"I'm afraid you misinterpreted what I told you long ago, Christina. I told you that I hadn't brought you to my camp to bear my children. I never told you I wouldn't want a child if you happened to conceive," Philip replied calmly.

"But I —"

Christina was cut off when John came to the door. "What is all this yelling about?" he asked sternly. Then he saw Philip standing just inside the door, and he smiled warmly. "Philip — I didn't expect to see you again so soon. But I'm glad you decided to accept my invitation to visit us. Estelle will be delighted to see you."

"Good Lord! Has everyone here gone crazy?" Tommy blurted out. "Don't you know who this man is, John? He's the father of Christina's child!"

John's smile faded. "Is this true, Christina?" he said.

"Yes," she whispered tensely.

John slammed his fist into the wall. "Damn it, Christina! I became friends with this man! You told me your child's father was an Arab!"

"But Philip is half-Arab, and I told you he had another name!" Christina yelled back at him.

"And *you!*" John stormed, turning to Philip again. "You come with me."

"John!" Christina screamed. "You gave me your word!"

"I well remember the promise you extracted from me, Crissy. I am just going to talk with Philip privately in my study," John said more calmly, and they left the room.

John poured two brandies and handed one to Philip. Then he sank into his black-leather desk chair.

"Why did you come here? Good God, Philip! I have every right to call you out for ruining my sister!"

228

"I hope it will not come to that," Philip replied. "I learned about my son from my brother, and I came here to marry Christina and take her and the boy to my home in Benfleet. But I overheard her accepting that belligerent puppy's proposal, so marriage is now out of the question. But I still want my son."

"Christina will never give up her child!"

"Then I must ask that you let me stay here to try to persuade her otherwise. You can understand how I feel. The boy is my heir, and I am a rich man. He would have more to gain if I raised him."

"I just don't understand it. You are a gentleman, yet you kidnap a lady and keep her as your mistress. How could you do such a thing?" John asked.

Philip was amused that John asked the same thing his own brother had asked.

"I wanted your sister more than I have ever wanted a woman before. She's so beautiful, you can hardly blame me. I am used to taking what I want, and I asked her to marry me when we first met in London. When she refused, I had you sent to Egypt, my father's land."

"So *you* were the one!"

"Yes, and you probably know the rest."

John nodded. He was amazed at the lengths to which this man had gone to obtain Christina. He would probably go just as far to get his son. So Crissy was wrong — Philip did want her and the child, and he had come here to marry her. John felt guilty for persuading her to marry Tommy. He might have ruined Crissy's one chance for happiness. But if he let Philip stay here, he and Crissy might be able to work things out between themselves. John decided not to interfere again.

"You may stay here as long as you like, Philip, although it will probably cause quite a commotion. As you know, Estelle is also here, and she fancies herself in love with you. I don't know how you feel about her, but please handle the situation carefully — for Christina's

229

sake." John stood up and walked to the door. "I'm sure you want to see your son now. I'll try to explain things to Tommy Huntington while Christina takes you to the nursery."

"I am grateful for your understanding," Philip returned.

Standing outside the study with Philip beside him, John called Christina, and she appeared in the hallway, her face a mask of trepidation.

"I've decided to let Philip stay for a while," John said.

"But John —"

"It's already settled, Crissy. Now take Philip up to the nursery. It's about time he met his son."

"Oh!" She turned and started for the stairs, not waiting for Philip.

"You didn't expect it to go easily, did you?" John asked.

"Nothing is ever easy where Christina is concerned," Philip replied, and followed her up the stairs.

She waited for him at the door to the nursery. She felt tense and angry, and when Philip reached her, she could no longer control her temper.

"What do you expect to gain by staying here?" she said harshly. "Haven't you caused enough misery as it is?"

"I've already told you, Christina. I came here for my son."

"You can't be serious! After what you did to me, you expect me to hand over my son? Well, you can't have him!"

"Is he in this room?"

"Yes, but —"

Philip opened the door and walked past Christina into the nursery. He went directly to the bassinet and stood there looking down at his son.

Christina came up beside him, but she didn't say anything when she saw his proud smile as he gazed at Philip Junior.

"He is a handsome lad, Tina — thank you," Philip said warmly, and Christina melted again at the softness in his voice. Philip picked up his son gently. Surprisingly, the baby didn't cry, but stared curiously at the stubble of whiskers on his father's face. "What did you name him?"

Christina hesitated and averted her eyes. What could she tell him?

"Junior," she whispered.

"Junior! What kind of name is that for my son?" Philip stormed, and Philip Junior began to cry.

She quickly took her baby from Philip's arms, as he stood there helplessly. "Hush, darling, it's all right — mama's here," she soothed. He stopped crying immediately, and Christina glared at Philip. "The name was my choice, since you weren't here. Oh — why did you have to come?"

"I came here with good intentions, but then I overheard you agreeing to marry your lover," Philip returned, his eyes dark and menacing.

"My lover!"

"Oh, come now, Christina — spare me your denials. I of all people know what a passionate woman you are. After all these months, I expected to find you in another man's arms."

"I hate you!" Christina cried, her eyes turning a dark, shadowy blue.

"I am well aware of how you feel about me, madam. If you hate me so, why do you wish to keep my son? Every time you look at him, you will see me."

"He is also my son! I carried him for nine months. I suffered the pain of bringing him into this world. I will not give him up! He is a part of me, and I love him!"

"There is another matter that puzzles me. If you hate me so, why did you go to Victory to bear my son?"

"I didn't know it was your home until after I arrived. I didn't want to stay here, and so Johnsy, my old nanny, suggested I go to her sister, who happens to be your cook. I went to Victory. How was I to know it was your estate?"

"That must have been quite a surprise," Philip sneered. "Why

231

didn't you leave when you found out the truth?"

"Emma insisted I stay. Now I don't want to discuss it any longer," she replied. "You will have to leave now, Philip. It's time for his feeding."

"Then feed him. It's rather late for false modesty on your part, Christina. I'm well acquainted with the body hidden underneath your dress."

"You are impossible! You haven't changed one damn bit."

"No — but you have. You used to be more honest."

"I don't know what you're talking about." She walked toward her bedroom door. "I suggest you have someone show you to your room. You may see your son later — if you wish."

She sat down in a chair in the far corner of her room and rested Philip Junior on her lap while unbuttoning her bodice. But she still felt Philip's presence and looked up to see him leaning against the doorframe, watching her intently.

"Please, Philip! You are welcome in the nursery, but this is my room. I would like some privacy — if you don't mind."

"Do I embarrass you, Christina? You have never bared your breasts in front of a man before?" he taunted. "I suggest you stop acting indignant, and feed my son. He is hungry, is he not?"

"Oh!" She decided to ignore him, and hoped he would leave. She pulled one side of her dress open and gave Philip Junior her breast. He sucked greedily, resting one tiny fist against her. She was fully aware that Philip still watched her.

"Christina, what are you doin'?" Johnsy shrieked, coming into the room from the other entrance and seeing Philip.

"It's all right, Johnsy. Calm yourself," Christina said irritably. "This is Philip Caxton."

"So you be Philip Junior's father," Johnsy snapped, turning to face Philip. "Well, you 'ave your nerve comin' 'ere after what you did to my baby."

"Oh, hush, Johnsy! You've said enough already," Christina bit off.

Philip started laughing, and she cringed, knowing full well what he found so amusing. "It's a common name, damn it! I need not explain myself to you!" Philip Junior began crying again.

"You get yourself out of 'ere, Mr. Caxton. You're disturbin' Crissy an' your son," Johnsy scolded. She closed the door behind Philip, but Christina could still hear him laughing. She quietly closed the other door, then looked at Christina, shaking her head. "So 'e did come — I knew 'e would. Does Master John know?"

"Yes. John has decided to let Philip stay here. And Tommy knows, too. Philip walked in just when I was agreeing to marry Tommy. Oh, Johnsy, what am I going to do?" Christina started crying. "He came here for his son — not me! Philip is so cold to me, and how can I bear seeing him and Estelle together?"

"It will be all right, Miss Crissy — you'll see. Now you stop your cryin', or that little one will never settle down."

Christina closed the door to the nursery very quietly and turned to see Philip coming out of the next room. She had to walk toward him to get to the stairs, but he blocked her way.

"Is *Philip* junior asleep?" he asked teasingly.

"Yes," she replied, avoiding his eyes. "Is your room satisfactory?"

"It will do," he returned, and tilted her face up to his. "But I'd prefer to share yours."

Philip pulled her against him, molding her body against his, and his lips covered hers, demanding a response. She gave it willingly. All the long, lonely months disappeared.

"Ah, Tina — why didn't you tell me you were carrying my child?" he murmured huskily.

"I didn't know I had conceived until I was three months' pregnant. And it was too late then — you had already married Nura."

"Nura!" he laughed, looking down into her soft blue eyes. "I —"

But then he stiffened. So — she had gone back to her brother because she wanted to. Philip thought she might already have known

233

of her pregnancy, and been afraid he would be angry. When would he learn that the woman hated him!

"Philip, what's the matter with you?" Christina asked, seeing the coldness in his eyes.

"You had best go to your lover, madam. I'm sure you prefer his kisses to mine!" Philip said harshly, and pushed her away.

Christina watched him walk away and felt as if her knees would give way. What had she said to make him hurt her so cruelly? She had been deliriously happy only a moment before, and now she felt like dying.

"Philip! Oh, I knew you would come!"

Christina heard Estelle's happy voice coming from the hall downstairs.

"I was hoping you'd still be here, my sweet. You'll make my stay here much more pleasant," Philip's deep voice answered cheerfully.

The tears came easily to Christina's eyes as she walked slowly back to her room and closed the door behind her. She fell onto the bed and buried her face in the pillow.

She couldn't bear to go downstairs and watch Philip flirting with Estelle. Why did he hate her so? Why couldn't he still desire her? How could she bear seeing them together, when her own heart was breaking?

Chapter 31

Philip stood in the open doorway watching Christina sleep. He had watched her many times before, but then he could have made love to her, as he wanted to now. She was so beautiful, her golden hair spread across the pillow, a sweet, innocent look on her face. If only she cared for him, he would be the happiest man alive.

He wondered why Christina hadn't come down to dinner the night before. He had been prepared to show her he could be as indifferent as she, and had planned to devote his attention to Estelle. He'd been disappointed by Christina's absence. Estelle was a lovely girl, but she couldn't compare to Christina — no one could compare to Christina. Why did she have to be such a deceitful bitch?

Philip Junior started crying, and Philip moved behind the door so he could observe Christina unseen when she came into the nursery. She walked into the room, and he was surprised to see her wearing the black robe she had made in Egypt. Why hadn't she burned it? Apparently it carried no memories for her, as it did for him.

She went directly to the cradle, her long golden curls streaming down her back, and Philip Junior stopped crying as soon as he saw her.

"Good morning, my love. You let mommy sleep late this morning, didn't you? You're the joy of my life, Philip. What would I do without you?"

Philip was warmed by her love for the child. But it puzzled him why she'd named the boy after him.

Christina turned suddenly, sensing Philip's presence in the room, but said nothing when she saw him standing beside the door. She turned back to Philip Junior, lifted him from the cradle, and sat down in a blue-cushioned rocker in the corner of the room. She slowly unbuttoned her nightdress.

Philip became irritated by her silence. He would rather she shout at him than ignore him.

"It didn't take you long to lose your modesty again," he remarked cruelly.

"You made your point yesterday, Philip. I have nothing to show you that you haven't already seen," Christina said calmly, giving him a half-smile that didn't reach her remarkably blue eyes.

He laughed. He wouldn't be able to make her lose her temper this morning. He watched his son suck greedily on Christina's breast, and felt deeply moved by the sight. This was his child and the woman he still wanted. He refused to accept defeat. He would find a way to have them both.

"He has a strong appetite. You don't need a wet nurse?" Philip asked.

"I have sufficient milk to satisfy his needs. Philip Junior is well cared for," she said tensely.

Philip sighed heavily. It seemed he didn't have to search to find a biting remark to make her angry — a simple question did the trick.

"I didn't mean to insinuate that you're not a good mother. Indeed, motherhood seems to suit you, Christina. You've done exceedingly well with my son," Philip said slowly, lifting a stray lock of her hair that had fallen behind the chair, and rubbing it delicately between his fingers.

"Thank you," she whispered.

"Where did you have him baptized?" Philip asked conversationally. He didn't want to leave, and thought he should say something or he would make her nervous just standing behind her.

"He hasn't been baptized yet," Christina said.

"Good Lord, Christina! He should have been baptized one month after birth. What have you been waiting for?" he stormed, coming around the chair to face her.

236

"Damn it — stop yelling at me! I just didn't think about it, that's all. I'm not used to having children," she replied just as angrily, her eyes turning a dark, sapphire blue.

With long strides, Philip reached the nursery door, but turned to face her again, his body stiff with rage.

"He will be baptized today — this morning! Prepare yourself and my son, and be ready to leave in an hour."

"This my home, Philip, not your camp in the mountains. You can't tell me what to do here."

"Be ready, or I will take him myself." Then he turned and left the room.

Christina knew he meant every word. She calmed herself down and finished feeding Philip Junior, then she put him down in his bassinet and called one of the upstairs maids to help her get ready. She couldn't trust Philip to take her son out alone — he might not come back.

She threw her robe onto the bed, and noticed that it was her black Arab one. She had unconsciously picked it up when Philip Junior started crying. Christina wondered if Philip had noticed. But no — he probably didn't even remember it, or he would have made some sly remark.

Christina pinned her hair up into a mass of curls, then hurriedly chose a plain cotton lilac dress with long sleeves and a high-collared neck that would be appropriate for the occasion. With time to spare, she slowly dressed Philip Junior, and an hour later descended the stairs.

Philip was waiting alone and took his son from her arms.

"Where is John?" she asked nervously.

"He left early this morning to go into Halstead on business. He said he'd try to be back before noon," Philip replied, and started for the door.

"But — we're not going by ourselves — are we?"

"Oh, come now, Christina," he laughed. "I will not kidnap you

237

again if that's what's bothering you. Although the thought did cross my mind."

Oh! How could he lie so easily, she thought angrily. "The next time you plan an abduction, Philip, your victim will probably be Estelle!" Christina snapped.

"Why — Christina, you actually sound jealous," he teased.

"I am not jealous!" she said curtly. "I'm thankful that your attentions have gone elsewhere."

It didn't take them long to arrive at the small church near Wakefield. Christina waited in the open carriage while Philip went into the church to find out if the priest was available. He came back soon and helped her down from the carriage.

"Is everything arranged?" she asked as he took Philip Junior from her again.

"Yes. It will only take a minute," he replied, and escorted her into the small, gloomy church.

A short, ruddy man waited for them at the end of the aisle, and Philip handed the boy to him. Philip Junior didn't cry when the water was dribbled on his forehead, but Christina gasped when she heard the clear words echoing in the dark room.

"I baptize thee — Philip Caxton, Junior."

Philip took his son back and grasped Christina's arm to lead her from the church. She said nothing until they were in the carriage and the driver had started back to Wakefield Manor.

"You had no right to do that, Philip!" she snapped, glowering at him.

"I had every right — I am his father," Philip grinned.

"You are not his legal father — no vows were spoken between us. Damn it! His name is Philip Junior Wakefield, as it appears on his birth record."

"That can be changed very easily, Christina."

"You'd have to find the original document first. He is my son, and he will carry my name, not yours!"

"And when you marry, do you intend giving him your husband's name?"

"I haven't really thought about it, but if Tommy wants to adopt him, then yes, he will carry his name."

"I will not have that young fop raising my son," Philip scowled at her.

"You will have nothing to say in the matter, Philip. Besides, Tommy will make a good father." But she didn't really believe her own words.

"We shall see," Philip murmured, and they said no more as the carriage pulled up in front of Wakefield Manor.

John met them at the door, his face a mask of anger. "Where the hell have you been! I've been worried sick!"

"We had Philip Junior baptized, John. There was nothing to be upset about," Christina replied. She looked quizzically at Philip, who had started laughing.

"Why didn't you tell someone where you were going? When I came home and found both of you gone, including the baby, I thought —"

"We know what you thought, John," she laughed. "But, as you can see, you were wrong. I'm sorry you were upset — it won't happen again."

Christina went upstairs to put Philip Junior down for a nap. After changing him, she closed the nursery doors so he wouldn't be disturbed, then went into her own room to remove her bonnet. Through her open door, Christina heard Philip going into his room. His voice drifted clearly to her, causing her to stand motionless.

"What are you doing in here? Your sister would have a fit if she found you in a gentleman's bedroom."

"Don't look so shocked, Philip. You must be used to entertaining ladies in your bedroom," Estelle said sweetly. "I've been waiting here so I could talk to you alone. Why don't you close the door and come over here where it's much more comfortable."

"That won't be necessary — you won't be here that long. I have no intention of being asked to leave this house simply because you wish to play games, Estelle."

Christina didn't want to listen to any more, but she couldn't help herself.

"I am not playing games, Philip Caxton! I came here for an answer. Do you still love Christina? I have a right to know!"

"Love! What has love to do with it? I desired her then, just as I desire you now," Philip said, with very little emotion in his deep voice.

"Then she doesn't mean anything to you now?" Estelle asked.

"Christina is the mother of my son — that's all. Now I must ask you to leave, Estelle, before someone finds you here. The next time you wish to talk to me privately, find a more suitable place."

"Anything you say, Philip," Estelle giggled, obviously pleased with herself. "Will I see you for lunch?"

"I'll be down shortly."

Christina sat down on the edge of her bed feeling as if a knife had been plunged into her heart. She had been famished, but now all thoughts of food vanished. She had to get away!

She tore off her dress, put on her riding habit, and ran down the stairs and out of the house.

Christina had a stableboy saddle Dax while she waited impatiently. Then she took off down the path leading to the open fields, and the tears finally came.

The wind pushed the salty drops to the sides of her eyes as Christina urged Dax faster and faster. The pins fell from her hair and it tumbled down her back, streaming in the wind behind her. She wanted to end it all, but remembered Philip Junior. She couldn't leave her baby. She had to face the fact that she still loved Philip but she would never have him again. She would just have to accept it and take what joy she could in her son. Tommy loved her, and perhaps someday she could feel content with him.

It had been dark for two hours when Christina finally came in the front door and leaned back against it, exhausted. Philip came out of the drawing room, an angry, concerned expression on his face, but he relaxed and grinned when he saw her. John and Kareen were right behind him, Kareen worried and John filled with rage.

"Where the hell have you been, Christina?" John fumed. "This makes twice in the same day you've gone off without a word. What's gotten into you?"

"Is Philip Junior all right?" Christina asked.

"He's fine. Johnsy had to send for a wet nurse when you didn't come back. He was a bit fretful, but he's sleeping now. Crissy, are you hurt?" John asked. "You look as if you've taken a fall."

Christina looked down at herself. She was a mess. Her hair was in tangles, falling over her shoulders and down to her waist. Her dark-green velvet riding habit was torn in many places from riding wildly through the woods.

She pushed herself away from the door and straightened her back proudly.

"I'm fine, John. Just tired and hungry."

She started to walk away, but John pulled her back. "Just a minute, young lady. You haven't answered my questions. Where have you been all this time? The whole household has been out searching for you."

Christina glanced at Philip's amused expression and became angry. "Damn it! I'm not a child anymore, John — I can take care of myself! Just because I go off by myself for a few hours is no reason for you to send out a search party."

"A few hours! You've been gone all day."

"I've been riding — that's all! And you of all people should understand why!"

John knew why. It seemed Philip's presence in this house troubled Christina more than he had thought it would.

241

"Crissy, I want to talk you — privately," John said.

"Not tonight, John — I told you, I'm tired."

He walked with her toward the stairs and out of the others' hearing. "Crissy, if Philip is upsetting you this much, then I'll ask him to leave."

"No!" she shouted, then said more softly, "I don't want him to leave, John. I can't deny him the right to be with his son. I've come to terms with myself — I'll be able to handle his presence from now on." She hoped she was telling the truth.

John walked solemnly back to Kareen after Christina went upstairs.

"I'll have someone take a tray of food to her room, and hot water for a bath," Kareen said, looking worriedly at her husband. "Did you find out what made her go off this afternoon?"

"I know why," John replied, giving Philip a disapproving glance. "But I don't know what to do about it."

242

Chapter 32

It was the fifth day of the new year, 1885. The last seven days had been filled with tension for everyone at Wakefield Manor, but for Christina most of all. Estelle snubbed her rudely whenever they met, while Philip looked on with an amused smile. But the supper table every evening was the worst time to endure. Poor John and Kareen sat at the head and foot, waiting nervously for an explosion. Christina and Tommy sat on one side of the table, Tommy glowering at Philip. And Philip and Estelle sat on the other side, Estelle openly showing contempt for Christina. They were sitting on a powder keg.

Philip had changed since Christina's disappearance a week ago. He no longer bantered with her, but treated her coldly and politely. He never mentioned the past, which unnerved Christina, for she was continually waiting for some biting remark that didn't come.

She tried to avoid being alone with Philip, but was always left alone with him in the nursery. Christina insisted that Johnsy stay with her, but as soon as Philip walked into the nursery, Johnsy would make some lame excuse and depart quickly.

However, Philip seemed interested only in his son, and he kept his distance from Christina. He watched her bathe Philip Junior, or played with him on the soft, carpeted floor. But whenever it was time for his feeding, Philip left tactfully. And that completely baffled her.

Tommy had become the worst of her problems. He had grown very demanding since Philip's arrival. He constantly pressed Christina to set a date for their marriage, although so far she had avoided doing so.

But today, Christina had finally found something to rejoice about.

Kareen came into the dining room while Christina was eating a late lunch.

"Estelle has finally decided to go home — she's upstairs packing right now," she said.

Christina said nothing, although she felt like jumping for joy.

"Even though she is my sister and I love her dearly," Kareen continued, "I don't mind admitting I'm glad she's leaving. But it puzzles me why — and she won't tell me. Only yesterday I tried to talk her into leaving, and she was flatly against it. Then she went riding with Philip this morning, and when she returned just a little while ago, she stated angrily that she wouldn't stay here another minute. It's better this way, for I know she was heading for a big letdown, but I still don't understand it."

Neither did Christina. But it didn't matter why Estelle was leaving — so long as she left. Now Christina wouldn't have to suffer seeing another woman clinging to Philip's side. But Philip might leave now that Estelle was going. Suddenly Christina didn't feel quite so happy.

With his hands clasped behind his head, Philip reclined on the big brass bed listening intently to the sounds coming from the room next to his. He glanced at the antique clock on the mantel above the fireplace. Five minutes to ten — he wouldn't have much longer to wait.

Philip grimaced when he recalled what had happened that morning. He had tired of the game he was playing with Christina and Estelle, and had been trying to think of a way to end it. Estelle's boldness had provided the solution to his problem.

Estelle had cornered him after breakfast and asked him to take her riding. Philip saw no reason not to, since Christina was upstairs feeding Philip Junior. But after they had ridden some distance from the house, Estelle had dismounted under a large oak tree. She had sat down under the tree and taken off her riding hat, shaking her thick black hair loose, and beckoned to Philip seductively.

"Estelle, get back on your horse. I have no time for playing games," he had said harshly.

"Games!" Estelle had cried. She had scrambled to her feet and faced him, her arms akimbo. "Do you intend to marry me or not?"

Philip had been surprised, but had seen the answer to his problem. He could end it all by saying no.

"I have no intention of marrying you, Estelle, and I'm sorry if I've led you to believe I would."

"But you said you desired me!" she had retorted angrily.

"I had a selfish reason for telling you that. Besides, it was what you wanted to hear. There's only one woman I will ever desire or want to marry."

"And she's engaged to someone else," Estelle had laughed bitterly. She had thrown herself onto her horse and galloped off toward Wakefield Manor.

At dinner that evening, Philip had been amused to find that Tommy Huntington was extremely agitated. The younger man knew that with Estelle gone Philip would have more time to devote to Christina. Philip wondered how he would react if the situation were reversed — if his fiancée's former lover were living in the same house she was, and he were helpless to do anything.

Well, he felt no pity for Huntington. Indeed, he hated the younger man. He couldn't bear to think that Huntington would soon be Christina's husband. He would have the right to hold her and make love to her. Philip shook the thoughts away. He would be damned if he'd let that happen! And if Tommy Huntington had already lain with Christina, he would kill him!

Knowing that Christina slept in the next room with only a thin wall between them was driving him beyond endurance. Hearing her move about her room, listening to her sweet voice — he wouldn't be able to stand it much longer. He must win her back before her wedding day, or kidnap her again. He would rather live with her hate than without her.

245

Philip heard the maid finally leave Christina's room. He opened his door and saw that the dimly lit corridor was empty. John and Kareen's bedroom was at the opposite end of the house, and he hoped they were already asleep.

He walked the few feet to Christina's door and opened it quietly. She was taking her bath before the brightly lit fireplace, unaware of his presence. He stood for a long moment watching her as she raised a sponge and let the water dribble down her arm. Her back was to him, and all he could see was the soft white contour of her shoulders above the rim of the large tub. Her hair was pinned up into countless ringlets shining like liquid gold, and the firelight danced around her.

Christina's towel and robe were lying on the footstool next to the tub. Philip edged his way over to them and picked them up. Christina gasped.

"What are you doing here?" she cried, sinking lower into the tub. She glanced angrily at his amused expression, then down at the robe and towel he was holding. "Put those down, Philip. Now! And get out of here!"

"What, these?" he asked teasingly, the firelight dancing in his gold-flecked eyes. "Anything you say, madam." He tossed the articles onto her bed, far from her reach.

He walked around the tub and over to the chair in the corner of the room. She stared stupidly at her robe and towel on the bed. Then she swung her head around fiercely and glared at him. He was sitting in the chair watching her, his legs spread out before him and his hands clasped across his middle.

"Just what the hell do you think you're doing, Philip Caxton? Damn it! Are you trying to get yourself thrown out of this house? Do you need an excuse to leave now that Estelle is gone? Is that it?"

Philip chuckled without taking his deep-green eyes from her angry face.

"I don't wish to leave this house, Christina, and I wouldn't need an excuse if I did. If you will kindly refrain from raising your voice,

246

no one will be the wiser and I won't be discovered."

Confusion overcame her. Philip was partially hidden in the shadows, but Christina could still see the smoldering look in his eyes. He wanted her, of that she was sure, and a tingling sensation coursed through her body. She wanted him with all her heart, but she knew their love would be only for tonight. Tomorrow he would be as cold and indifferent as before, and she wouldn't be able to stand it.

"Get out of my room, Philip. You have no right to be here."

"You look exceptionally beautiful tonight, Tina," Philip murmured. "You could tempt a man to do anything you wanted — except leave you."

He laughed heartily.

She turned around in the tub. She couldn't bear to look at him, his jet-black hair tousled and his crisp white shirt open to the waist baring his bronzed chest with its curls of black hair. He was the temptation! She was hard pressed not to go to him, soaking wet, and make love to him! It was what she wanted, it was what he wanted, but she couldn't. She couldn't bear to love him and then face his hatred again in the morning.

Twenty minutes passed. Philip said nothing, nor did Christina. Her back was to him, but she knew he still watched her.

"Philip, please — this water is getting cold," she pleaded.

"I suggest that you get out of it," he replied softly.

"Then leave so I can!" Christina snapped.

"You amaze me, Tina. I've watched you bathe a hundred times and emerge naked. You weren't shy then, so why do you pretend to be now? We even made love once lying on the hard earth beside the bathing pond. It was you who came to me that day and —"

"Stop it!" she cried, slamming her fist down into the water. "There's no point in talking about the past, Philip. It's over and done with. Now leave this minute before I catch cold."

"Was your body marred in giving birth to my son?" Philip asked. "Is that why you refuse to stand before me?"

"Of course not! My figure has regained its former shape!"

"Then stand up and prove it, Tina," he murmured huskily.

Christina almost took the bait and started to stand up, but then she sank back down in the water even lower than before, cursing Philip under her breath. The soap bubbles had all dissolved, leaving her body open to view. Her only hope was that he wouldn't come near her, but leave! If he so much as touched her, she knew she would give in.

Just then they heard footsteps in the corridor, and Christina froze when a light tap sounded at her door.

"Christina, I must talk to you. Christina, are you awake?"

She turned her head to look at Philip, but he was still sprawled at ease in his chair, clearly amused at her new predicament.

"Tommy, for heaven's sake, go home! I am taking my bath now — I'll talk to you in the morning!" she said loudly.

"I'll wait until you are through," Tommy called out.

"No, you won't, Tommy Huntington!" She was more afraid than angry now. "It's late at night. I will see you in the morning — not now!"

"Christina, this can't wait, damn it! I will not stand that man in the house with you any longer. He has to go!"

Philip's deep laughter rang through the room. The door swung open forcefully, slamming against the wall, and Tommy stalked into the room. Philip was still in the shadows, and Tommy had to glance about the room twice before he saw him.

Tommy, outraged, clenched his lists tightly at his sides as he looked at her, then at Philip, then back at her again. Before she could think of anything to say, Tommy let out a sickening cry and started toward Philip.

She stood up, splashing water onto the thick blue carpet.

"Stop it, Tommy!" she screamed.

Tommy halted in his tracks. His mouth fell open at the sight of her, and he completely forgot that Philip was in the room. But Philip, who had half risen to brace himself against Tommy's attack, scowled darkly at Christina.

"Sit down, woman," Philip growled angrily.

She did so immediately, splashing water over the sides of the tub again, and a hot blush spread across her face.

"What the hell are you doing in here, Caxton?" Tommy demanded.

"There is nothing for you to be upset about, Tommy," Christina said soothingly. "Philip came in here just before you did — to talk to me about his son. He didn't know that I was taking my bath when he walked in."

"Then why was he sitting over there watching you bathe? How could you let him in here, Christina, or has this been going on all along?"

"Don't be absurd! I tell you it was perfectly innocent. Heavens! The man has seen me bathe a hundred times in the past. If you will remember, Philip came here for his son — not me. And he sat down only long enough to ask me a few questions — that's all. I was in this tub the whole time, Tommy. He didn't see me until you forced me to stand up with your foolishness."

"But he has no right to be in here at all, damn it!"

"Lower your voice, Tommy, before you wake John!" Christina snapped.

"Wake John — that's exactly what I intend to do. You won't be here much longer, Caxton." Tommy laughed bitterly, and rushed out of the room.

"Now look what you've done!" Christina cried. "Why couldn't you just leave me alone? Now John will be forced to ask you to leave this house. You did this on purpose, didn't you?"

"It was not my intention to be discovered, Christina," Philip said calmly. "This is your house as much as John's. I won't have to leave unless you also wish it. If you want our son to grow up without knowing his real father, that's up to you."

It was the first time Philip had called him "our son," and Christina was surprised and yet pleased to hear him say it.

"Quickly — hand me my robe before John gets here!" she said frantically. "Well, turn around, damn it!"

"Oh, for God's sake, Christina!" But he turned around and moved far away from her to stand by the window.

Stepping out of the tub, Christina managed to slip the robe over her wet body and tie it about her waist just as John rushed into the room with Tommy right behind him.

"What the hell is going on, Christina?" John demanded.

Philip turned to face them, and Tommy glowered at him.

"I told you it was God's truth. This is an outrage, John, and I demand that Caxton leave this house immediately!" Tommy stormed.

"That's enough, Tommy. I'm going to have to ask you to go home now. I will handle this matter," John returned.

"I will not!"

"Tommy — now! I wish to talk to Christina alone. I'll do whatever is necessary."

Tommy turned and stormed from the room.

"I will also take my leave if you wish to talk privately," said Philip.

"Yes," John replied curtly. "I'll tell you of my decision in the morning."

"In the morning, then. Good night, Tina." Philip closed the door behind him.

Christina knew that he was asking her to fight for him so he could stay with his son. She relaxed a bit and sat down on the edge of her bed.

"Crissy, what could have possessed you to let Philip come into your room this late at night?" asked John. "Have you and Philip finally settled matters between you? Is that it?"

"I don't know what you're talking about, John. There's nothing to settle between us. What we had once is finished — it won't come back. And I didn't invite Philip into my room, he just walked in and wouldn't leave."

"Did he —"

250

Christina smiled weakly. "Philip sat in the corner the whole time he was here, but I knew he wanted me. And I know I can't shock you more than I have in the past by telling you that I wanted him, too, more than anything," she whispered, afraid that Philip might hear her from his room. "But I resisted him, for I knew he'd only want me tonight. Tomorrow he would hate me again."

"But Crissy, Philip has never stopped wanting you."

"He has, too!" she snapped.

There was no point in arguing with her when she turned stubborn. John shook his head. "Well, I'm going to have to ask him to leave, Crissy. Had it been any man but Philip, he would be dead now."

"I don't want him to leave, John."

"You can't be serious! You just got through telling me that you won't be able to resist him if he — Crissy, this *will* happen again if he stays."

"It won't happen again, John, I know it won't. And besides, I'll lock my door from now on. I want Philip to stay until he's ready to leave. I will not deny him the right to know his son."

"And what about Tommy? He won't understand why Philip is still here." John paused, shaking his head. "This is all my fault, Crissy. I should never have talked you into marrying Tommy."

"That doesn't matter now. I'll talk to Tommy in the morning. I'll make him understand this was just an innocent meeting."

"I doubt he'll believe that. What do you intend to do when you marry Tommy? He'll never allow Philip in his house."

"I don't know. I'll handle that when the time comes. And when you speak with Philip, tell him I said we spoke about Philip Junior. And although it was improper, you'll forget about the matter as long as it doesn't happen again."

"Is that what you told Tommy tonight? No wonder he was so angry. Did yon think Tommy was naive enough to believe that? He's not a fool."

"Well, I'll just have to insist it's true," said Christina. "I don't

251

want any more confrontations between Philip and Tommy."

"Just you talk to Tommy before I run into him. I wouldn't know how to explain why Philip is still staying here. I don't really understand it myself." John came over and kissed her lightly on the cheek. "I imagine Tommy will be over early, so you had best get some rest. Good night, little sister. I hope you know what you're doing."

She smiled weakly but didn't answer him. After John left, Christina glanced about the empty room and felt a pang of regret. She wondered what would have happened if Tommy hadn't burst in. She slipped into her nightdress, crawled into bed, and a burning desire came over her as it had so many nights before. She wanted Philip — his hands exploring her body, his lips taking her will away, the feel of his muscles rippling across his back when she caressed him. She turned over and cried softly into her pillow for what could never be.

Chapter 33

Christina awoke to her son's loud crying. She grabbed her robe and ran into the nursery. She glanced about the room to make sure Philip wasn't there, then walked to the bassinet. Philip Junior stopped crying when he saw her, but still thrashed his arms and legs. She had been blessed with a son who slept through the night. But when morning came, he would not be kept waiting any longer, and he made sure she knew it.

She changed him, then sat down in the rocker to satisfy his hunger. While he suckled, Christina thought again of what Philip had called him. *Our son.* It had such a natural ring to it. She had always thought of Philip Junior as her son, or as Philip's son.

She put Philip Junior back in his bassinet and moved it into the sunlight streaming through the window. She gave him a few toys to keep him happy until it was time for his bath, and went into her own room to prepare for her confrontation with Tommy.

The small clock on the mantel showed ten after seven, but Christina had no doubt that Tommy would be downstairs any second. She chose a low-cut, deep-violet satin dress with long, tight-fitting sleeves. Hardly a dress for morning wear, but she hoped it would distract Tommy from his anger.

Christina decided on her ruby-studded pins to hold her curls in place, and her long, dangling earrings of small rubies. She didn't wear the matching necklace for fear it would hide what she wanted Tommy to see. With a last turn before her full-length mirror, Christina was satisfied with her appearance.

Christina went downstairs and was glad to find that Tommy hadn't arrived yet. At least she would be able to have breakfast in peace.

253

She went directly to the counter filled with covered serving dishes in the dining room, and filled a plate. From the half-emptied dishes she judged that John and Philip had already eaten, and had probably left the house.

After Christina finished her meal, she got up to pour another cup of tea. When she turned around again, Tommy was standing in the doorway. He was handsomely dressed in a suede riding outfit and held a crop in his right hand. As she'd hoped, his brown eyes were drawn straight to the low neckline barely concealing her full, rounded breasts.

She smiled warmly. "I didn't hear you come in, Tommy, but never mind. Come and join me for a cup of tea."

"What?" He finally looked up to meet her eyes.

"I said, come and have a cup of tea."

"Yes." He came over to her, gazing hungrily at her breasts. "Christina, how can you wear such a dress in the morning? It's —"

"Don't you like my dress, Tommy?" She smiled beguilingly. "I wore it just for you."

Tommy melted. He pulled her into an embrace. His lips searched hers, yet she felt no deep trembling of excitement. She didn't feel the fires that surfaced every time Philip kissed her.

"It is a beautiful dress, Crissy." He held her at arms' length and studied her from head to foot. "I don't mind your wearing it now Caxton is gone."

"Tommy."

"God, Crissy, you don't know what I've been going through since that man came. It's been hell! I couldn't sleep, I couldn't eat, I couldn't do a damn thing. I could only think that he'd been your lover."

"Tommy."

"But everything is going to be just fine now. Tell me, did John kick him out last night, or did he leave this morning?"

Christina sighed wearily. "Philip isn't leaving, Tommy."

He looked as if he'd been slapped unexpectedly across the face, but she went on quickly.

"John believed me when I told him that nothing happened last night. It was all perfectly innocent, Tommy — nothing did happen. Philip Caxton doesn't want me anymore — You've seen how he acts with Estelle. There's no reason for you to be upset."

"No reason!" Tommy stormed. "He was in your room, and you were — you were *undressed!* Do you call that nothing? I won't have him here any longer, Christina. I won't have it!"

"Now, Tommy, stop it! Philip has a right to stay here. His son is here."

"I'll talk to John about this! That man is not going to remain in this house with you!"

"This is my house as much as it is John's!" Christina yelled. "And I say Philip can stay here."

"Damn it!" He slammed the riding crop down on the table.

"Tommy," she said, "Philip is here only because of his son — not because of me. Can't you understand that?"

"Then why in God's name don't you give him his son?"

"You can't be serious," Christina laughed.

"If all Caxton wants is his son, give him to the man. I never wanted the brat, anyway," Tommy said bitterly. "We'll have sons of our own, Christina, just as soon as we're married. *My* sons!"

Slowly Christina said, "I'm thankful you told me how you feel about Philip Junior before we were married. Now there will be no marriage. If you don't want my son, I can't possibly marry you, Tommy."

"Christina!"

"You don't understand how I feel about my child, do you? He is my baby, Tommy, and I love him with all my heart. Nothing on this earth could make me give him up."

"You never intended to marry me, did you?" Tommy screamed, his face contorted. A cold chill went down Christina's spine. "You've

255

loved that man all along! Well, you won't have him, Christina. Mark my words! Philip Caxton will regret the day he ever came into this house. And so will you!"

"Tommy!" she screamed. But he ran from the house, slamming the entrance door behind him.

Christina started to shake uncontrollably. What was she going to do? What was Tommy going to do? She had to find Philip and warn him, but she had no idea where he was.

Christina ran up the stairs two at a time. She went straight into Philip's room and closed the door. She would wait for him here. Oh, Philip — please hurry! Tommy was like a madman!

Twenty minutes passed while Christina paced the floor in Philip's room. They seemed like hours. She kept going over what Tommy had said, wondering what he had meant. When she heard footsteps in the corridor, she held her breath, praying it was Philip. When the door opened, she almost fainted with relief.

"What the devil are you doing here? Are you trying to pay me back for last night?" Philip asked coldly. He came into the room taking off his heavy riding jacket.

Christina was stung by his harshness, but she remembered why she was here.

"Philip, I came here to warn you. Tommy made a threat against you, and he was acting so oddly that I —"

"Don't be absurd, Christina!" Philip cut her off. "You asked me to leave your room last night, and now I am asking you to leave mine. Your brother has made it quite clear that he doesn't want us alone again."

"Did he say that?"

"Not exactly, but it amounted to the same thing," he returned.

"But Philip, Tommy said he would make you regret ever coming here. He —"

"Do you actually imagine that I give a damn what Huntington says? I assure you, madam, I can take care of myself." He turned

256

away from her, leaving her in a state of confusion. "If your young lover attempts anything, I will try not to hurt him. Now kindly get out of my room!"

Christina grabbed Philip's arm and turned him back to face her, her stormy blue eyes clashing with his angry green ones.

"I think he means to kill you! Can't you get that through your thick head, damn it?"

"Quite right, Christina, that is exactly what I intend to do," said Tommy.

Christina felt suddenly sick, and she felt the muscles tense in Philip's arm. She turned slowly to look at Tommy standing in the doorway. He held two pistols pointed directly at Philip.

"I knew I'd find you two together. Well, your warning was a little too late, Christina. Nothing is going to save your lover now." He laughed shortly.

She forced herself to speak despite the feeling that she would faint at any moment. "Tommy, you can't do this! It's — it's murder! You are throwing your own life away."

"Do you think I give a damn about my life anymore? I don't care what happens to me as long as he dies. And he is going to die, Christina — right before your eyes. Do you think I don't know you have been sleeping with him all the time we were engaged? Do you think I'm that much of a fool?"

"It's not true, Tommy!" Christina cried. She edged around in front of Philip, but he pushed her aside forcefully and she fell back against the bed.

"Just stay out of the way, Christina. This is between Huntington and myself," Philip said harshly.

"Very touching," Tommy laughed. "But I don't intend to shoot Christina."

"Tommy, listen to me!" Christina pleaded. She had to stop him! She pushed herself off the bed and faced Tommy, her breasts heaving. "I'll go away with you, Tommy. I'll marry you today. Only please,

please, put the pistols down."

"You're lying. You've always lied to me!"

"I'm not lying, Tommy. This is insane! You have no reason to be jealous of Philip. I don't love him, Tommy. He doesn't want me and I don't want him. How could I want him after what he did to me? Please — you've got to listen to reason! I'll leave with you today, and we'll never mention this again. Tommy, please!"

"That's enough, Christina! You're playing me for a fool again, and I won't have it. You have always wanted him, so don't try to tell me otherwise!" Tommy raged, the muscles twitching in his cheek. "All the time we were engaged you wouldn't even let me touch you, but you've let *him* put his hands on you, haven't you? Well, no more! You won't have him, Christina — nor his son." Tommy laughed again when he heard her gasp, but he kept a steady eye on the motionless Philip. "Did you think I would leave that brat alive to remind you of him? No, Christina — they will both die! I have two bullets, one for each of them."

"You will have to use them both on me, Huntington. And even then I will tear you apart." Philip's voice was calm but deadly.

"I doubt that, Caxton — I am an excellent shot. My first bullet will find your heart, and that will leave me one to kill that bastard son of yours. She will have nothing left of you." He paused and stared blankly at the floor. "You were all I ever wanted, Crissy, but they took you away from me." He looked up at Philip, and the madness returned to his eyes.

Tommy raised one of the pistols and aimed straight at Philip's heart. A bloodcurdling scream escaped Christina, and she plunged forward just as Tommy fired. Philip had stepped aside to avoid the bullet, but he was able to catch Christina in his arms as she collapsed, blood pouring from a head wound.

Christina felt that she was falling, falling in slow motion and spinning around and around. Everything flashed red before her eyes — and then blackness engulfed her.

"Oh my God. What have I done? I've killed her!" Tommy cried. The color drained from his face, and with a sickening cry he turned and ran down the stairs. But before he'd reached the front door, John came tearing through the dining room, with Kareen and Johnsy right behind him.

"Tommy!" John yelled, halting him at the door. Tommy turned slowly around, and John paled at the sight of the two pistols in his hands. "My God! What have you done?"

Tommy dropped the weapons instantly, as if they burned his hands. But one pistol was still loaded, and it exploded with a horrible sound when it hit the floor. An anguished scream echoed from upstairs. Tommy fell to his knees, tears streaming down his cheeks.

"She's come to haunt me already!" Tommy cried. "Oh, God, Crissy, I didn't mean to hurt you. I loved you."

"Stay where you are, Tommy," John commanded in a choked voice before he ran up the stairs, the women right behind him.

"Where will I go?" Tommy mumbled to himself in the empty hall. "Why doesn't Caxton come after me? Justice must be done! Oh, God, how could I have been so blind as not to see how much she loved him — so much that she would run into my line of fire to protect him? I can't live with what I've done — I want to die!"

259

Chapter 34

"Damn it, Doctor, why won't she wake up? It's been three days now, and you said it was only a superficial wound — it didn't even need bandaging!" John paced the floor in Christina's bedroom as old Dr. Willis closed his bag.

"From what Mr. Caxton tells me, I'm afraid Christina's condition is mental, not physical. When she awoke from the first faint and heard the second shot, she instantly assumed her son had been killed. There is absolutely no reason why she shouldn't wake up — she just doesn't want to."

"But she has every reason to live!"

"We know that, but she doesn't. All I can suggest is that you sit here and talk to her — try to bring her out of it. And don't fret so much, John. In all my years, I have never lost a patient who died of plain stubbornness. Except your mother. But she was awake, she willed herself to die. Talk to Christina. Tell her that boy of hers needs her — tell her anything that might make her come out of it. Once she's awake, she will be fine."

After Doctor Willis left, Philip came into the room and stood beside the bed.

"What did Willis have to say?" Philip asked soberly.

"That there is no reason why she shouldn't wake up, she just doesn't want to!" John replied heatedly. "Damn it! She's willing herself to die from grief, just as our mother did."

Late that night, after John had spent the whole day talking to her, Christina finally opened her eyes.

She looked at John, who was sitting in a chair beside her bed, and she wondered why he was there. Then she remembered what had happened.

"Oh, God, no — no!" she cried hysterically.

"It's all right, Crissy — Philip Junior is all right! He is alive, I swear it!" John said quickly.

"Don't — don't lie to me, John," Christina implored him through her sobs.

"I swear, Crissy, no harm came to your son. He is in the next room sleeping."

She couldn't stop crying. "I heard the shot. I heard it!"

"The shot you heard came from downstairs, Crissy, when Tommy dropped his pistols on the floor. No one was hurt by it — Philip Junior is all right."

Christina threw back the covers and started to get out of bed. But a blinding pain shot through her head, and she fell back onto the pillow. "I have to see for myself."

"Very well, Crissy, if you won't believe me. But sit up slowly this time. You've been in bed for three days."

John finally had to carry her into the nursery. He set her down gently beside the bassinet and held her so she wouldn't fall. Christina looked down at her sleeping son. She put her hand close to his small face and felt his warm breath, then she caressed his cheek. He stirred and turned his head.

"He is alive," she whispered happily. John picked her up and carried her back to her bed. She started crying again from sheer joy.

"I'll have some food brought up, Crissy. And then you should rest some more."

"But you said I'd been sleeping for three days. The last thing I need is more rest. I want to know what happened, John," Christina said soberly.

"One of the Huntington servants found me in the stables. Lord Huntington had sent the lad over to warn me that Tommy was coming here armed. I heard the first shot before I reached the house. I found

261

Tommy in the hall. The second shot was fired accidentally. You screamed, and I thought Tommy had already killed Philip. But when I got upstairs, I found that you'd been shot. Crissy — I thought you were dead. But Philip assured me you had only fainted on hearing the second shot. If you hadn't blacked out, you would have known that Philip Junior was all right. The first shot didn't bother him, but the second shot echoing through the house scared him and he was screaming his lungs out. He wouldn't even stop crying for Johnsy."

"Philip is all right, too?"

"Yes. You both would have been all right if you hadn't run into the line of fire. I know why you did it, Crissy, but I didn't think it my place to tell Philip. Thank God the bullet only grazed you."

"Where is Philip now?"

"I believe he's downstairs getting drunk, as he has done these last three nights."

"And Tommy — is he all right?"

"Tommy, I think, was more shaken than the rest of us. He really thought he'd killed you. He cried like a baby when I told him you were only unconscious. But I'm afraid he was arrested. After all, he did shoot you."

"But I'm all right — it was only an accident. I don't want him in jail, John. Tommy went crazy because I broke off our engagement. I want you to have him released — tonight."

"I'll see what I can do, but first I'll get you some food."

"Miss Crissy, love, wake up. There's someone 'ere who'd like to see 'is mama."

Christina turned over in bed to see Johnsy rocking Philip Junior in her arms. She smiled, for even though he was being cuddled, he was still fidgeting. She unbuttoned her nightgown, then put him to her breast while she watched Johnsy, who was obviously agitated, straightening the room.

"Whatever is the matter with you?" Christina asked.

"I don't mind sayin' you scared the wits out of me — you lyin' up 'ere in bed three days. And your brother, of all things, tells me to come and ask you if you're up to seein' Master Tommy. If 'e'd asked me, I'd'a said no, but nobody asks me anything anymore."

"Oh, stop your grumbling, Johnsy. I'll see Tommy as soon as I'm finished feeding Philip Junior."

"Perhaps you're not up to it yet?" Johnsy ventured hopefully.

"There's nothing wrong with me. Now get along with you and tell Tommy I'll see him shortly."

A while later, Tommy knocked on the door as Christina came back from putting Philip Junior in his bassinet. She opened the door and noticed that Tommy was wearing traveling clothes. She invited him into the room.

"Crissy, I —"

"It's all right, Tommy," she interrupted. "You don't have to say anything about it."

"But I want to," he said, taking her hands in his. "I'm so sorry, Crissy. You've got to believe that. I wouldn't have hurt you for the world."

"I know that, Tommy."

"I realize now how much you love Philip Caxton. I should have seen it sooner, but I was too obsessed with my own feelings. When Caxton came here, I saw him only as a rival. But now I know you were never mine to have — you were always his. Tell him I'm sorry for what happened. He's still sleeping or I'd attempt to tell him myself."

"You can tell him later."

"No, I won't be here. I'm leaving this morning."

"But where are you going?"

"I have decided to enter the military, as John did," Tommy said sheepishly.

"But what about your lands? Your father will need you," Christina said. But she could tell that Tommy had already made up his mind.

"My father is still a young man. There's nothing for me here. I'm like you were, Crissy, living all my life here. It's time I saw a bit of the world." He kissed her lightly on the cheek, his brown eyes warm with friendship. "I'll never find anyone like you, but perhaps there will be someone."

"I hope so, Tommy, I really do. And I wish you all the luck in the world."

Christina stood in the middle of the room for a long time after Tommy left. She felt very sad and lonely, as if a little piece of her heart had just been chipped away. The Tommy she'd just spoken to was the old Tommy, the Tommy she loved as a brother, and she would miss him sorely.

Chapter 35

Philip woke with a splitting headache. The sunlight streaming into the room didn't help matters any. He pressed his hands against his temples to ease the pain, but it didn't help. He glanced down at his fully clothed body, minus one shoe, and groaned slightly.

John had said last night that Christina had finally awakened. Or had he dreamed it all? Well, there was one way to find out. He stood up. A sharp pain shot through his head again, and he vowed he wouldn't touch another glass of whiskey for a long time. He splashed water liberally on his face, then stood there holding onto the dresser until the pain eased somewhat.

After a while, Philip was able to kindle the fire that he hadn't bothered to light the night before. He shaved the stubble off his face and changed his clothes. He began to feel almost human again, and decided this was as good a time as any to see Christina.

He walked the few feet to her room and went in unannounced, to find her propped up in bed and wearing her black-velvet robe, of all things, over a white-lace nightdress. Her long hair was spread out on the pillow behind her framing her in a golden halo of beauty.

"Don't you ever knock?" she asked curtly.

"You would only tell me to come in, anyway, so why should I waste both your time and mine?" Philip closed the door and sat down in the chair that John had pulled up beside the bed. "So — you are finally awake. What the devil do you mean by sleeping three days, madam, and leaving my son to the mercy of a wet nurse?"

By the tone of his voice, Christina didn't know whether Philip was chaffing her or if he was serious. She chose the latter and became annoyed.

"I'm sorry if my delay in waking has upset you, but I have seen *my* son this morning. And he seems to have fared rather well. And since you appear to have a dislike for wet nurses, tell me, Philip, how would you have managed if I'd agreed to give you my son?"

"Damn it, woman!" he bellowed, then groaned at the sound of his own voice.

Christina realized what was the matter with him, and she started to giggle.

"What the hell is so damn funny?" He scowled at her through reddened eyes.

"You are," Christina said, repressing her laughter. "What could have possessed you to drown yourself in liquor three nights straight? I know you were upset about nearly losing Philip Junior, but is that any reason to make yourself sick? He wasn't harmed."

"You are up here in bed in an unconscious state, and I don't know if you are going to live or die — and you ask me what possessed me to drink!"

"What would it matter to you if I lived or died? I am sure that if I hadn't come through, John would have given you Philip Junior. You should have been quite happy at the prospect of getting what you wanted. I'm sorry I disappointed you."

Philip leaned back in the chair and stared at Christina. "I ought to tan your hide for that remark! Ah, hell — never mind. I shouldn't have come to see you this soon. I should have realized you'd be upset knowing your lover is in jail."

"He was not my lover, damn it!" Christina snapped angrily. "For the record, Mr. Caxton, you are the only lover I've ever had."

"You don't have to shout, damn it!" he shouted himself.

"Don't I? It would seem that is the only way I can reach you. And furthermore, Tommy is no longer in jail. He was —"

"Did I hear you correctly?" Philip cut her off, his green eyes turning a shade darker.

"You did," she replied, ignoring his rising anger. "Tommy was released last night — at my insistence."

"For the love of God!" Philip exploded, forgetting his headache. "After what he did to you, you turn him loose as if nothing happened?"

"He didn't mean to shoot me."

"I know! It was *me* he was aiming at. Did it occur to you, madam, that I might want to press charges?"

"I wish you wouldn't, Philip," Christina said quietly. "Tommy regrets what he did. He asked me to apologize to you. He —"

"You've talked to him already?" Philip interrupted.

"Yes. He came to see me this morning."

"And now you're pleading with me for his freedom." Philip leaned back in the chair as if a heavy weight pressed him against it. "You must really love him."

"I grew up with Tommy. We were close friends until he decided he loved me. But I didn't love him in the same way."

"But you were going to be wed?"

"He asked me to marry him the first day I came home and every day after that until I couldn't stand it anymore. I told him no, but he wouldn't give up. I went to Victory to get away from Tommy, but he started all over again when I returned home. I asked John to make Tommy leave me alone, but he took Tommy's side. I never expected to see you again, so I gave up. I agreed to marry Tommy because everyone wanted me to. We were friends and I loved him as a friend — I still do. When he came to say good-bye this morning, he was like his old self again."

"Good-bye?"

"Yes, he's gone to join the army. I'll miss him. When I broke off our engagement he went crazy from jealousy, but he's all right now. Do you still wish to press charges against him?"

"No. If he's gone, I wish him luck. So you only thought of him as a close friend?"

"Yes."

267

Philip laughed boisterously. He leaned forward in the chair.

"I'm going to tell you what I should have told you a long time ago. I love you, Tina, I always have. My life isn't worth living without you. I want to take you home with me — to Victory. I will understand if you say no, but I have to ask you. And if you agree, I won't press you for anything. I know you hate me for the misery I've caused you, but I can live with your hatred as long as I can live with you."

Christina started crying. She couldn't believe it.

"You don't have to give me an answer now, Tina."

She flew off the bed and knelt before him. Her arms circled his waist as if she would never let go. Philip lifted her face to his and stroked her hair gently, his eyes soft and searching.

"Does this mean you will come with me?"

"Philip, how could you think otherwise? How can you believe I hated you? I love you with all my being. I guess I have from the beginning, but I didn't realize it until Ali Hejaz stole me away from you. I would have stayed with you in Egypt forever if you hadn't sent me away. And when you did, I went through all the anguish of hell until I learned I was carrying your child. Philip Junior gave me a reason to go on living."

"Please, Tina, don't lie to me. I didn't send you away. You left me!"

"But I'm not lying, Philip. I still have the note Rashid gave me after you left for Yamaid Alhabbal's camp. I didn't believe it at first. But when Rashid told me that you wanted to marry Nura, I gave up and went with him."

"I left you no note, Tina. I went to Yamaid's camp to invite his tribe to our wedding. When I came back —"

"Our wedding!"

"Yes — I had begun to think you really cared for me. I wanted to marry you to make sure that I would never lose you. I planned our wedding as a surprise. But when I came back, I found you gone, and — Let me see that note."

268

Christina reluctantly let go of him and went to her dresser. From the top drawer she took out the crumpled piece of paper and handed it to him.

"Rashid!" Philip bellowed after reading the note. "I should have known! If it's the last thing I do, I'll go back to Egypt and kill that bastard."

"I don't understand."

"Rashid wrote this note! He left me one signed with your name asking me not to follow you. I thought you had tricked me that last month. I thought you'd only pretended to be happy so I'd trust you alone and you could make your escape."

"How could you believe that, Philip? I was never more happy in my life than I was that last month with you. I couldn't have pretended that kind of happiness." She smiled lovingly and caressed the back of his neck. "But why would Rashid do such a thing?"

"He must have hoped I would follow you back to England and not return. Rashid has always hated me because I was our father's favorite and because I became leader of the tribe. Being sheik meant more to him than anything. I understood this, and I let him have his way in many things. But he went too far to gain what he wanted. He planned your abduction and my death at Sheik Ali's hands. When I learned the truth from Amine's brother, I searched for Rashid everywhere, but he was not to be found. I finally gave up. I just couldn't stand living in that land anymore with your memory haunting me everywhere I looked. But Rashid cannot be forgiven. He made us waste a whole year of loving each other."

"It would have been pretty difficult during part of that year," Christina laughed. "But it doesn't matter — as long as we have each other now, and forever." She paused. "But what about Estelle? You told her you desired her."

Philip laughed. "Only because I knew you were listening, my sweet. Why do you think I left the door open?"

Philip stood up and pulled Christina into his arms. Their lips met in a passionate kiss, and Christina thought she would faint with ecstasy. Philip held her face between his hands and kissed her eyes, her cheeks, her lips.

"Will you marry me, Tina? Will you live with me and share my life and love me always?"

"Oh, yes, my love, forever. And I will never hide my feelings from you again."

"Nor I from you."

"But something still puzzles me, Philip. Why have you treated me so coldly from the first moment you came here?"

"Because, my sweet, I came here to marry you, but walked in to hear you accepting a proposal from another man. I was so filled with rage that I couldn't see straight."

"You were jealous?" she asked merrily, running her finger along his cheek.

"Jealous! I've never been jealous!" He walked away and locked her bedroom doors. He pulled her roughly against him again. "If I ever catch you looking sideways at another man, I will beat the daylights out of you!"

"Will you really?" She looked surprised.

"No," he murmured. His eyes were dancing with devilry as he slid the black robe off her shoulders. "You won't be out of bed long enough to give me reason."

Chapter 36

They had been married six months, six blissful months. Christina still found it hard to believe Philip was hers. She wanted to be near him every minute, to touch him, to hear his sweet words of love filling her heart with happiness.

"Have you forgotten the wager I made you last night?" Philip asked when she came into their bedroom carrying a breakfast tray. "I believe the stakes were a morning spent leisurely in bed — and I won."

"I haven't forgotten, my love, but you were still sleeping when I awoke. I thought you might like something to tide you over until lunch."

"More likely you wanted something to tide *you* over. The way you've been eating lately, I'm beginning to think you care more for food than for me," he teased. He took the tray from her hands and set it on the black-marble table in front of the couch.

"That's not true, and you know it," Christina said, pretending to pout.

"Well, you shouldn't have carried the tray up yourself. In the future, let the servants earn their wages."

"You know very well, my lord, that the servants are not allowed to come near your bedroom when the door is closed. You gave the order yourself, the second day of our honeymoon. A maid came in to change the linens and found us still abed. Your rage scared the wits out of the poor girl."

"And with good reason," Philip chuckled. "But what kept you so long? I've been up for almost an hour and was about to come after you. When I win a wager, I expect to collect in full, not just half measure."

"Every time we've played poker these last months, I've lost. I'm beginning to think you let me win intentionally when you taught me the game back in Egypt."

"You wouldn't wager with me then, if you'll remember. But now that the stakes are well worth winning, I prefer to win. Then again, perhaps you prefer to lose."

"You'd like to believe that, wouldn't you?" she teased, reclining on the velvet couch.

"Isn't it so?" he asked, sitting beside her.

"My love, you don't need a deck of cards and a game of chance to get me to spend the morning in bed with you — or the entire day, for that matter. You should know that by now."

"I spent so many months thinking you hated me, Tina, that now it's hard to believe our happiness is real," Philip said.

He took her face in his hands and looked at her with glowing warmth in his eyes. "No man has the right to be as happy as you've made me by giving me your love. I can't believe you are really mine."

Christina came into Philip's arms, clinging to him tightly.

"We must forget about the eleven months we were separated," she whispered, "forget about the doubt we once shared. We were both fools not to speak of our love then. But I know now that you love me as I do you. I will never, never leave you."

She leaned back and looked at him, a spark suddenly coming to her eyes. "And if another woman should ever capture your fancy, let me inform you now, Philip Caxton, that I would fight for you! You told me once that nobody takes what is yours. Well, no woman will ever take what is mine!"

"Such a spitfire I have married," he chuckled. "Why didn't you tell me you were going to be a jealous and possessive wife?"

"Are you sorry you married me?" she asked.

"You know the answer to that. Now tell me what kept you so long downstairs. You're not trying to avoid my bed, are you, my sweet?"

"*That* I will never do. I just stopped for a few minutes to see Philip

Junior. He was trying to walk again without holding onto anything. He's so cute when he does that. Emma also gave me a letter — from Kareen."

"And I suppose you want to read it right now? Go ahead," he said.

She smiled and quickly opened the letter. After she had read it silently for a few minutes, she started to laugh. "Well, it's about time."

"What is?" Philip asked.

"Kareen is going to have a baby. John must be so happy, and I imagine Johnsy is, too. She was so upset when we left taking away *her* baby, as she called Philip Junior. She'll be glad to have another one in the house."

"That's good news, and I'm happy for them. But it's about time we enlarged our own little family." Philip grinned devilishly. "And we can start working on it right now."

He picked her up and carried her to their big four-postered bed still tousled from the night's sleep. He kissed her tenderly, his lips soft, pliant, moving ever so slowly over hers. He kissed her throat, her shoulder, and lowered her onto the bed.

His smoldering green eyes were alight with anticipation. He slipped out of his velvet robe and helped Christina take off her dress. She opened her arms to him, and their bodies entwined closely. He kissed her again, with the fiery temper of love.

Suddenly he raised himself on one elbow and smiled lazily at her.

"I rather like the idea of having a big family," he said. "You won't mind having another child so soon, will you?"

"You should have asked me that question a month ago. I have no choice in the matter now. In eight months there will be an addition to our family," Christina grinned.

"But why didn't you tell me sooner?" he asked joyfully.

"I was waiting for the right moment. I hope we have a girl this time."

"No, that won't do. We'll have three or four boys first — then you can have the girl you want."

"But why?"

"Because if our daughter looks anything like you, my sweet, she's going to need all the protection she can get."

"Well, let's just wait and see. I'm afraid we won't have much say in the matter."

"I suppose this is why you've been eating so much lately," he said. "Well, this time I'll be around to watch you bloom with motherhood."

Christina frowned slightly, remembering how big she'd grown with Philip Junior. But Philip smiled.

"It's our child that will grow within you. And in my eyes you will be more beautiful than you are now — if that is possible. I love you, Tina."

He kissed her then, passionately, and their bodies molded together. The ardent flames of love possessed them, and Christina knew this was the way it would always be between them. She knew her love for Philip would never die.